CH00482595

MAUREEN CHILD

Strictly Lonergan's Business

Harlequin
Mills & Boon

Desire

DID YOU PURCHASE THIS BOOK WITHOUT A COVER?
If you did, you should be aware it is **stolen property** as it was
reported 'unsold and destroyed' by a retailer.
Neither the author nor the publisher has received any payment
for this book.

First Published 2006
First Australian Paperback Edition 2006
ISBN 0 733 56915 3

STRICTLY LONERGAN'S BUSINESS © 2006 by Maureen Child
Philippine Copyright 2006
Australian Copyright 2006
New Zealand Copyright 2006
Except for use in any review, the reproduction or utilisation of this work in
whole or in part in any form by any electronic, mechanical or other means,
now known or hereafter invented, including xerography, photocopying and
recording, or in any information storage or retrieval system, is forbidden
without the permission of the publisher, Harlequin Mills & Boon, Locked Bag
7002, Chatswood D.C. N.S.W., Australia 2067.

All the characters in this book have no existence outside the imagination of
the author, and have no relation whatsoever to anyone bearing the same
name or names. They are not even distantly inspired by any individual
known or unknown to the author, and all the incidents are pure invention.

This book is sold subject to the condition that it shall not, by way of trade or
otherwise, be lent, resold, hired out or otherwise circulated without the prior
consent of the publisher in any form of binding or cover other than that in
which it is published and without a similar condition including this condition
being imposed on the subsequent purchaser.

All rights reserved including the right of reproduction in whole or in part in
any form. This edition is published by arrangement with Harlequin
Enterprises II B.V.

Published by
Harlequin Mills & Boon
3 Gibbes Street
CHATSWOOD NSW 2067
AUSTRALIA

HARLEQUIN MILLS & BOON DESIRE and the Rose Device are trademarks
used under license and registered in Australia, New Zealand, Philippines,
United States Patent & Trademark Office and in other countries.

Printed and bound in Australia by
McPherson's Printing Group

MAUREEN CHILD

is a California native who loves to travel. Every chance they get, she and her husband are taking off on another research trip. The author of more than sixty books, Maureen loves a happy ending and still swears that she has the best job in the world. She lives in Southern California with her husband, two children and a golden retriever with delusions of grandeur.

To my "other" mother—Mary Ann Child

For everything you've given me.
For everything you've been to me.

I couldn't love you more.

One

"It's really easy," Kara Sloan told herself, giving her own reflection a narrow eyed glare in the rear view mirror. "He opens the door, you say 'I quit.'"

Right.

If it was that easy, she'd have said those two little words six months ago. Heck. A *year* ago.

The minute she'd realized she'd made the huge mistake of falling in love with her employer.

The trouble was, every time she was anywhere near her boss, Cooper Lonergan, her brain shut down and her emotions took over. One look from the man's dark brown eyes and she turned into a puddle of goo.

She still wasn't sure how this had happened.

Heaven knew she hadn't planned it. She'd been the man's assistant for five years, and for four of those five, everything had been great. They'd had a comfortable friendship and easy working relationship. Until it suddenly dawned on her nearly a year ago, that she was in *love* with him.

And ever since that day, she'd been miserable.

She couldn't even get mad at Cooper for not noticing that her feelings had changed. Why would he? To him, she was as familiar a sight in his life as the dark red leather sofa in his living room at home. And just as comfortable.

This situation was her own fault. She'd changed the rules and he didn't even know it. She was in love and he was in like.

Not a good thing.

"Which is *why*," she said sternly, still meeting her own wide green eyes in the rental car mirror, "you have to quit. Just suck it up, face him down and say it."

She inhaled sharply, blew out a breath and nodded grimly. She could do this. She *would* do this.

Muttering darkly, she swung her legs out of the car, slammed the door and then stared up at the big yellow Victorian farmhouse Cooper had rented for the summer. It looked…welcoming, somehow. As if the house had been waiting for her.

Silly, but she was sorry she wouldn't be staying. Sorry she'd have to leave and go back to New York in just two weeks. There was something about this place that 'spoke' to her.

It sat far back on a wide, manicured green lawn and several old shade trees surrounded the structure. Window panes glinted in the morning sunlight, fresh flowers in terra cotta pots lined the porch, their bright summer colors dazzling in the morning light.

She inhaled sharply, deeply, enjoying the scents of freshly mowed grass and the hint of the ocean, just a few miles away. Kara had always considered herself a city girl. Happy in Manhattan, she loved the rush and crush of the crowds, the blaring symphony of horns and shouted insults from the cabbies who drove as if every mile made was a personal victory.

But, she thought, there was something to be said for this, too. The quiet. The color. The lazier pace.

No point in getting used to it, though.

Her three inch heels wobbled slightly on the crushed gravel driveway, and she thought that was only appropriate. Hadn't she been off balance around Cooper all year? Besides, if she'd had any sense, she'd have traveled in jeans and sneakers. But no…she'd had to look *good* when she saw him. Not that he ever noticed what she was wearing.

Gritting her teeth, Kara silently admitted that Cooper wouldn't notice if she had shown up naked.

Which, she reminded herself sternly, was *exactly* why she had to quit her job. It was just too hard. Too miserable to be in love with a man who only saw you as the world's most efficient assistant.

"My own fault," she muttered, turning her back on the house to walk to the rear of the car. She pushed a button on the rental car key ring and the trunk slowly opened like a coffin lid in an old Dracula movie.

They worked well together, had a lot of laughs, and Kara had had the satisfaction of knowing that she did her job so well, he couldn't get along without her. Then she'd messed it all up by changing the rules.

She wasn't even sure when it had happened. When she'd stopped looking at Cooper like an employer and started having X-rated dreams about him. He'd slipped up on her. Sneaked under her defenses. Damn it, he'd made her fall in love with him without even trying and didn't even have the decency to *notice*.

That's why she had to quit. Had to get out while she still could. It was, as her best friend Gina had put it just the night before, *a freaking emergency*.

Gina had taken her out for drinks and given Kara the pep talk that apparently was considered the best friend's duty.

"You know darn well that man is never going to change."

"Why should he?" Kara challenged, stabbing the olive in her martini as if it were an alien out to take over the world. "As far as he's concerned everything is great. Fabulous."

"Exactly my point." Gina blinked at her, lifted one hand to signal the bartender for another round, then turned back to look at her friend again. "He's been in California what? Three days?"

"Yesss…"

"And he's called you like a hundred times already."

True. Her cell phone, always on so that Cooper could get in touch with her whenever he needed to, had been ringing with alarming regularity. Kara checked her watch. Twenty minutes since his last call. He was due. "I work for him."

"Oh, it's way beyond that, Kara," Gina said, leaning across the glossy bar table until her long blond hair brushed the polished surface. "Last time he called, the man asked you how to make *coffee*. He's thirty something and can't make a cup of coffee without your help?"

Kara laughed. "He's thirty one and he can too make coffee. It's just terrible."

Gina was not amused. Shaking her head, she sat back. "You did this to yourself, girlfriend. You made yourself indispensable."

"That's a *bad* thing?" Kara reached for her fresh drink and turned her attention to the new olive.

"It is when Cooper Lonergan sees you like a well-programmed robot." Gina took a gulp of her apple-tini and then waved the glass in the air. "He doesn't see *you*. He never will."

"That's harsh."

"But true."

"Probably."

"So," Gina demanded, "What are you going to do about it? Stick around until you're old and alone and wondering what the hell happened to your life? Or get out now while you still can?"

And *that*, Kara thought now, reaching into the trunk, is the million dollar question. She knew Gina was right. Heck, she'd known the truth for the last year. She had no future with Cooper. At least, nothing beyond what she had now. And that just wasn't enough.

Not anymore.

A crisp, cool wind with the scent of the sea on it, swept across the yard, set the leaves on the trees dancing, and tossed her dark brown hair across her eyes. She plucked it back, blew out a breath and grabbed up both her suitcase, the small carry-on bag she'd filled with fresh bagels from Cooper's favorite deli, the gourmet coffee he couldn't write without, and five bags of marshmallow cookies.

The man had the palate of a ten-year-old. She smiled to herself, thinking, as she always did, that it was kind of cute how Cooper had to have his favorite cookies on hand at all times.

But she caught herself an instant later. Not cute. Annoying. Right.

Nodding to herself, she pledged that the minute she saw Cooper, she'd give him notice. Two weeks.

He could hire someone temporarily for this summer in California, then when he went home to Manhattan, he could find a more permanent replacement.

As for Kara, the sooner she got back to New York and what was left of her life…the better.

Grim determination fed her steps as she started toward the big house at the end of drive. With every wobble of her heels, she told herself over and over, *It's just a job. You can find another, better one. You don't need Cooper.*

She'd almost convinced herself when the front door flew open, the ancient screen door slapped against the wall of the house and Cooper Lonergan stepped out onto the wide front porch.

Tall and lean, he was wearing his New York uniform of black pants and black shirt. His features were sharp, angular and his black hair, just long enough to touch his shoulders, flew about his face like a dirty halo. His dark eyes glinted in the sun and when he smiled, Kara felt it deliver a solid punch to her belly. Probably had more impact because he didn't really smile all that often. But brother, when he did…

The man was mouthwatering.

Damn it.

"Kara!" He took the five steps down to the yard in two long strides and crossed to where she was still standing, dumbstruck by the force of her own emotions. He swept her up into a brief, hard hug that lit up her insides like Times Square on New Year's Eve, then let her go so abruptly, she staggered back a step.

"Thank God you're here."

A brief flash of something that might have been hope darted through her. "You missed me?"

"Boy, did I," he said. "You have no idea. I made coffee this morning and it pretty much tasted like I think motor oil with a dash of cinnamon would taste."

Right. Hope dissolved into reality. Of course he hadn't actually missed her. When she took her three weeks of vacation every year, he didn't miss *her*. He missed the convenience of having her around. Why should this time be any different?

"Please tell me you brought real coffee and my cookies."

She sighed, accepting the truth. "Yes Cooper, you too tall four-year-old. I have the coffee and I brought your cookies."

"Excellent." He ignored her jibe, just as he pretty much ignored her, Kara thought. Then he took her suitcase from her and started for the house. "Did you get the dry cleaning for me, too?"

"It's in the trunk."

"And bagels. Oh God, tell me you remembered the bagels."

She shook her head and kept pace with him. Ten seconds with him and she fell into the old, familiar pattern. What had happened to her vow? Where had her backbone gone? Why wasn't she looking into those dark chocolate eyes of his and telling him that she quit?

She took a breath and almost groaned. He even *smelled* delicious.

"Yes, I remembered the bagels," she muttered, disgusted with both of them. "When in the last five years have I *not* remembered?"

"Never," he said with a quick wink that weakened her knees even as it stiffened what was left of her resolve. "That's why I can't live without you."

Words spoken so easily, so lightly. She knew it meant nothing to him, but if they were only true, what those words would mean to her.

Cooper ushered Kara into the house, standing back to let her pass in front of him. Her heels clicked against the wood floor and she flipped her long, dark brown hair back over her shoulder as she turned in a circle to look around the room.

He took his first good look at the same time. Sure, he'd been there three days already, but he'd spent most of his time in the master bedroom, sitting at a makeshift desk, working.

Well, *trying* to work. In reality, he'd played about three thousand games of solitaire. Which wouldn't help him meet the deadline that was already flying at him.

"It's a great place," Kara said, studying an old brass chandelier hanging in the center of the living room.

He glanced around, noting the big, overstuffed

chairs in faded cabbage rose upholstery. A braided rug covered most of the scarred wood floor and the pale yellow walls looked bright and cheerful, even to him. The property management company who'd leased the place to him had done a first-rate job keeping the old house in shape.

"People say it's haunted."

She whipped around and stared at him, her green eyes wide and fascinated. "It is?"

He nodded. "When I was a kid, I spent every summer here in Coleville with my grandfather and my cousins." Memories rushed in, nearly strangling him with the force of the accompanying emotions. He pushed them down, deliberately shut the door on the feelings rising in him as he said, "We'd ride our bikes over here at night and watch this house, tell each other scary stories and wait to see something otherworldly floating by." He shrugged and smiled. "We never saw a damn thing."

"And since you've been here...?"

"Nada."

"Well that's disappointing," Kara said.

He smiled at the whine in her voice. No matter what, he could always count on Kara to see the same possibilities that he could. As a horror novelist, he'd really enjoyed the idea of renting the same haunted house that had fascinated him as a kid.

But he should have known that the only ghosts he'd find this summer were those in his own past. Instinctively, Cooper cut that thought off neatly. He wasn't going to go there.

"Anyway," Cooper said with a shrug, "It's only a couple of miles from my grandfather's place, so it was handy."

"Oh! How is your grandfather?"

"Long story. But he's actually fine."

"But his doctor said he was dying…"

"Like I said," Cooper repeated, not really wanting to go into it all at the moment. "Long story. First, tell me what took you so long to get here. I expected you yesterday."

"I told you it would take three days to close up your condo and take care of all the details—"

"You're right, you did. Just felt like a really *long* three days. You're the best, Kara. Have I given you a raise lately?"

"No," she chided.

"Put that on your list—" he cut her off before she could say anything else. "The important thing is you're here now."

She smiled at him and Cooper added, "With you here, I can finally work. I'm telling you, I haven't had a decent meal since I left home."

Her smile slowly faded.

"The grocery store in Coleville doesn't deliver, so you'll need to make a trip over there to stock up." He picked up her suitcase and headed for the stairs. "I'll put your bags away. You're in the room across from mine. It's big, got a nice view of the fields. We have to share the bathroom, but we'll work it out. You could make up a schedule and—"

"Cooper!"

He paused, looked back at her and sent her another one of those rare, genuine smiles. "It really is good to see you, Kara. And it's okay. I know what you're gonna say."

"Really?"

"Absolutely," he said. "I feel the same way. Good to have things back to normal."

Two

A few hours later, Kara had been to the grocery store, had a chicken roasting in the oven and had even managed to arrange for a fax machine to be delivered and set up first thing tomorrow.

Cooper was upstairs working and down here, in the square, farmhouse style kitchen, Kara was wondering what the heck had happened to her plan.

She hitched one hip against the worn, Formica countertop and folded both arms across her chest. Wearing her favorite pair of faded, nearly threadbare jeans, a pale blue T-shirt and wonderful, comfortable sneakers, she shook her head and said aloud, "You're a wimp, Kara. A spineless wiener dog. A disgrace to assistants everywhere."

Late afternoon sunlight slanted through the curtained window, making lacy shadows on the round, pedestal table and the gleaming wood floor. Kara watched as a soft breeze ruffled the curtains, sending those shadows into a lazy dance.

Walking across the room, she pulled out one of the captain's chairs and plopped down onto it. Bracing her elbows on the table, she stared out through a gap in the curtains at the rolling back lawn that stretched out to a wide green field. Then she heaved a dramatic sigh of complete disgust. Oh, she wasn't disgusted with Cooper so much as she was with herself.

Back to normal. Abruptly, she shifted in the chair, leaned back and stretched out her fingertips. Her nails tapped against the table like a frantic heartbeat. "Not his fault he fell right back into the same pattern we've been in for years. You *knew* this was going to happen, Kara. The question is…why didn't you quit?"

But she knew the answer to that already. Because one look at Cooper and her fantasies took over. Her reasonable, intelligent, logical brain went right to sleep and into Fantasy Land.

She'd imagined it all so perfectly, her dreams were even filled with the dialogue her brain had provided. And sitting right there at the kitchen table, she indulged herself yet one more time. She'd walk into a room, a stray beam of sunlight would strike her just so and...

Cooper glances up. His gaze meets hers. And for one, heart-stopping moment, the two of them are lost in the suddenly discovered rush of love.

He crosses the room to her, cups her face in his big, wonderful hands and says, "My God, Kara. How could I have been so stupid? How could I not have seen the real you for so long? Can you ever forgive me?"

And Kara smiles, reaches up to cover his hands with her own and says, "There's nothing to forgive. It's enough that we're finally together. I love you, Cooper."

He whispers "I love you, too," just before he kisses her with more passion than she could have imagined.

"Right," she muttered now, coming up out of her daydream like a drowning diver frantically breaching the water's surface to find air. "*Nothing to forgive?* What am I? An idiot?"

Yes, she thought. An idiot in love with a man who was clueless enough to not even notice what was right in front of him. A man who would *never* see her until it was too late.

A sigh swept through the room.

Kara jolted upright and twisted her head from side to side, glancing around the empty kitchen, futilely trying to find the source of that heartbreaking sound. But there was nothing. She stiffened, waiting for it to come again. It didn't. There was just a sunny kitchen, empty but for her. Chills snaked along Kara's spine and tingled at the base of her neck.

A ghost?

Cooper did tell her the house was supposedly haunted. But then he'd also said he hadn't felt a thing in three days.

"Imagination," she whispered, standing up slowly, carefully. She chuckled softly, and pretended that her laughter didn't sound quite as shaky as it felt. Swallowing hard, she rubbed her hands up and down her arms, dispelling the sensation of every nerve in her body standing on end.

Then, blaming the weird feeling on her own day-dreaming, Kara shut down her brain and finished getting dinner ready.

Cooper spent his day with a murderous demon.

His mind raced just a few beats ahead of his fingers, furiously typing at the keyboard. He knew what he wanted to capture. What he wanted his reader to feel. What surprised him was that this was the first piece of decent writing he'd managed to accomplish since arriving in California. It felt good. Good to be lost in his own imagination. Good to be caught up by the characters forming on his computer screen.

Good to let go—however briefly—of the memories that had been choking him for three long days.

A silent shroud of snow covered the walkway to the old hotel, but David hardly noticed. The cold seeped into his bones, down to his soul and a ribbon of dread slowly unwound in the pit of his stomach. His shoulders hunched against the icy wind, he shuffled his steps, reluctant to approach, as if every cell in his body was trying to warn him to stay away...

Cooper finally lifted his fingers from the computer keyboard and leaned back in his desk chair. He knew exactly how the hero of his latest novel felt. Hadn't he himself only reluctantly returned to Coleville? Wasn't every cell in *his* body still telling him to get the hell out?

But he was trapped for the summer. No getting out of it. He'd given his word to his grandfather, and a Lonergan never went back on his word. Even to sneaky old men who lie to their grandsons about being at death's door on a skateboard.

Not that he was pissed off about that, he assured himself. He was glad Jeremiah wasn't dying. Glad the old man was as healthy and apparently, as slippery as he'd always been. But damn it, Cooper hadn't been back to Coleville in fifteen years. And if Jeremiah hadn't pulled one over on him, he doubted he ever would have returned.

It was too hard. Too many memories, constantly

fluttering through his mind like swarms of gnats—annoying and impossible to ignore.

His screen saver flicked on, a haunted house complete with bats, ghosts and vampires. Usually, that was enough to motivate him to get back to writing. To delve into whatever story he had going. Today though, he ignored the animated cartoon drawing filling the screen.

From downstairs came the clank of pans and the rush of water through old pipes. The scent of something delicious wafted up the stairs and he took a deep breath, enjoying not only the mingled aromas of garlic and sage, but the realization that Kara was right downstairs.

Damn, it was good having Kara here. And for more reasons than her cooking abilities.

Since arriving in Coleville for the first time in fifteen years, Cooper had never felt so alone. Sure, his family was right down the road a couple of miles, but here, in this house, he lay alone at night and felt emptiness crowding in on him.

Ordinarily, he liked being alone. In New York, he spent most days working, avoiding the phone, the doorbell, and e-mail. Kara kept the world at bay, affording him plenty of time to lose himself in his stories. When he needed a distraction, the city was just beyond his doorstep and there were any number of women he could call.

Here though, the quiet reigned supreme. There

were no hustling throngs of people. No loud crash and scream of cabs darting in and out of vicious traffic. No sirens or street peddlers. Just the quiet— and too much time to think.

Pushing his chair back, Cooper stood up and walked across his bedroom to the window overlooking the front of the house. He wasn't seeing the neatly tended yard, or the shade trees, or even the green field sweeping down the narrow two lane road toward his grandfather's ranch.

As he had the last three days, he looked beyond, to a lake he couldn't even see from here. He'd thought that renting a house a couple of miles away would be enough. That not being able to actually *see* the water would make being here easier.

But he should have known better.

Hell, he'd been living in Manhattan for years, and every night in his dreams, he saw that lake. Every day when he sat down to write the horror novels that had given him fame and fortune, he saw that lake. Saw again how that summer day fifteen years ago had become a nightmare.

If he closed his eyes now, it would all come racing back. The feel of the sun on bare shoulders. The rush of laughter from his cousins. The sigh of wind in the trees. The splash as he and his cousins had taken turns jumping for distance into the icy water.

The numbing shock that followed.

So he didn't close his eyes, but the memories clung to the edges of his mind, taunting him, pushing at him. He reached up, scraped one hand through his hair, then rubbed his eyes as if he could rub away the images that felt as though they were burned on his retinas.

"Hey!"

Startled, he spun around and found Kara standing in the open doorway staring at him. Heart pounding, he shook his head and scowled at her. "Trying to give me a heart attack?"

"It wasn't on the schedule for tonight, no," she said and stepped into the room, still watching him curiously. "Everything okay?"

No.

"Why wouldn't it be?" he hedged and turned his back on her to walk back to the desk and his laptop. He never left the lid up when someone else was around. Call it superstition or whatever, he didn't like anyone getting a peek at what he was working on.

"Well, because I called your name three times and you didn't hear me."

"I was…thinking," he said and at least it wasn't a lie.

"New book giving you trouble?"

"Yeah." His fingertips smoothed over the gray lid of the computer as if caressing the words hidden inside. "At least, it was. Until today." He forced a smile as he looked at her. "You must have brought me some luck."

"Uh-huh." She crossed the room, threw the curtains back and opened the window. A cold sharp breeze raced into the room as if it had been crouched just outside, waiting its chance. "So, translation is, you didn't work before because I wasn't here."

"Right." Cooper watched her as she wandered the room, efficiently tidying up the space, folding the old quilt at the foot of his bed, straightening a framed landscape, then turning to the desk, where she shuffled papers into neat stacks.

He felt calmer just watching her. Damn, Kara was good for him. She always had been. Her voice, her even temper, her cool logic, her no-nonsense way of looking at the world was exactly the right leash he needed to keep him grounded.

"So I'm guessing," she said, glancing at him with a knowing gleam in her eye, "that means you killed me horribly again."

One corner of his mouth quirked into a half smile. God, she knew him better than anyone ever had. Part of the fun of being a writer was being able to kill off whomever happened to be bugging you at the time. And when Kara wasn't around, it was lowering to admit just how lost he felt without her. Hence the catharsis of killing off a secretary/assistant in one of his stories.

"How'd I die this time?" she asked, planting both hands on her hips. "Drowning?"

"I told you before," he said, his voice going as stiff as his spine. "*You* never drown."

"Okay," she said, lifting both hands in mock surrender. "Sheesh. Just asked."

"Right. Sorry." He pushed one hand through his hair again and willed the tremor inside into stillness.

In every one of his books, at least one character drowned. But it was always someone Cooper didn't like. Someone he thought the readers wouldn't be too invested in. Death by drowning was something Cooper could never take lightly. Not with his memories. Not with the past that was always so close.

"You sure you're okay?"

"Yeah," he said, nodding as if to confirm his own word. "I'm fine. Did you come up here for something in particular?"

"Dinner's ready."

He glanced at the window. The sun was just setting. Turning his gaze back to her he asked, "This early?"

"Shoot me, I'm hungry." Shrugging, Kara headed for the door and said over her shoulder, "You can wait till later if you want to."

"No," he said, sweeping his gaze around the room that without her suddenly seemed way too empty. "I'll join you."

"Great. You can open the bottle of chardonnay I got at the market."

He chuckled as he followed her downstairs.

"Mmm. Chardonnay from Al's market in Coleville, California. Can't wait."

"Snob."

"Peasant."

Kara was still laughing as they walked into the kitchen. She took a seat at the table and watched him as he grabbed the wine and the bottle opener. They'd already settled back into the familiar routine. And damn it, it felt good. And right.

God, she would miss this so much when she left. And she *had* to leave. That was more apparent by the moment. They'd become too comfortable together.

He sat down and his long legs bumped into hers. Kara felt a flash of something hot and dazzling skyrocket inside, and only just managed to keep from yelping.

Naturally, Cooper didn't notice.

While he poured clear, straw colored wine into the pink antique glasses she'd found in a cupboard, Kara looked around at the homey old kitchen. The cabinets were painted white, the appliances looked as though they were new in the fifties, and the windows overlooked a huge backyard lined by ancient shade trees.

It all should have been…soothing somehow. Cozy. Instead though, Kara felt a sensation of…waiting. She hadn't heard anything weird since that sigh earlier in the afternoon and she'd almost convinced herself that hadn't really happened.

"This smells great," Cooper said, helping himself to a serving of chicken, potatoes and fresh broccoli.

"You know you could have found the grocery store yourself," Kara pointed out, taking a sip of her wine. Cool, tart, wonderful.

"Oh, I did," he said, reaching for a slice of wheat bread from the plate in the center of the table. "I bought coffee and a couple boxes of doughnuts. Oh," he added, "and a few frozen burritos."

"Pitiful." And somehow, cute. How twisted was she?

"We go with our strengths," he said around a bite of chicken. Then his dark eyes closed and he sighed, obviously in pure heaven. "At home, I can call a restaurant. Here—let's just say that the Burger Hut doesn't deliver." He swallowed and groaned. "Man, Kara. I owe you. Big."

She didn't want him to owe her.

She wanted him to *love* her.

But she might as well wish for a ten pound weight loss and a spanking new wardrobe by morning. Neither wish was going to happen.

Outside, late afternoon slid into twilight, the sky softly darkening. Inside, a familiar, comfortable silence settled between them and Kara found herself taking mental pictures that she would be able to pull out and look at later—after she left.

At that thought, her gaze landed on Cooper and a twinge of regret pinged off her chest, bouncing off her heart, leaving it feeling bruised. She hated the notion of walking out of Cooper's life, but at the same time, she had to, if she ever expected to get a life of her own.

Still, she wanted to enjoy what time she did have with him, so she pushed those thoughts to the back of her mind and asked, "So, what's the story on your grandfather?"

He grabbed his wineglass and took a long drink. Then he eyed the liquid in surprise. "Pretty good."

"Uh-huh," she said, sensing a stall tactic. "Talk."

"Right." While he ate, he told her the story of Jeremiah's tricky maneuvers to get his grandsons back home for the summer. Not only had Jeremiah faked a bad heart, he'd even convinced his own doctor to go along with the deception. He'd worried them all, just to get them to come back to Coleville.

"That's terrible," Kara said.

"Yeah," Cooper agreed, taking another bite of chicken. "Jeremiah's a wily old goat. But this was pretty low. He scared the hell out of us."

"No," Kara said, glaring at him because he couldn't see what she was trying to say. "I *meant* it was terrible that your grandfather felt as though he had no choice but to coerce his grandsons into a visit."

"Huh?" His dark eyes fixed on her in confusion.

"How could you all do that to him, Cooper?" She set her fork down on her plate and the quiet *clink* it made sounded overly loud in the suddenly still room.

The silence only lasted for a moment or two.

"*We* didn't do anything," he pointed out defensively, waving his own fork at her for emphasis.

"That's the point," she said, taking a gulp of wine and letting the icy liquid slide down her throat to form a nice warm ball in the pit of her stomach. "You didn't do anything. None of you."

"Hey."

"You said you haven't been back here in fifteen years, Cooper."

"There were reasons."

"*Reasons?* For breaking an old man's heart?" Sympathy welled inside her and along with it came anger. "You went away and stayed away. The poor man. No wonder he was desperate enough to lie."

He sighed and sat back in his chair, gripping his wineglass as if it were a life rope. "You're right."

"What?" She thunked the heel of her hand above her right ear. "I mean, excuse me?"

"Funny," he acknowledged with a nod. "But you heard me. I know we were wrong to stay away so long. Trust me, it wasn't easy on any of us, either. Don't you think we missed Jeremiah? Don't you think it was hard for us to stay away?"

"Then why?" she whispered, leaning on the table to watch him carefully. "Why did it take you so long to come home for a visit?"

"Because, Kara," he said softly, shifting his gaze from hers to the surface of the pale wine in his glass.

"As hard as it was to stay away, it was even harder to come back here."

There was something distant about Cooper. As if he had emotionally taken one giant step back from her. As if he were deliberately trying to shut her out. And it hurt. They'd been close for five years. She'd thought they were, if not lovers, then at least friends.

"Cooper..." she waited for him to look at her. As stubborn as he could be, she kept quiet, counting the ticking seconds as they passed before, at last, his gaze lifted to hers. Those dark brown eyes looked shadowed by old pain and instantly she felt an answering ache inside her. "What could be so important that it would keep you from someone you love for so long?"

He took a sip of wine, swallowed, then set the glass carefully onto the table as if afraid it would shatter.

"Sometimes love's just not enough, Kara." He sighed, scraped one hand across his face, then forced a smile that did nothing to ease the shadows in his eyes. "Sometimes love is the problem."

An icy draft slipped through the kitchen, twining itself around Kara, reaching out for Cooper and then holding them both in a chill embrace.

"Whoa," Cooper said as Kara shivered, "these old places really let in the cold." He stood up and started across the kitchen. "I'll close the living room windows."

The cold eased away and Kara sent a disquieted glance around the empty room. Old houses were drafty, yes. But Cooper's errand was a fruitless one. She'd closed the windows herself an hour ago.

Three

Kara woke up with a jolt.

Heart pounding, lungs heaving, she shook off the last of the nightmare still clinging to the edges of her mind. She swallowed hard and grabbed at the quilt pooled at her waist in an effort to steady herself.

She couldn't remember what she'd been dreaming. Couldn't remember what had chased her from that dream into wakefulness. All she *did* know was that goose bumps were racing up and down her spine and air was still hard to come by.

Then she heard it.

Sobbing.

Someone in the old house was crying as if their

heart was breaking. The sound lifted, rising, filling the house with pain that was nearly tangible. Then an instant later, the sobs quieted, becoming a whisper that Kara strained to hear.

Mouth dry, heartbeat frantic, she tossed the quilt back and swung her legs to the floor. The polished wooden floorboards felt cold against her bare feet, but she hardly noticed. She moved to the door, determined to follow the desperate sobs to their source.

Fear tugged at her insides, but curiosity was stronger. Grabbing hold of the icy brass knob, she opened her door, stepped into the hallway and stopped dead. The sorrow filled wails rose again, and with them, the small hairs at the back of Kara's neck.

Moonlight filtered in through the arch-shaped window at the end of the hall, painting a pale silver glow on the walls and the faded carpet runner stretched down the center of the hallway. Outside, trees danced in the wind and their shadows dipped and swayed wildly.

Kara could have sworn she jumped three feet, straight up, when the door across from hers suddenly swung open. Heart in her throat now, she grabbed hold of the doorjamb as Cooper appeared on the threshold. His long black hair mussed from sleep, he glared at the empty hallway, then at her.

"What the hell is going on around here?" he demanded, voice raw.

She had to swallow hard before she could be sure

her voice would work. He wore dark red cotton drawstring pants that hung low on his hips and the hems stacked up on his bare feet. In the moonlight, his sculpted chest looked as if it had been lovingly molded from a sheet of bronze and Kara's palms itched to touch it. Touch him.

"Kara?" He waved one hand in front of her face to get her attention. "Hello?"

She shook her head, told her hormones to take a vacation and snapped, "Get your hand out of my face, Cooper."

"You zoned out on me."

"I did not *zone out*," she argued, though she was pretty sure she had. Heck, one long look at Cooper, fresh from bed, was enough to conquer the strongest of women. And Kara had already admitted to being a spineless wiener dog.

The sobbing rose again, swelling up from below the stairs like a slowly inflating balloon taking to the sky. And a new set of goose pimples ice-skated up and down Kara's arms.

Cooper turned his head and stared at the head of the stairs for a long minute, before turning his gaze back to her. "Tell me you heard that."

She huffed out an anxious breath. "Oh, yeah."

"Good."

"*Good?*" she repeated. "What's *good* about that?"

"I thought I was dreaming it," he whispered, stepping further into the hall and throwing another glance at the stairs. "Then I figured it was a hallucination. But if we're both hearing it, then that means it's real." His voice dropped even further and he leaned in close so she could hear him above the mournful weeping that seemed to be dripping from the walls. "And if it's real, then somebody's trying to pull something funny."

Kara swallowed hard. Cooper's breath came warm against her cheek and she had to fight to concentrate on what he was saying instead of the way he made her feel, leaning in so darn close. Closing her eyes briefly, she gulped at air then asked, "Who would think this kind of thing is funny?"

He shot her a look. "My cousin Jake for one, but as far as I know he's still in Spain." Then he smiled. "Mike Haney."

"Who?" Kara followed him quietly, walking right behind him as he started down the center of the hall toward the stairs.

He turned around quickly and she nearly yelped.

"Shhh…" he said, dropping both hands onto her shoulders. "Mike Haney's an old friend. We all grew up together. My cousin Sam told me he saw ol' Mike in town the other day. And trust me, this is *just* the kind of thing Mike would think up."

She didn't think so. But then, her brain wasn't really working on all cylinders at the moment. His big hands, with those talented, long fingers, held her firmly and felt so warm on her skin. Everything inside her hummed with an electrical sort of awakening that couldn't be quenched—even by the goose bumps that were still rippling along her spine.

Focus, Kara, focus.

"Cooper—"

"Stay here," he warned, lifting one hand to hold up his index finger like he was signaling a recalcitrant puppy to sit.

"Excuse me?"

He scowled. "Kara, will you just stay here while I go down and beat the crap outta Mike?"

"No, I'm not staying here," she said and waved a hand, silently telling him to get going and she'd be right behind him. "What? Are we in a 1950s movie? Big strong man leaves the little woman behind while he stalks off to danger?"

He snorted. "The only one in danger around here is Mike Haney."

"That sobbing does *not* sound like a guy."

He looked about to argue, so she added, "Besides, what if you're wrong? You think I want to be up here all by myself? No freakin' way."

The crying continued, rolling on and on, lifting and falling like waves cresting on the shore, then sliding back out to sea. The very air seemed thicker, heavier somehow and Kara—for just a second and who could really blame her—almost wanted to be in that old movie. Hiding under a bed while Cooper went to check things out.

Then a terrible, wrenching moan swept through the house and Kara's heart twisted in empathy.

"Stay behind me," Cooper muttered, starting down the stairs at a dead creep, carefully putting one foot gently down before moving the other.

"No problem there," she murmured and stayed as close to him as his shadow at high noon.

He reached behind him, grabbed her hand in his and held on tight. Kara clung to him like he was the last eighty percent off sweater at a clearance sale at Bloomie's.

At the bottom of the stairs, the sound was all around them, reverberating off the walls, the floor, the ceilings, until it seemed to echo over and over again.

"Cooper…"

"Come on…"

His legs were a lot longer than hers, so Kara practically had to trot to keep up with him as he sprinted for the main parlor.

"It's centered there," he whispered. "You hear it? Louder the closer we get."

And now that they were almost on top of the sound, Kara wondered why in the devil she'd wanted to come down here to investigate it in the first place. If it *was* a friend of Cooper's, then there was nothing to worry about. And if it *wasn't?* Oh, she so didn't want to think about that at the moment.

"Ready?" He glanced at her as his left hand curled around the brass knob of the parlor door.

"No."

He shot her a wicked grin that quieted her fear and stirred up other, far more interesting things. She nodded jerkily. "Fine. Just open it."

He did. Throwing the door wide open, Cooper dragged Kara into the room behind him.

Instantly, the sobbing stopped.

Moonlight slanted through the wide front windows, illuminating the tiny room like someone in heaven was focusing a spotlight on the place. Deep shadows crouched in the corners, but when Cooper flicked on the overhead chandelier, they disappeared. Kara and Cooper were alone in the room.

Loosening his grip on her hand, Cooper stalked around the perimeter of the small, old fashioned parlor. He pulled back the drapes at either side of the windows and even opened an old armoire, as if expecting to find Mike Haney and a tape recorder, crouched inside.

When he found nothing, he turned around and looked at Kara. "Okay, I admit it; I'm stumped."

Kara wandered the room more slowly, touching the little china dog on an end table, smoothing her fingertips across the fringe on a lampshade. Thoughtfully, she asked, "You said the place was haunted, right?"

Cooper frowned, folded his arms across his chest and watched her. He'd been so sure that either Sam or Mike was at the bottom of this night's little spookfest. Hadn't they all enjoyed scaring the crap out of each other when they were kids? And what better thing to do to a horror writer then give him his very own personal ghost?

But if his cousin and friend were behind it, where was the proof? Of course, he'd have to give the room a thorough going over in the morning, but at the moment, he couldn't figure out how that voice was pumped through the whole damn house and then cut off in an instant.

"Just because I didn't find Mike hiding in here," Cooper said, "doesn't mean there's a ghost in the house."

"Uh-huh."

She didn't look convinced. As she wandered around the room, studying the spines of the worn leather books tucked into a bookcase, Cooper studied her. He hadn't noticed before—now, he couldn't imagine why not—but, Kara's sleep ruffled dark brown hair hung in unruly waves to her shoulders. The summery, pale green silk nightgown she wore had thin straps and dipped low across her breasts before skimming a surprisingly taut, tempting body and ending just beneath the curve of her behind. Her legs were bare and her toenails were painted a brilliant scarlet.

Heat slammed into him and Cooper whooshed out a breath in reaction. His gaze locked on her as she stooped down to inspect a book on a lower shelf and he caught himself hoping she'd simply bend over.

Man.

Where the hell had that come from?

In the five years he'd known and worked with Kara Sloane, Cooper could honestly say he'd never once been slapped with the notion of tossing her over his shoulder and throwing her onto the nearest bed.

Now, it was the only thought in his fevered mind.

"Are you okay?"

"Hmm?" He shook his head and scowled even more fiercely when he found her watching him curiously. Great. Could she tell he'd been wondering if she was wearing anything underneath that nightgown? "Of course I'm okay. Why wouldn't I be?"

"No reason," she said, in a tone that clearly contradicted her words, "you were just...looking at me weird."

He forced a laugh that grated his throat and sounded overly loud. "No I wasn't."

"Yeah, you were."

Smooth, Cooper. Really smooth. He stabbed both hands through his hair and gave it a tug while he was at it. Anything to distract him from the thoughts that were now racing uncontrollably through his brain. Kara in that nightgown. Kara *out* of that nightgown. Geez.

"Didn't mean to," he said with a careless shrug, "it's just, you look...different."

"*Different?*" She folded her arms beneath her breasts, thereby pushing them high enough to peek over the top of that low scooped neck.

Cooper felt what was left of the blood in his brain rush southward.

"Never mind," he muttered and turned to check all the windows, making sure the latches were closed. *Keep busy. Don't think. Don't…*

"Different how?"

He glanced at her over his shoulder and immediately turned back around. She was suddenly looking *way* too good. And his own body was starting to get *very* appreciative. "Leave it alone, will ya?"

"Nope. *Different how?*" Amusement colored her voice and Cooper winced.

Sighing, he admitted stiffly, "The nightgown."

She chuckled and he turned to look at her, keeping his gaze locked with hers, for his own peace of mind.

"My nightgown? Honestly, Cooper," she said, skimming her hands along the silky fabric barely covering her. "It's not like I'm wearing black lace."

Mmm. A picture burst into life in his mind and he enjoyed it far too much.

"Besides," she added, "I was sleeping. What? Did you really think I wore high heels to bed?"

Yet *another* interesting image filled his brain and left him inwardly groaning. Seriously. Between the weird noises and the new visuals of Kara, he was probably going to be awake all night.

He blew out a long breath and determinedly shifted the subject away from Kara's nightgown. "We're not going to figure out what's happening tonight and I'm too tired—" translation, *horny*, "—to talk about this anymore. Let's just forget about it and go back to sleep."

The smile slid off her face as her gaze swept the quiet, empty room. "You think it'll start up again?"

"I sincerely hope not," he muttered and led the way out of the room. He heard her walking behind him, the soft fall of her small bare feet against the floorboards. At the foot of the stairs, he started taking them two at a time. No way was he going to climb those stairs behind Kara.

The view would kill him.

The next day, as Kara sat beside Cooper in his enormous SUV, she was still enjoying the sensation of having finally won his attention. However briefly it had lasted. She'd seen his face the night before. Watched him watch her and though she knew nothing would come of it, she'd relished the few moments when he'd looked at her and really seen her.

Of course it wouldn't happen again.

Without the quiet intimacy of a shadow filled house in the middle of the night, everything was back to normal. Cooper, kind but distracted, Kara, wishing things were different.

He'd avoided her all morning. When he came down for coffee, he'd simply nodded at her, then filled a thermal jug so he wouldn't have to face her again. She'd heard his fingers flying across the keyboard, but except for that constant sound, whispering in the background, she might as well have been alone in the house. Well, just she and whoever had done all the crying the night before.

And now, though he was sitting less than a foot away from her, he still wasn't talking. Instead, he kept his gaze locked on the road and determinedly away from her.

She simply could not go on like this forever.

She wanted a man to love her. She wanted children before she was old enough to be a grandmother.

Slanting a look at him now as he steered his car into the driveway of his grandfather's ranch, she watched as his features tightened. His dark eyes narrowed and a muscle in his jaw twitched as if he were gritting his teeth.

What was it? Why was he so reluctant to be here? To see an old man she knew he loved?

And why wouldn't he tell her?

The SUV sailed smoothly over the rutted road with hardly a bump to the occupants. Cooper drove around behind the edge of the house and parked the car under the shade of a giant tree that looked as though it had been there since the beginning of time.

Wind scuttled across the open yard, lifting dust and tossing it into tiny tornadoes while it fluttered the laundry dancing on the clothesline. Ancient shade trees lined the property, swaying in that same wind, sliding in from the nearby ocean.

There was a small guesthouse at the edge of the yard and even from a distance, Kara could see the sunlight glinting off shining window panes. Pansies in shades of deep purple and blue tumbled from a window box near the tidy front porch and a grapevine wreath with a tiny Welcome sign attached hung on the door.

About a hundred yards from the main house, a barn stood proudly, its double doors standing open, inviting visitors into the cool, shadowy interior.

But the house itself caught Kara's attention. It was old and proud and wide. It sprawled across the land like a lazy old man stretched out for a nap. Stone pillars guarded the four corners of the house and bright red and white geraniums crowded the outside edges of the structure. It looked, Kara thought, permanent. Cozy.

Apparently though, it looked like something else entirely to Cooper. Shutting off the engine, he pulled the keys from the car and jangled them in his palm for a second or two.

They'd been invited to his grandfather's house for lunch, but never had a man looked less willing to go inside a relative's home.

Finally, Kara asked, "Are you okay?"

"Fine," he said shortly. "Why?"

"I don't know," she answered, "because there's enough tension rolling off of you right now to make diamonds out of charcoal?"

He sighed and leaned back, unbuckling his seat belt but making no move to get out of the car. Turning his head, he looked at her for the first time that morning. In his eyes, Kara saw a tumult of emotions that appeared and disappeared so quickly, she couldn't identify them all.

And for the first time since she'd known him, she was worried about Cooper. There was something here. Something that was tearing at him.

"It's not something I want to talk about."

Intrigued, and a little unsettled, Kara unsnapped her own seat belt and shifted in her seat to look at him. "But if there's something I should know before I meet your family…"

He smiled briefly, the slightest curve of his lips and then it was gone again. "Don't worry," he said, opening the car door. "They don't want to talk about it, either."

Four

Cooper watched his cousin Sam wink at his new fiancée Maggie and felt a twinge of something suspiciously like envy. Which didn't really make any sense at all, because he'd never wanted the whole "wife and family" thing anyway. And yet...

Lunch had been awkward, despite Jeremiah's repeated attempts to keep everyone talking, laughing. Cooper had been uneasy from the moment he'd stepped into his grandfather's house. For some insane reason, he'd kept waiting for a sixteen-year-old Mac to come running into the room—and when he didn't, the pain roared through Cooper, as hot and fresh as it had been fifteen years before.

Now that he was outside, sitting in a lawn chair at the back of the house, Cooper at least felt as though he could breathe again. But the memories here were just as thick. Still watching Sam, in the chair beside him, he blurted suddenly, "How can you do it?"

"Do what?" Sam reluctantly tore his gaze from Maggie, hanging damp sheets on the clothesline.

"Be here," Cooper said, clutching his beer bottle in one tight fist and sweeping his arm out to encompass the ranch. "*Live* here."

The smile in Sam's dark eyes dimmed a bit as he took a sip of his own beer before answering. "Wasn't easy at first," he admitted. "So many memories."

"Exactly." Cooper sighed with relief. Good to know he wasn't the only one wrestling with the images of the past. "Just sitting here, I can see us all clearly, playing over the line."

Sam smiled sadly as he, too, thought about those days. "You remember when Mac hit the home run through Gran's kitchen window?"

Cooper chuckled. "And it landed in her pot of spaghetti sauce? Who could forget?" The memories took hold of his throat and squeezed. To ease the tension, he added, "By the way, you should have had that ball."

"Right. It was miles out of my reach."

"Too lazy to jump for it," Cooper said, and took another sip of cold, frothy beer.

"Mac always could hit a ball like a bullet."

"Yeah." The beer suddenly tasted flat, bitter. "Damn it, Sam, I keep expecting to see him. Hear him."

"I did, too, at first," Sam said softly. "Then I realized Mac's gone. He's not here, Cooper. He's not hanging around trying to make us all feel bad about what happened."

"He doesn't have to," Cooper muttered and stood up, because he couldn't sit still another minute. Knots formed in his guts, his throat tightened and his mouth was suddenly dry. "God. Every day of my life I remember. And I feel bad. Guilty."

Sam looked up at him, understanding shining in his calm brown eyes. "There's no reason to."

"No reason? Mac *died*." Cooper kicked at the dirt and watched pebbles skitter. "While we stood there like morons, Mac *died*."

"We were kids, too," Sam reminded him and pushed his hair out of his eyes, when the wind blew it across his face.

"Yeah," Cooper said stiffly, "but we didn't die at sixteen."

And just like that, he was back there. On that long-ago summer day.

Playing one of their favorite games, the four cousins had lined up along the ridge above the ranch lake. One at a time, they ran and jumped in, while the guys on the bank timed them. You got points, not only for how far out you could jump, but for how long you stayed underwater.

Jake always won.

Mac though, had been determined to be the winner this time. He had outjumped Jake by a mile and Jake was seriously pissed. But to win, Mac had to stay underwater longer than he had, too.

Sam had the stopwatch and Cooper and Jake stood on either side of him while he timed Mac's turn. Jake got madder by the second, sure his best time was going to be beaten. Cooper hooted with glee that one of them had finally taken Jake down.

When Mac was underwater two minutes though, Sam started worrying. Wanted to go in after him. Cooper urged him to give Mac a few more seconds. Make sure Jake lost for a change.

And God, even now, Cooper could feel the wind in his face, the sun on his back. He heard Jake's muttered cursing and the note of worry in Sam's voice. Most of all though, he heard himself saying, "Don't be such an old woman, Sam. Mac's fine. He'll come up in a second."

Except he never did.

The three of them had—at last—jumped into the icy water after Mac and they'd found him. On the bottom of the lake. They'd dragged him out, tried mouth-to-mouth, but Mac was gone. The doctor said later he'd broken his neck in the fall and unconscious, had drowned.

And nothing since that day had ever been right again.

Cooper had avoided this ranch like the plague

ever since. Hell, they all had. Punishing themselves and each other. Now he was here again and damn it, he could hardly draw a breath without strangling on it.

Sam stood up and took a white-knuckled grip on his beer bottle. "Do you really think you have to remind me of what happened? Do you honestly believe that Mac's death hasn't chased me through the years as hard as it's chased you?"

In the cool shade of the old oak where they'd once played on a tire swing, Cooper stared at his cousin and saw the same torment in his eyes that he faced every morning in the mirror.

"No." He shook his head. "No, I don't. It's just…" he looked around, at the yard, the house, the barn, and felt the memories pulling at him as strong as a riptide. "I don't understand how you got past it. How you can live here and not choke on every breath?"

"I couldn't at first. Hell, I had my plans all laid out." He laughed shortly and took another drink of beer. "I was going to stay the summer, since Jeremiah had tricked me into giving my word—"

Cooper nodded wryly, since he, too, was caught by the same wily old man.

"—then," Sam continued, "I was going to hit the road again. Get as far from Coleville and the memories of Mac that I could."

"So what happened?" Cooper asked, then held up one hand. "Never mind. I know what happened."

He shot a glance at Maggie, now in a desperate tug-of-war with a golden retriever puppy over a wet pillowcase. "I like her, by the way."

Sam grinned. "Thanks. Me, too." His smile faded as he added, "It wasn't just falling in love with Maggie though. It was finding a way to make peace with Mac." His gaze locked on the woman he loved as she laughed, dropped to the ground and gathered the tiny dog to her chest. "Maggie helped me do that. Helped me see that Mac wouldn't want us torturing ourselves forever."

Cooper didn't know if he agreed with that or not, but he was willing to admit that the belief had certainly helped Sam. "Special woman."

"Beyond special," Sam said quietly. "She's everything."

Envy swept through Cooper again and was just as quickly brushed aside. After all, he wasn't interested in loving anybody. Too much risk came with love. Too high a chance at pain. And he'd already had enough pain to last a lifetime.

No. The only romance he was interested in, was the kind he wrote about. The kind he gave whatever hero and heroine he was dealing with in his latest book. And when he wrote their "happily ever after," his readers didn't know or care if he believed in it or not.

But unthinkingly, his gaze drifted to the edge of the field, where Kara walked with Jeremiah.

* * *

"It's good to have Cooper back home," Jeremiah said as he followed Kara's gaze to the two men standing beneath the oak tree at the far end of the yard.

"I can't believe he stayed away so long."

"They all had reason," he said on a sigh. "Or so they thought. Which amounts to the same thing, really."

Kara turned her gaze on the older man. His skin was leathery from a lifetime spent outdoors. Only a fringe of gray hair remained on his head, but his dark eyes, so much like Cooper's, sparkled with intensity.

She liked him a lot. Just as she liked Sam and Maggie. Kara had spent most of the afternoon trying not to be jealous of the other woman as she talked excitedly about her wedding plans and her pregnancy. In just a few weeks, Sam and Maggie would be getting married and moving into the main ranch house together.

Sam was taking over the local doctor's practice and Maggie was finishing school and…Kara's life felt emptier with every word Maggie had spoken. Terrible, she thought, immediately ashamed of herself. She should be happy for them. And she was. They seemed like perfectly nice people. But wasn't it only natural that she'd be just a little bit sorry for herself?

What did she have to show for her life?

A nicely balanced checkbook? A good apartment

and a tidy savings account? She was nearly thirty and beyond her mother, who made a point of calling at least once a week to remind her that she wasn't getting any younger, Kara had no one to care about. Or to care about her.

Something was definitely wrong with this picture.

She walked alongside Jeremiah, but only half listened as he talked about the ranch and what he and Sam were planning for it. Instead, her brain raced and though she didn't much like the decisions it was reaching, she had to admit that they were the right ones.

She'd put off quitting when she knew Cooper was having a hard time getting his latest book going. But she wasn't doing herself any favors by stretching this out. Better to just suck it up and make the move.

Her gaze shot to Cooper again, standing in the shade, laughing at something Sam had just said. And while her heart broke a little, she filled her mind with these pictures of him. Etched them into her brain so that years from now, she'd always be able to see him as he was today.

Then mentally, she started packing.

"Man, you're a great cook," Cooper said, leaning back in his chair at the kitchen table and grinning at Kara.

"Thanks, but steaks? They don't exactly require gourmet training."

"I've burned enough of 'em in my time to know that it takes a knack."

Kara shook her head. "Cooper, you are the only human being I know who could actually burn water."

"Sad, but true," he admitted and didn't look the least bit ashamed of himself. "I don't know what I'd do without you, Kara," he said and stood up to carry both plates to the sink. "Seriously," he went on when she didn't say anything, "you're the best."

"That's nice Cooper, but—"

He set the plates into the sink with a clatter. "You know though, you don't have to cook while we're here. You could hire someone locally to come in and do the cooking and cleaning."

All she had to do now was work up the nerve to tell him he was going to need not only a cook and a maid—but a new assistant. "Now that you mention it—"

A knock on the back door interrupted Kara and Cooper paused in clearing the table to go and open it. His grandfather stood on the porch, holding a foil covered plate.

Cooper grinned at the older man. "Didn't we just see you a few hours ago?"

"Sure did," Jeremiah said and pushed past his grandson without waiting for an invitation. Right on his heels came the puppy, its claws scrambling for traction on the old wood floor. It shot across the room, then put on the brakes and slid into the underside of the cabinet.

Jeremiah chuckled. "Told Maggie I'd take Sheba there for a walk and she loaded me down with a plate of her chocolate chip cookies to bring you two."

"Cookies? Always welcome," Cooper said, already reaching for the plate. "Oh, you can come in too, Jeremiah."

The older man laughed and stepped inside, taking a seat at the kitchen table. He reached out to pat Kara's hand and whispered, "Don't suppose you could spare an old man a cup of coffee? Maggie's got me drinking that decaffeinated stuff at night. Like to kill me."

"You bet," Kara said, pathetically grateful for the interruption and the chance to stall a few more minutes. *Why* couldn't she tell Cooper she was quitting? *Why* couldn't she bring herself to leave him? It was the right thing to do and she knew it. So why was it so hard?

In a few seconds, Cooper had the rest of the table cleared and Kara poured three cups of coffee.

The puppy lay under the table, contentedly chewing on the laces of Cooper's sneakers.

"So," Jeremiah said after a hearty sigh with his first sip of coffee, "you two see any ghosts yet?"

Cooper laughed and took a cookie for himself. "Haven't seen anything, but did hear something last night. Crying."

"More like sobbing," Kara corrected and cradled her own cup of coffee between her palms as if to ward off a chill she knew was coming.

"Yeah?"

Cooper laughed at his grandfather's eager expression. "Don't get excited. It's more likely somebody's playing a trick on us than it is for there to be a ghost in this house."

"Hell, boy," Jeremiah scoffed, "you write scary stories for a living and you don't believe in ghosts?"

Cooper's expression hardened. "Not the kind who make noises in old houses."

Kara watched as Cooper, in a heartbeat, distanced himself, even though he hadn't budged from his chair. It was as if he'd taken an emotional step back and she was clueless about what had caused it. But as she always did, she stepped in to help him out.

"Do you know anything about this house?" Kara asked, dissolving the taut silence and shifting his grandfather's attention from Cooper to her.

The older man sighed heavily, then gave her a small smile, as if to say he knew she was trying to smooth things over and he appreciated it. He gave her hand another friendly pat, took a sip of his coffee and said, "Everyone around here knows the story of this old house."

Cooper didn't say a word, so Kara urged, "Tell me."

Jeremiah nodded. "It was back during the gold rush era," he said, his deep voice slipping into storytelling mode as if he were born to it.

As he painted a vivid picture of the times, Kara

realized that Cooper had inherited his gift with words from his grandfather.

"Weren't many ranches here then. Most of the land was still owned by Spanish dons who weren't real happy about the yankees streaming into California by the boatload." He looked around the kitchen, took a sip of coffee and continued. "This house was built by one of the first to find gold. Bought the land from the local don, built this place and brought his wife out from back east. They had one daughter and when he died, he left the house to her—who, as young women will, fell in love with a scoundrel of a man."

"Oh, this doesn't have a happy ending, does it?" Kara murmured.

"If it did, it wouldn't be a ghost story, now would it?" Cooper took a drink of coffee and leaned back in his chair, his gaze fixed on his grandfather, sitting across from him.

Jeremiah ignored him and focused instead on Kara. "Oh, the young man loved her, but he was ambitious. He wanted to make his fortune more than he wanted to settle down. He left for the gold fields, promising to come back for her."

"He didn't?" Kara's heart hurt for the long-dead woman.

"She waited here for him," Jeremiah said, "for two long, lonely years. Desolate, she stood at the parlor window, crying for her lost love while she watched the road, hoping for a sign of him."

Pain swelled inside Kara and she could almost feel that poor woman's misery shivering in the air around her. Outside, the wind kicked up, spattering the window panes with dust and pebbles. A frigid puff of air scuttled through the kitchen and beneath the table, little Sheba growled, low in her throat.

"She died," Jeremiah said softly, almost reverently, "of a broken heart."

Cooper snorted.

Kara glared at him.

Jeremiah ignored him completely. "Without the love of her life, she simply couldn't go on."

Kara felt, rather than heard, a sigh.

"Every tenant since then never stays long in this place. It's not a happy house. Shame, really," Jeremiah said.

"What happened to her young man?"

The older man looked at her. "He finally did come for her, a few weeks after she died. But he was too late."

A shutter slapped against the side of the house and Kara jumped, startled.

Cooper laughed. "God, Kara, you should see your face. Jeremiah really got you going on that story, didn't he?"

His grandfather scowled at him, gray brows beetling. "Boy," he growled, sounding a lot like the puppy still restive beneath the table, "don't you think love is worth dying for?"

Cooper shook his head, got up and went for the coffeepot over on the counter. He refilled everyone's cup, then returned the pot before answering. "Jeremiah, the moral to that story is simple. Love isn't worth it."

"You got it all wrong, Coop," his grandfather said with a slow shake of his head. "Love is the only worthwhile thing there is."

Kara's heart sunk as she listened to the two men argue over the value of love. Emptiness opened up inside her and she felt a cold that went down deep into her bones. Her instincts had been right. Cooper would never love her. Never see her as anything more than an uber-efficient assistant and a pretty good cook.

It didn't matter how long she put off her decision, nothing was going to change. So what was the point of hanging around and torturing herself?

None.

An hour later, Jeremiah and the puppy were gone and the two of them were alone in the kitchen again. Working together, Kara dried the dishes as Cooper washed them. The silence was companionable, the task ordinary, and she knew there would never be a better time to say what she had to say.

"Cooper?"

"Yeah?" He turned to hand her another plate.

"I quit."

Five

"Very funny." Cooper gave her the plate and chuckling, turned back to the dirty dishes. "But don't joke about stuff like that."

"I'm not joking, Cooper."

"You'd better be, because you can't quit."

"Yes, I can. I just did. Consider this my two weeks' notice."

Cooper shut off the water and turned to face her. Her dark brown hair was pulled back from her face and held by one of those clip things that opened like an alligator's jaws. In the overhead light, her big green eyes were shadowed as she looked at him, and there wasn't so much as a hint of a smile on her face.

A solitary thread of worry slithered through him.

"Is this about the ghost thing? And the crying last night? Because if it is, don't worry about it—I swear it's just somebody playing a dumb joke."

"It's not about the crying, or the ghost story. It's about us."

Now he was really confused. "*Us?* What about us?"

She tossed the yellow-and-white striped dish-towel onto the counter, then folded her arms under her breasts, tipped her head to one side and glared at him. "You don't get it at all, do you?"

"Apparently not."

"So typical."

"What'd I do?"

She unfolded her arms, slapped her hands on her hips and said, "Nothing. Ever. Just nothing." Before he could speak, she held up one hand for silence, took a deep breath and said shortly, "Never mind. Let's just say that I'm quitting because we can't keep going on like this."

"Like what?" Why did he suddenly feel like he was speaking Greek in a Chinese restaurant?

"Like we are, Cooper."

"What's wrong with it?" And why was she suddenly not making any sense to him at all?

"It's like we're married, Cooper. Only without any of the good stuff. Like sex."

Instantly, the memory of her in that pretty silk nightie popped into his brain and set fire to a com-

pletely different part of his anatomy. He had to admit that up until the night before, he'd never really thought about Kara and sex in the same sentence. But now, he wasn't so sure. "You want us to have sex?"

Kara blew out a frustrated breath, reached up and tugged the clip from her hair then shook her head and rubbed at the spot where it had been. All of that thick, dark brown hair flew about her face in soft waves and made Cooper want to reach out and comb his fingers through it.

Hey, maybe sex was a good idea.

"Of course I want sex. But I want more than that, too." Sighing, she said, "I want a husband. Kids. A home. I've been working for you for five years and all I've got to show for it is a nice savings account and a few new recipes."

"So you've been miserable working for me? Is that it?"

"No, that's not it at all. Just the opposite, in fact," she said irritably. "I got so comfortable that I didn't notice that I wasn't getting anywhere."

"What's so bad about comfortable?" he demanded, suddenly realizing that she might just be serious about quitting. Her eyes shone with regret, but there was no going back with Kara. He knew that already. Once she'd made up her mind about something, that was it.

And the thought of losing Kara hit him hard.

"Nothing," she said, "if that's all you're looking

for, then comfortable is great. But it's not enough for me. Not anymore."

"Hold on," he countered, feeling his heart jolt in his chest. "This is all coming out of the blue for me, Kara. As far as I knew, everything between us was working great."

"Well sure," she snapped, throwing both hands high and letting them slap to her sides again. "Why wouldn't it be great from your point of view? I take care of everything for you. I pay your bills, talk to your editors, handle your publicity, pick up your dry cleaning…you can't even make a decent pot of coffee on your own."

"Hey!" Insulted, and not just because most of what she said was true, Cooper stared at her like he'd never seen her before. In the five years they'd been together, Kara had always been calm, cool, reasonable. This Kara had sparks flying from her eyes.

Which he was just twisted enough to actually think sexy.

"It's not entirely your fault," she conceded. "God knows, I worked hard at making myself indispensable."

"Did a good job of it, too." Cooper tried a smile out on her and felt a quick stab of disappointment when it didn't warm her eyes. "How about a raise? Would that make you feel differently?"

"No!" Frustration ringing in her voice, she said loudly, "It's not about the money, Cooper. It never was."

He reached for her, but she took a quick half step back. "Kara, you can't quit. I need you too much."

"That's exactly why I have to go!" She inhaled sharply, deeply and blew the air out again in a rush. "Don't you get it? If I keep acting like your wife, I'll never get to really *be* one."

Those sparks in her eyes were flashing like warning lights at the edge of a cliff. And Cooper was bright enough to back off fast. "You're tired. Why don't you sleep on it and we can talk about this in the morning when you're calmer?"

"Grrrrrr…" Kara tugged at her hair again and shouted, "I'm perfectly calm."

"Yeah," he assured her, keeping a wary distance between them. "I can see that."

"Honestly Cooper, you can be the most infuriating man…" She turned on her heel, stomped across the kitchen and marched into the living room. Just before she turned for the stairs, she stopped dead, turned her head and fried him with a look. "Just so you know. I'm not going to change my mind. I *am* quitting."

Then she stomped up the stairs, managing to sound like an invading army, which just proved to Cooper that she was too upset to be making major decisions. He walked to the doorway and winced when she slammed her bedroom door. She'd feel differently in the morning.

He could talk his way around Kara.

She'd see reason.

So why, he wondered, was he suddenly so worried?

When the sobbing started in the middle of the night, Kara was already awake. The muffled crying seemed to weep from the walls, surrounding her in a sea of pain that was strong enough to bridge the centuries. Cold crept through the bedroom and sighed around Kara.

Despite what Cooper might like to think, this was no joke. And Kara knew she should be terrified. Should be running screaming from the old house, putting as much distance between her and the ghost as she possibly could. But she didn't feel *fear.* She felt…compassion.

Sitting up in bed, she rubbed her bare arms as tears welled up in her eyes. Empathy for the long-dead woman filled her and Kara realized that she and the ghost had a lot in common.

Okay, not *a lot.*

After all, Kara was still alive.

But the ghost had waited for love until it was too late—Kara had waited, too, hoping that Cooper would see how good they could be together. The sobbing woman had allowed the longing for love to kill her. Kara wouldn't make the same mistake.

"I'm so sorry," she whispered, glancing around the shadow-filled room as tears rolled unheeded down her cheeks. "I'm sorry for both of us."

* * *

Cooper, wide awake and trying to work, jolted as the sobbing began. Already, he was on edge since he hadn't been able to write a single coherent sentence since Kara had told him she quit. All he could think about was her. And how in the hell he could convince her to change that stubborn mind of hers.

The crying was just what he needed as a distraction. He jumped up and headed for his bedroom door. Yanking it open, he stepped into the hall and paused, waiting for Kara to appear as she had the night before. In his mind, he saw her again, hair tumbled about her face, that silky nightgown and all of her bare, tanned skin. But her door didn't open. Did she not hear the crying? Unlikely. She was simply trying to avoid him. That simple truth jabbed at him and he scowled at her closed door. Damn it, how could she quit? How could she walk away from him?

Cooper muttered darkly, then headed down the hall alone, following the crying as it seemed to float through the house. He didn't care what Jeremiah said, Cooper didn't believe in ghosts and he was going to find the damn joker behind these nightly visits.

He didn't bother with turning on the lights, finding his way with no problem, since moonlight filtered through the windows. The wood floor cool beneath his bare feet, Cooper moved soundlessly through the house, determined to put an end to this ghost stuff once and for all.

Only last night, he thought, he and Kara had been in this together. And a part of him missed having her with him. Missed the feel of her hand in his as they slipped through the shadows. Missed the sense of…teamwork, they'd always shared.

Damn. How could she *quit?*

Pushing that furious thought out of his head, he concentrated instead on the mournful cries reverberating around him. The night before, when Kara had been with him, the sobs had led them to the parlor. Tonight, the terrible crying took him to the front door.

Smirking to himself, he muttered, "Trick me into opening the front door? Bet Mike Haney's crouched on the porch laughing himself sick over this."

Grabbing the brass doorknob, Cooper threw the door open, expecting to come face-to-face with some practical joker.

But no one was there.

He took a step forward and stopped dead.

A wall of icy cold blocked the doorway.

Cooper sucked in air like a drowning man. His heartbeat jumped into a frantic beat that felt as though it was going to burst through his chest. Chills snaked along his spine. His throat squeezed shut and his mouth went dry.

The cold was immovable. Solid. As if it had always been there.

Around him, the sobs grew harsher, louder, more desperate.

Moonlight spilled onto the lawn, spearing through the trees, laying down lacy patterns that dipped and swayed in the wind.

"Mike Haney's not behind *this*," he whispered, scrubbing one hand across his face as his heartbeat slowly returned to normal.

This was no joke. The wall of cold was too real to be ignored or explained. He watched as his breath formed tiny clouds of mist in front of his face. Nope. No joke. This was yet another ghost.

The too late lover?

The cold pressed forward, trying to enter. Trying to get into the house, even if it had to go through Cooper. He felt the pressure against his chest as if someone were pushing him. The small hairs at the back of his neck stood straight up as the sobbing in the house became a moaning wail and then nearly a shriek of desperation fueled by fury.

It was one thing to *write* about ghosts. It was totally another to actually *live* with one.

"Is that what this is all about?" he asked, not really expecting an answer. "She's been waiting for you and you're finally trying to get into the house?"

His breath misted. Chills raced up and down his spine, but he fought off the instinct to close the door. If he could solve this ghost problem, maybe the long-dead lady would stop crying in the night. So instead, he opened it wider, stood back and waved one arm in silent invitation. "Come on then. Come find your woman and apologize or whatever it is you're trying to do and—"

The door was snatched free of his grip and slammed closed with a force that rattled the window panes.

Cooper blew out a breath and looked around the suddenly silent room. The cold was locked outside, the crying ghost was quiet—and apparently pissed off—and he was just as confused as ever. According to Jeremiah, this ghost had been waiting for her lover for a hundred and fifty years. Now that he's come she won't let him in?

Women.

"He's the most stubborn man on the face of the planet," Kara said grimly and snapped a green bean neatly in half.

"Believe me," Maggie said with a quiet smile. "I totally understand."

"No, you couldn't possibly." Kara pushed up from the table set under the oak tree in the backyard of Cooper's grandfather's ranch. She'd come to talk to Maggie, Sam's fiancée, because frankly, she was going a little stir crazy.

The last few days had crawled past.

Cooper wouldn't talk to her. Wouldn't even *acknowledge* the fact that she'd quit her job. Whenever she tried to talk to him about arranging for a temp until he could find someone permanent, he only gave her a patient smile. He wasn't listening. Wasn't taking her seriously.

Heck, she was going to have to actually leave to convince him she meant business.

"Trust me," Maggie said as she leaned back in her chair and stretched her legs out in front of her. "I think stubborn is a Lonergan family trait."

Kara shook her hair back out of her face as a quick wind kicked up out of nowhere, carrying on it the scent of the sea. She took a deep breath, blew it out and made a concentrated effort to calm herself.

It didn't work.

Lifting one hand, she rubbed her aching eyes. The headache that had been creeping up on her for hours was now in full bloom and every muscle in her body hurt. It was lack of sleep, she knew. Had to be.

The ghost had been in fine voice the last three nights. And every night, Kara sat in her room alone, listening to a long-dead woman cry for her lost love. It was as if the ghost were trying to tell Kara something. Warn her. *Don't let this happen to you,* she seemed to be saying.

"Are you okay?"

Turning around to look at the other woman, Kara swallowed hard, forced a smile she didn't feel and said, "Yes. I'm fine. Just…tired."

"The ghost?"

Kara smiled again. "You don't have any trouble believing?"

"No." Maggie stood up and walked to Kara's side. Dappled shade from the tree swept across her face in a lacy pattern. "Love's the strongest emotion there is. Why shouldn't it be able to linger long after we've gone?"

"I feel so bad for her," Kara said, "it's not just hearing her. I can feel her pain. Her sorrow is so profound, so all encompassing that—" What? That she was beginning to think the ghost was trying to communicate with her? Kara shook her head at her own crazy thoughts and chuckled. "Though I could really use some sleep."

"You sure you're only tired?" Maggie's dark gaze fixed on her with concern. "You sort of look feverish. I could take you into town, have Sam give you a checkup."

Kara's stomach turned and she sucked in a gulp of air to steady it. She didn't want to see a doctor. She just wanted to go. To leave Coleville and Cooper behind so she could start the big plan of getting over him.

"Honest. I'm fine." She tried another smile and added, "I actually came over here to ask you for a favor, Maggie."

"Sure, what is it?"

"I told you that Cooper won't admit that I quit my job?"

"Uh-huh."

"Well, I've decided the only way to prove it to him is to just go."

"You're leaving?"

"I have to," she said firmly, not really sure if she was trying to convince Maggie, or herself. But did it matter? "I wanted to give him two weeks' notice, but he's not listening to me, so what's the point? Anyway, until I can arrange for a temporary assistant for him, Cooper's going to be on his own—and he'll probably starve if someone doesn't remind him to eat occasionally."

"You're worried about him."

"Only natural," Kara said, trying to shrug off Maggie's words. "I've been running his world for five years. Without me, he's going to be lost." Just as she would be without him. "So I was wondering if you'd mind checking up on him once in awhile. You know, just…make sure he goes grocery shopping for more than frozen burritos?"

Maggie watched her for several long seconds and Kara wanted to squirm under the woman's steady regard. Finally though, Maggie said, "I'll be happy to—if you answer one question for me."

Kara sighed. "What is it?"

"Why don't you tell Cooper that you're in love with him?"

Surprised, Kara thought briefly about denying the truth. Then, looking into Maggie's understanding gaze, she figured, why bother? Rubbing at her forehead again in an attempt to quiet the pounding just behind her eyes, she said softly, "Because he doesn't want to know."

"But loving him, can you really walk away?" Maggie asked, reaching out to lay one hand on Kara's forearm.

"I have to," she said, wishing things were different. "While I still can."

Cooper was waiting for her.

Twilight filled the kitchen. Candles on the old table stood straight and tall, their flames dipping and swaying in the breeze. From the living room came the quiet, smooth sound of old jazz playing on the stereo. Everything was set. He had dinner made— even he could make pasta—and a bottle of wine open and breathing on the table.

Over the last few days, he'd done a lot of thinking— mostly because he hadn't been able to do anything else. He couldn't concentrate enough to write and couldn't talk to Kara without her talking about leaving him. This afternoon, he'd decided on a plan of action.

She walked inside, closed the door, then turned to face him.

Cooper looked her over, head to toe. Her dark brown hair had been tossed by the wind and her green eyes glittered in the reflected sunlight. She wore denim shorts, a pale yellow tank top and white sandals. She looked...*beautiful.*

Why had he never really noticed before? When had he become the kind of man who didn't pay attention to the people around him? Had he really become so secluded that he didn't even take notice of the woman who kept his entire life running on schedule?

"What's wrong?" she asked.

"What?"

"What's wrong, Cooper?"

"Nothing." He shook his head, told himself to quit with the self-analysis and get down to the plan. "Nothing's wrong."

"Good." She sniffed the air. "You *cooked?*"

"Contrary to popular belief, I'm not a complete moron."

"Pasta?" she asked, giving him a half smile.

"With chicken this time."

"Ah, innovation." She smiled a bit, then asked, "What's this about?"

He stepped up close and laid both hands on her shoulders. She looked up into his eyes and something inside Cooper clicked. He didn't know what the hell it was, but it was there and it was…important.

Don't think about it now, he told himself.

"What're you doing, Cooper?"

"I've been thinking."

She gave him a half smile. "I'll alert the media."

"Ha-ha." He pulled her closer and enjoyed the hell out of the look of surprise that flickered in her eyes. "I think I figured out what the problem is between us—"

She huffed out a breath. "You mean the problem where I quit and you don't believe me?"

"No, the other one."

"There's another one? This should be good."

"I think so."

"Okay, tell me," she said, squirming a little in an attempt to either get closer or move away—he wasn't entirely sure which.

"It's unrelieved sexual tension, Kara," he murmured, his gaze moving over her face before settling briefly on her mouth, her full bottom lip and that top lip that she always chewed on when she was worried about something.

Like she was doing now.

He smiled. "Why don't you let me chew on that lip for you?"

She went perfectly still and blinked up at him. "Are you *serious?*"

He pulled her hips tight against him so she could feel just how serious he really was. Her green eyes went wide and she huffed in a quick breath. His gaze dropped to the swell of her breasts, barely visible over the edge of her tank top.

A rush of need, much stronger, hotter, deeper than he'd expected, pumped through him and he drew her even closer, dipping his head to hers. She fit perfectly against him and he wondered why he'd never noticed that, either. And wondered why the hell it had taken him so long to come up with this plan.

She wanted him, he could see it in her eyes. He wanted her too. So what could be simpler than having each other? And once they'd had sex, she'd quit talking about leaving and things could go back to normal.

Brilliant.

"Well?" He lifted one hand to smooth her hair back from her face, then trailed his fingertips along the line of her jaw. She shivered and he smiled. "What do you say we get rid of all this tension?"

"I should warn you, I'm feeling pretty tense," she said, slowly sliding her hands up his chest until she could hook her arms around his neck. "This could take awhile."

He smiled and brushed his mouth against hers, once, twice, experiencing a surprising jolt of something hot and amazing each time. Then he met her gaze and promised, "Work, work, work."

Six

Kara's head was spinning, the headache behind her eyes was pounding and even her stomach wasn't very happy.

But all of that paled into nothingness the minute Cooper's mouth came down on hers. It was everything she'd been dreaming about...and so much more.

She sighed into him and gave herself up to the spiraling sensations unwinding inside her. He parted her lips with his tongue and she gasped at the sensual invasion. Their tongues met in an erotic dance that began smoothly, softly and quickly escalated into erupting need.

His arms came around her waist and he held her

tightly to him. So tightly, she felt his erection against her abdomen and her muscles quivered in anticipation. She'd wanted this, needed this for so very long, she could hardly believe it was finally happening.

Maybe she shouldn't give into the urges clamoring inside her. Maybe she should back up, step out of his arms, end this moment of fantasy. But the instant that thought raced through her brain, she greedily shut it down.

He slid one of his hands up her spine to cup the back of her head, fingers spearing through her hair. She moaned and leaned into him, taking more, giving more.

One corner of her brain screamed at her to be logical. Rational. To *think* for heaven's sake.

But she didn't want to think.

Not anymore.

Now, all she wanted, was to *feel*.

It didn't matter that she was a little woozy, that her headache had already begun slipping back up on her or that her stomach was none too steady.

If she had *bubonic plague*, she wouldn't have been too sick to have sex with Cooper. Not after she'd spent so much time over the last year imagining it, dreaming about it.

And oh boy, so far, it was *way* better than her dreams.

He tore his mouth from hers and dropped his head to the curve of her neck. His teeth and tongue slid over her flesh, sending ripples of something hot and delicious crashing through her.

His breath hot on her skin, his voice came muffled, strained. "Dinner can wait. Let's go upstairs."

Upstairs.

To a bed.

Oh, boy.

Once he stood back from her and took her hand to lead her from the kitchen, Kara's brain woke up with a new set of warning signals. *You're planning to leave. You've already quit. Is this really the right thing to do? Won't this only make it even harder for you to live without him?*

Probably, she acknowledged to the voice in her brain she was seriously starting to hate. But loving him, could she really not take the opportunity to have him for herself? If only for one night?

Not a chance.

He hit the stairs at a dead run and pulled her along in his wake. Kara stumbled a bit, but kept up, her much shorter legs having to move twice as fast. At the landing, he made a sharp right turn to his bedroom and when he'd pulled her in behind him, he slammed the door, enclosing them both in the big room.

A soft breeze rippled the curtains over the windows and the spicy scent of geraniums, mingled with the richer scent of summer roses, filled the air. She hardly noticed. All Kara knew was that Cooper was looking at her as she'd always wanted him to and nothing else mattered.

His dark eyes shone with a fire Kara had never seen before and it was all for her. It didn't matter that he didn't feel for her what she did for him. Not at the moment anyway. All that mattered now was this minute. This room. This man.

Cooper reached for the hem of her pale yellow tank top and in one smooth, practiced move, pulled it up and over her head before tossing it onto the floor.

"Gorgeous," he murmured and as Kara swayed unsteadily, he undid the front clasp of her bra and pushed it off her shoulders. His hands cupped her breasts and when his thumbs and forefingers tweaked her nipples, Kara heard a groan and only belatedly realized it had come from her.

Abruptly, his hands dropped to her waist. He scooped her up, tossed her onto the bed, then stood looking down at her with a smile. "Can't think why we never did this before, Kara."

"Me neither," she said, lifting both arms in welcome.

He grinned, reached down and pulled her denim shorts off, then paused a second or two to admire her white lace thong. "Man, if I'd known you were wearing something like that under your sensible clothes, I swear, it wouldn't have taken me five years to see it."

That nagging ache behind her eyes dulled a bit as she enjoyed the rush of his admiration.

She'd wanted this so long, hoped for it, dreamed

about it, that she wanted to remember every second. Every feeling. Every image. She wanted to imprint on her brain the sensation of Cooper's hands on her skin. She wanted to commit to memory the rough sound of his voice and the hot flash in his eyes.

Oh, she wanted it all.

For one night, she wanted it all.

Delicately, Cooper slid his fingers beneath the fragile elastic band of her thong and slowly, sensually, slid it off, caressing her thighs, her calves, as he went.

Kara chewed at her top lip and shifted impatiently on the quilt covered mattress. She watched him with hungry eyes as he quickly tore his own clothes off and then loomed over her on the bed.

He was simply amazing.

Body sculpted by the gods, his skin was bronzed, and her fingers itched to caress him. Reaching up, she smoothed her palms across his chest and over his shoulders and he sucked in a breath through gritted teeth at her touch. Then he dipped his head and took first one of her hardened nipples into his mouth and then the other.

Dizzying sensations rocked her and she held onto him as if it meant her life. Arching into him, she sighed breathlessly as his mouth worked her flesh into a tingling mass of nerves. His hands kept moving, sweeping up and down the length of her body, exploring, caressing, stroking. Wave after wave of desire crashed inside her, leaving Kara a whimpering mass of need.

Cooper shifted over her, raising his head just enough to kiss her, to take her mouth with a hunger that matched her own. His left hand dropped to her center and his fingertips slid across her damp folds, sliding back and forth with a sure, tender touch that spiked her desire into a frenzy.

Rocking her hips into his hand, she sighed into his mouth as he dipped his fingers deep within her. He used first one, then two fingers, to tantalize her, to push her to the very brink of climax—only to pull her back, demanding she stay hungry.

"Cooper," she whispered, tearing her mouth from his long enough to snatch at desperately needed air. "Cooper, I need…"

"So do I, Kara," he murmured, looking down into her eyes. His breath came in short, sharp gulps as he watched anticipation crest and recede on her features. "Let me watch you go over."

"No," she said, twisting her head from side to side, and smiling, though it cost her. "No, I want you. Inside me. Now. Now, Cooper."

"You're killing me, Kara," he said, dipping his head long enough to steal a kiss and taste her need.

She managed a short laugh, then lifted both hands to cup his face, even as his thumb brushed across a most sensitive nub at her center. "Oh, not yet. Definitely, not yet."

He swallowed hard and pulled away from her. Kara wanted to drag him back instantly, but she watched him reach over to the bedside table and yank open the drawer. He pulled a box of condoms out, then tore the package apart, grabbed one foil packet and quickly took care of the necessities of sex in the twenty-first century.

In seconds, he was back, touching her, stroking her, moving to position himself between her thighs. She moved with him, eager now to feel him inside her. To feel him take her deep and fast and hard.

While his fingers worked that one tender bud, he pushed his body into hers, and Kara gasped as she stretched to accommodate him. Her body awakened in a series of sparkling jolts of awareness. He rocked his hips against hers, pushing deeper with every thrust.

"Cooper..." She tipped her head back, into the mattress, closed her eyes and concentrated solely on the amazing sensations peaking inside her. She smiled, gasped and smiled again. "So...good. So...good."

"Let go, Kara," he said, pushing himself deeper into her body, shuddering with the force of his own all encompassing need. For the first time in his life, Cooper felt connected to the act of sex. To the wonder of it. To the incredible sense of expectation crowding at the edges of his brain.

He fought for control—despite knowing he wouldn't find it. He'd never before so lost himself in the moment. Never experienced this rush of tenderness and passion so completely commingled before.

And staring down into Kara's passion glazed green eyes, he knew that nothing would ever be simple between them again. Yet he couldn't bring himself to care.

He needed to hold her closer, deeper. To feel himself sliding so deeply within her that they would be locked together. Groaning, he leaned back, sitting on his heels and drawing Kara up with him, until she was on his lap, legs at either side of him, impaled on his body.

Her head fell back as she held onto his shoulders. His hands at her hips, he lifted her, moving her up and down on his body, drawing her up and down his length until neither of them could breathe. Until the passion was so thick in the room they were strangling on it.

He felt it when her climax rushed in. Knew the exact instant when she finally released the tension within and rode the first wave of completion.

Her body arched and she swiveled her hips on him, taking him even deeper. "Cooper! It's too much!"

"It's not," he told her brokenly. "It's not too much."

The air around them seemed to sigh, echoing softly in a tender whisper.

Their eyes met and locked and Kara's fingers dug into his shoulders as she groaned, trembling against him.

And holding her tightly to him, Cooper at last allowed himself to follow. Then when the tremors eased and the electricity arcing between them shimmered to an end, Cooper rested his forehead on her shoulder and tried to keep his thundering heart in his chest where it belonged.

Seconds ticked past, with the only sound in the room, their labored breathing. Then long before Cooper was willing to move, Kara shifted in his grasp and murmured, "Uh-oh."

"Hmm?" He tightened his grip on her and felt his body stir again. Sucking in air, even he was surprised by just how quickly he needed her again.

"Cooper," she whispered, "let me go."

"Not yet." He lifted his head, looked into her eyes and gave her a smile. "I kind of like you just where you are."

She shook her head, and inhaled sharply through her nose. "I need to—"

"Hey, I need something too and—"

"*No.*" Eyes suddenly wild, she clambered off his lap, pushed off the bed and staggered hurriedly out of the bedroom to the bathroom off the hall. She slapped the door open and in seconds, Cooper heard her being violently ill.

Frowning now, Cooper followed her into the bathroom and stood in the open doorway. As the first bout of sickness left her gasping for air, leaning back against the edge of the tub, he said, "You know, if this is a comment on my lovemaking skills, I want you to know I've never had this particular complaint before."

Clearly miserable, Kara swept her hair back out of her face and muttered thickly, "Go away, Cooper."

"Are you okay?" he asked, going down on one knee.

"*No* would be the short answer," she said, then gulped, "oh, no…"

Kara gripped the edges of the toilet and wished she could just open a hole to the center of the Earth and fall into it. How could her world go from glorious to miserable in the space of a couple minutes? And oh, *why* did she have to be so sick in front of Cooper?

"Take it easy," he whispered from just behind her. He held her hair back and soothed her with muttered nonsense as she turned inside out.

When she could take a breath, she tried again. "Cooper, if you care anything about me at all, you'll go away. Leave me to my misery in private."

He actually had the nerve to chuckle. Vaguely, she heard water running in the sink and then he was back, holding a cool damp cloth to her forehead while she was sick. And when she was at last finished, wanting only to curl up on the deliciously cold bathroom floor, he scooped her up in his arms and carried her back to the bedroom and to his bed.

Head pounding, mouth feeling like she'd been

sipping a sewer and a raceway for goose bumps forming on her spine, Kara wished absently that she were alive enough to enjoy being carried. But at the moment, that was simply beyond her.

She did try one more time to slink back to her own room. "Cooper, I just need to sleep," she said, trying to push up from the mattress on arms that suddenly felt too weak to support her.

"And you're going to," he said, helping her into a bathrobe and pulling the quilt out from under her, then draping it across her still form and tucking it tenderly in.

Damn it, he was being *nice*. And she was too weak and humiliated to protest. Apparently, the Fates had quite a sense of humor—and the joke was on her. She'd wanted him forever and it wasn't until *now* he paid attention. Now when she finally gets him into bed, she has to end the interlude by worshipping at the porcelain altar.

God.

Maybe she was weak enough to die.

"You're burning up," Cooper said, resting his hand on her forehead briefly.

"No I'm not," she argued, "I'm *freezing*." She burrowed deeper under the quilt and made a conscious effort to keep her teeth from chattering.

"Right. Okay. Stay put. I'm gonna call Sam."

"Sam?" She shook her head and looked up at him. He stood there beside the bed in all his naked glory and Kara couldn't even bring herself to care. She really was sick.

"He's a doctor. He'll know what to do."

"I don't need a doctor. Mortician, maybe."

"Funny." He grabbed his jeans off the floor and tugged them on, not bothering with the button fly. He scraped one hand through his hair and headed for the door. "I'll be back."

An hour later, Sam and Cooper stood in the kitchen. The candles he'd had burning when Kara came home had long since guttered out in their own wax puddles. The pasta was cold and congealed in a bowl on the table and the lingering scent of garlic still seasoned the air.

"You're sure she's okay?"

"Trust me," Sam said, snapping his black leather bag closed. "It's the flu. Kara will be fine in a couple of days. Just make sure she rests and gets lots of fluids."

"That's it?" Cooper demanded, glaring at his cousin. "You go to medical school for God knows how many years and the best you can do is *take a nap*?"

"Hey, you called me for my professional opinion, remember?"

"Right." Cooper blew out a breath. He didn't like this. He liked Kara up and annoying him. Ordering him around. Seeing her so weak and tired and…sick, worried him. "So should she eat anything?"

"Not till tomorrow at least. Then light stuff. Chicken soup, crackers." Sam studied him for a minute or two, then shook his head. "I can arrange for a nurse to come in and take care of her if you want."

Cooper's gaze snapped to his. "No. I'll do it."

"You sure?" Sam's voice was disbelieving and who could blame him?

Cooper couldn't remember a single time in his life when he'd voluntarily put himself out for someone else. Man. What did that say about him?

That he was a miserable, selfish jerk. Which he already knew. Hell, since that summer fifteen years ago, he'd done his best to keep a safe distance between himself and the human race. It had started deliberately. He even remembered making the choice to pull back, not only from his cousins, but from his parents, his grandfather, his friends.

Then after a few years, that distance had become a part of him. A part of his life that he'd grown so comfortable with, he'd never tried to change. Safer that way. Easier.

Until now.

But this was different.

This was Kara.

"It's not rocket science, Sam," he snapped, shoving both hands into his jeans pockets and rocking on his heels. "I can take care of the house and one sick woman."

"Okay," Sam nodded, eyeing him speculatively,

as if he wasn't quite sure Cooper meant what he was saying. Then he shrugged. "Maggie will probably want to come over tomorrow to check on her anyway, though."

"She doesn't have to, but thanks."

"Now, I'm going home." Sam turned for the back door, opened it, then stopped, looking at Cooper over his shoulder. "And while you're at it, you ought to get some rest, too. You look like hell."

Cooper shrugged off Sam's suggestion and once his cousin was gone, set the teakettle on the antique stove and turned on the burner. Rummaging through the kitchen cabinets, he located a coffee mug, then finally unearthed the jasmine tea bags that Kara had bought her first day in town.

Hitching one hip against the counter, he stared at the kitchen windows and the night crouched just beyond the circle of lamplight. He caught his own reflection in the glass and admitted that Sam had a point. He *did* look like hell. Worry etched itself into his eyes and bracketed his mouth.

Not too surprising. Of *course* he was worried about Kara. She was a part of his life. And tonight, she'd become an even bigger part.

A draft of cold air slipped past him and he shivered. Still staring at the glass, while the water in the teakettle began to stir, Cooper noticed a flash of movement. A white, shadowy film that moved across the glass and then disappeared.

He straightened up slowly and only absently heard the low pitch of the teakettle beginning to hum. He looked around the empty room and wasn't even surprised when he heard a heavy sigh reverberate around him.

The teakettle began shrieking, the sound driving into his head like a nail. He took the two steps to the stove, shut the fire off and flipped the cap off the kettle to end the noise. He poured a steaming stream of water into the cup, instantly releasing a flowery aroma.

While the tea steeped, he searched through the pantry for a couple of soda crackers. Despite what Sam had said, he figured Kara might be hungry and he wanted to be ready. When the tea was ready and the crackers on a small plate, he picked them up and looked around the room again.

"You still here?" Weird. Talking to a ghost. Weirder still, he was half expecting an answer. When nothing happened, he headed out to the stairs. At the door to his bedroom, he stopped. In the soft puddle of light from the bedside lamp, Kara lay, sound asleep.

He walked into the room, set the tea down on the dresser and placed the crackers alongside it. Then Cooper took a nearby armchair and dragged it to the side of the bed. He sat down and felt another cold chill brush along his shoulders and he stiffened reflexively.

Whispering into the quiet room, he said, "I'd appreciate it if you could skip the crying tonight. Kara's sick and she needs to sleep."

For several long moments, nothing happened, and then Cooper felt the chill in the room slide away, as if it had never been. Nodding to himself, he settled into the chair, got comfortable and prepared for a long night of keeping watch over Kara.

Seven

The cold was a living wall, surrounding him, devouring him. David felt it taking small bites of his heart, his soul. Helpless to stop it, he could only observe helplessly as the cold slowly, inexorably, eased into every corner of his being.

But there was something more, too. Something less substantial than the cold and yet far more insidious. Like an oil spill, it filled him, an inky blackness that was slowly obliterating who he had been before he'd first entered the hotel.

Worse, he couldn't fight it.

A scream slashed through the silence,

tearing it as a sharp blade would rend fragile silk. And...and... Damn it.

"Then what?" Cooper said aloud as he flopped back against the chair and glared at the screen of his laptop computer as if the machine itself were deliberately sabotaging him. A scream? Who the hell screamed? And why?

Usually, he worked through his books by the seat of his pants, believing strongly that if he ever sat down and plotted the thing out, scene by scene, he'd suck the heart of it out. The immediacy. And besides, he sort of enjoyed being surprised by whatever his characters got into.

But now...he couldn't think. Couldn't concentrate on his book because he couldn't stop thinking about the woman upstairs, lying in his bed. Sitting in a chair in his bedroom, he'd managed to doze off a couple times during the night. But every time Kara moaned or sighed in her fevered sleep, she'd brought him right out of it again.

His eyes felt like two marbles rolling in sand. Lifting both hands, he rubbed them, making the ache more pronounced. Then he braced his elbows on the tabletop and cupped his face in his palms. How was he supposed to come up with a fictional horror story while he was so concerned about Kara? Should the flu really be this hard on a person? Shouldn't she be feeling better by now?

Kara wouldn't drink any of the tea he brought her. Turned green at the offering of soda crackers and only spoke to tell him to go away.

As a nurse, he was a bust.

Or maybe Sam was a quack and she needed something more than rest.

Pushing up from the chair at the kitchen table, he stalked out of the room, across the living room and up the stairs, his long legs taking them two at a time. He turned for his bedroom and knocked quietly before opening the door.

Kara turned her head on the pillow to look at him as he entered. In the sunlight, her skin was too pale and lavender shadows lay beneath her eyes. She looked exhausted.

"Cooper, at least let me go back to my own bed."

"No," he said, giving her a smile she didn't want. "You're not getting out of that bed until you can do it without racing to the bathroom."

She tugged the quilt up to her chin and sulked. "I'm not a child," she pointed out.

"I remember," he said.

She groaned and pulled the quilt up over her face. Voice muffled, she said, "Oh, God, don't."

"Don't what?"

"Remember." She weakly pushed the quilt back down but closed her eyes as if she couldn't bear to look at him. "Put the whole night out of your mind. I have."

That stung more than he would have thought

possible. Amazing how much difference a few hours could make. Last night, he'd held her in his arms, locked himself inside her body and felt her quickening response. Today...they were like two polite strangers.

The easy camaraderie they used to share was gone. Friendship splintered by sex. Sex she didn't even want to think about. Great. By changing their relationship, he'd hoped to convince her not to quit. Now, it was starting to look like he'd only accelerated the process. Hell, she was lying there in his bed and already further away from him than she'd ever been. Disgusted with himself and the situation, he said, "I'm going into town. Pick up a few supplies."

"Good. Go away."

"Won't be gone long," he said, paying no attention to her crabbiness. "I'm going to ask Maggie to come sit with you. Make sure you stay in that bed."

Her eyes opened so she could glare at him briefly. "I'm not an infant. I can survive on my own for a couple of hours."

He ignored her tone, figuring a person was allowed to be crabby when they felt like hell. He always did. And the last time he was sick, he remembered suddenly, Kara had been at his side the whole time. He'd never questioned it, never even really taken the time to *appreciate* it. *God, what an idiot.* "Trust me, I don't think of you as an infant. But Maggie'll be here anyway."

"I don't need a sitter. I just need to get well."

"You will."

"When?"

"Okay," he said smiling, "now you're starting to sound like a baby."

"I can't help it," she snapped and flopped her arms down on top of the quilt. Her fingertips idly played with a loose thread. "I hate being sick and I don't want you taking care of me."

"You've been taking care of me for years," he reminded her. "Consider this payback."

"A debt." She sighed. "Great. Perfect."

Now what had he done? "I'll be back in awhile."

"Apparently, I'll be here."

He left her then and went to call Maggie.

"This'll be good for him," Maggie said, smoothing the fresh linen case on the plumped pillow behind Kara's head. As she moved along the bed, tugging at the quilt, she walked through a slash of sunlight that gilded the lighter streaks in her dark hair. Smiling, she glanced at Kara. "Maybe what Cooper needs is to feel needed."

Kara wasn't so sure about that. In the years she'd known him, he'd made a point of never being indispensable to anyone. He never had relationships that lasted more than a few months. And until this summer, he hadn't even seen his family in years.

He wanted to be needed?

No, Kara didn't see that. She'd always thought that Cooper did everything he could to keep from being needed.

"He's making me crazy," Kara admitted as her stomach did another wild pitch and roll. She slapped one hand to her abdomen and swallowed hard, determined to get through the rest of the day without ending up on her knees in the bathroom. Inhaling deeply, determinedly, she said, "He hovers. He brings me tea I can't drink and crackers that make me want to heave. And then he just sits there and stares at me. And I look *hideous.*"

Maggie chuckled then sat down in the chair beside the bed. "Apparently, Cooper doesn't agree. He's worried about you."

She'd like to think so, but reality kept rearing its ugly head to keep her from delving into fantasies best left alone. "It's not worry," she said on a sigh. "He said he's just paying me back for all the years I've been taking care of him."

Maggie shook her head, disbelieving. "Did he actually say that?"

"Yes. And," Kara added, "he feels bad for me because I got so sick right after—" Oops. No point in turning this little chat into a confessional.

But Maggie was too quick to be fooled. A pleased smile curved her mouth as she leaned back and lifted her feet to cross them on the edge of the bed. "Ah…so you finally managed to get him to *notice* you?"

Kara sighed again, this time in disgust. "Oh yeah. He noticed all right. Hard not to notice when the woman you're making love to suddenly has to make a break for the bathroom."

"Oh no." Maggie winced in sympathy. "Right in the middle?"

She shook her head. "Right after. In the middle of what was looking to be a truly great afterglow."

"Oh," Maggie said dreamily, "I do love the whole glow part."

"I wouldn't know," Kara said. "My glow was cut short."

"So, next time will be better."

"Next time?" Kara repeated on a disgusted groan. "There won't be a next time. He saw me sick as a dog. Held my head. Please. Any man who has to live through that is never going to look at that woman with passion again."

Maggie laughed.

Kara scowled at her. "So happy to give you your morning chuckle."

"Well come on, Kara." Still grinning, Maggie nudged her with her foot. "You think couples never see each other at their worst? Trust me. I'm sick every morning and every night, Sam's right there, pulling me in close and…" She cleared her throat. "Well, that's not the point."

"No you're right. It's not. That's completely different. You're *pregnant,*" Kara said, pointing an accusatory finger at her. "With Sam's child. Of course he's still sexually attracted to you. He *loves* you."

"Yeah," Maggie said with a contented sigh, "he really does. Are you so sure Cooper doesn't love you?"

Kara snorted and tugged a little harder at the loose string on the quilt, wrapping the thread around her index finger until the tip of it turned purple. "Love didn't have anything to do with it. At least not on his part. Trust me Maggie, I wish you were right. I wish he did love me. But he doesn't."

Another sigh wafted through the room. This one was deep, tormented, heartfelt. It came from nowhere. And everywhere.

Maggie dropped her feet to the floor and shot straight up in her chair, like someone had shoved a steel rod down the back of her tank top. "Was that...?"

Kara looked around the room and shrugged. "I'd introduce you but I don't know her name. So I'll just say, Maggie, meet our ghost. Ghost...Maggie."

He really had to get out of the frozen food section more often.

When left to his own devices, Cooper usually snatched up whatever edible looking frozen dinners he could find and called his shopping finished. Today, he'd gone up and down every aisle, the produce section and even the meat counter. Amazing really, what was out there.

He stacked a dozen grocery bags in the trunk of

his SUV, and slammed the lid shut. Then he looked around the quiet main street of Coleville and for the first time, really felt as though he'd come home.

Not much had changed and a part of him was grateful. Stupid really. He'd been avoiding this place for fifteen years because of the memories and now he was relieved to find it much as he'd left it.

A cool, sharp wind flew in off the ocean, dispelling some of the summer heat as Cooper walked toward the drugstore on the corner. Two kids rattled past him, surfing the sidewalks on skateboards whose wheels growled in their wake. An old woman lifted her suitcase-sized purse and shouted at them, but the kids didn't even slow down.

Cooper was still smiling to himself as he opened the door and heard the familiar clang and jangle of the old-fashioned bell over the door. God, when he and his cousins were kids, they'd been in and out of this store all summer. Candy bars, ice cold sodas and comic books were all he'd needed back then to make him happy.

And just for a second, Cooper wondered why life had to get so complicated.

He wandered through the aisles, nodding and smiling to the few people he passed. A refrigerated cabinet held a selection of flowers and before he could think twice about it, Cooper had the thing open and was reaching inside. Roses? He grabbed up a big bouquet of yellow roses, took a sniff, then stopped to think about it.

Did Kara like roses? He didn't know. And why the hell didn't he know? Five years they'd been together and he didn't know if she liked roses? He scowled down at the tight, colorful buds, then let his gaze sweep the interior of the case. There were a few mixed bouquets and a selection of carnations, daisies and some weird looking purple flower he couldn't identify.

"This shouldn't be so hard," he muttered, shifting his gaze from one bunch of flowers to the next as refrigerated air puffed out around him.

"Cooper Lonergan, shut that door! You think I'm paying to cool off the inside of the store?"

He jumped, startled and spun around to look down into Mrs. Russell's beady black eyes. The old woman had been a hundred and ten when Cooper was a boy, so he could only guess that she really had been an evil witch. Because she was still alive—and looking no friendlier than she had back in the old days.

"Sorry Mrs. Russell," he said and stepped back, still clutching the roses as he shut the glass doors. "Just trying to make up my mind."

She frowned at him and scuttled past toward the cash register behind the front counter. "Well, do your thinking with the door closed."

"Nice to see you, too," he muttered.

"Horrifying, isn't she?"

Cooper turned to face a tall pretty woman with

pale blond hair and deep blue eyes. She had a wire basket over one arm and a knowing smile on her face.

"Ah, yeah," he said, trying to figure out who she was. She looked at him as if he should know her, but for the life of him, he couldn't figure out how. "But then she always was."

The blond cast a quick glance to make sure Mrs. Russell was out of earshot before saying, "I think she's still holding a grudge against you and your cousins for the Fourth of July fiasco."

He smiled just thinking about it. Funny, he hadn't remembered that in years. He, Jake, Sam and Mac, eager for a little early celebration, had pooled their money and bought some illegal bottle rockets. They hadn't actually *planned* to launch one of them into the Russells' shed and burn it down.

Still smiling, he recalled, "And then Jeremiah made us spend the next three weeks building her a new shed."

"You got off easy," the blond said. "I was grounded for a month."

Cooper narrowed his gaze on her and just for a minute or two, the last fifteen years fell away and he saw her as she had been then. Tall and skinny, with wide blue eyes that were always locked on Mac. "Donna? Donna Barrett?"

"Hi, Cooper," she said, "it's good to see you again."

He swept her into a hard hug, then jumped back

as the bouquet of roses dripped water on her shoulder. "Sorry about that."

"No problem. I heard you and Sam had come home."

"Yeah. For the summer anyway. Jake's coming, too."

"All of you together again." Her voice went wistful, and her gaze dropped to the basket on her arm.

"Almost all of us," he said, knowing that Donna's thoughts were centered on Mac. And why wouldn't they be? Donna and Mac had lived in each other's pockets that last summer.

She'd become an unofficial part of their little group not just because the rest of them liked her, but because if they hadn't included her they wouldn't have seen much of Mac. In fact, the day Mac died, was only one of a handful of days Donna hadn't been with them. If she had been, maybe things would have been different. Maybe they wouldn't have waited so long to jump in after him. Maybe…

Silence stretched out between them as taut as an overextended rubber band as both of them drifted through the past, facing their regrets. Finally, he spoke up again, scrambling for something to say. "I heard you moved out of Coleville right after—"

Great. Perfect. Nice job, Cooper. Think of something else to say and go right back to that summer. But Donna played along.

"Yeah. I went to live with my aunt. In Colorado. Stayed there and went to school and now, well…" she shrugged and swept her hair back from her face. "It was time to come home." She waved one hand at the roses, now dripping water all over the linoleum. "So, hot date?"

He laughed uneasily. "No. Just trying to find flowers to bring to a…friend." *Friend?* Weak word. But what other word would do? *Lover?* Did one night together make them lovers? Not if Kara was to be believed. She was already trying to find a way to wipe that incident from her memory and his.

"She'll love them."

"You think?" He stared at them as if expecting them to change color or something. "All women like roses, right?"

One blond eyebrow lifted. "We're not interchangeable, Cooper."

"I know, I just meant—hell." He didn't know what he meant. Never before had he been so at a loss as to how to treat a woman. But Kara was different. She had a place in his life. She was…special.

Right. So special he didn't even know if she liked roses or not.

Well, he could solve that problem at least, he told himself and opened the refrigerated door again. Grabbing up all of the other bouquets, he figured that the one sure way to get Kara's favorite flower, would be to buy all of them.

"Making a statement?" she asked, laughing.

"No," he said, resisting the idea—even the vague hint of the idea—that he might be trying to win someone's heart. That wasn't what this was about. This was about being nice to someone he...cared for. About wanting to make Kara feel a little less crappy. "Just buying too many flowers," he said firmly.

From outside, a car horn blasted three or four times in short, impatient bursts. Donna threw a quick look over her shoulder at the wide windows overlooking the street. Then she turned back to Cooper, and said, "It was good to see you, but I've really got to run."

"Everything okay, Donna?" She looked...nervous all of a sudden.

"Fine." She hurried to Mrs. Russell at the cash register. "I hope your friend likes her flowers."

"Yeah, me, too." Thoughtfully, he watched her leave the store, and hurry to a pickup truck. There was someone in the passenger seat, but thanks to the sun's glare on the windshield, Cooper couldn't make out who it might be.

Then shaking his head, he told himself to forget about Donna Barrett. Whatever she had going on in her life now, he wished her well. But he had a sick woman at home and he didn't want to keep her waiting.

"Six bouquets?" Kara asked, astonished as Cooper carried in the last bunch of purple irises and set them across from her on top of the dresser.

He shrugged, shoved both hands into the pockets of his black slacks and said, "I didn't know—" he caught himself and started again. "They were all nice."

Kara smiled in spite of the disappointment she felt. Five years of knowing him, working with him every day and he didn't even know this one small thing about her. "You didn't know what kind of flowers I like."

He frowned and pulled one hand free long enough to stab his fingers through his hair. In a disgusted grumble he admitted, "No, I didn't. I did know you like flowers, though."

"Uh-huh." Thank God, her stomach had stopped its rumbling and spinning. Otherwise the combined scents of the fresh flowers would have had her running for the bathroom again. Now, it was just giving her a headache.

But he looked so pleased with himself, it was hard to burst his bubble.

"It was sweet of you to think of it," she said finally, trying to let go of her old dreams and see him as he really was. Did it matter that he didn't know what kind of flower she liked? Wasn't it more important that he'd thought of the act at all? "Thank you, Cooper."

He beamed at her, then reached for the shopping bag he'd dumped unceremoniously at the bedroom door. "I brought these, too. And stared Mrs. Russell, the old bat, right in the eye while I paid for them."

"What are you talking ab—" she broke off and smiled as he pulled five magazines from the bag and laid them on the bed beside her. Magazines about fashion and hair and gossip, he'd picked up exactly what he thought a woman would read. "Thanks, they're great."

"So how about soup?" he asked in a coaxing voice, "I bought chicken and stars."

"You don't have to fix my dinner, Cooper. Why don't you just go out and get something for yourself."

"Get something?" He managed to look both proud and insulted. "I bought steaks at the market and I'll be cooking my own dinner."

"Really?"

"I'm not completely useless, Kara."

"I never said *useless*," she corrected. "I believe the word I used was *hopeless*."

"Is that right?" He moved around the edge of her bed and straightened the quilt laying over her. "Well, I not only grocery shopped, but I did a couple of loads of laundry—did you know you can overfill a washing machine?"

"How big a mess was it?"

"The floors are clean."

"Cooper…"

"And, I even did some ironing."

She stared up at him, amazed and just a little sad. "You ironed?"

"Not for long," he admitted with a shrug. "The

plastic cover on that ironing board in the pantry? Why would they want you to put something hot on a covering that can melt?"

"You didn't."

"I'll buy a new iron," he said, brushing aside his little domestic disaster.

"Cooper," Kara said softly, "why are you doing all this? Really."

He stopped, looked down at her and gave her one of those smiles that could turn her inside out in a heartbeat. "Because I want to. Now, about that soup?"

Kara nodded, but didn't speak because she was just a little bit afraid that her voice might break if she tried. She watched him leave the room and when he was gone, she shifted her gaze to stare up at the late afternoon sunlight playing across the beamed ceiling. The scent of fresh flowers surrounded her and from somewhere in the room came the softest of sighs.

Not only was Cooper surviving without her...he appeared to be thriving.

Eight

"How're you holding up?" Sam set his medical bag onto the kitchen table and gave his cousin a stern look.

Morning sunlight shone in the room and Cooper squinted against the brightness while he cupped a full coffee mug between his palms. Lifting it for a sip, he shuddered at the taste and made a mental note to ask Kara *again* how to brew a decent pot of caffeine.

"I'm great," he said tightly, then dropped into a kitchen chair before he fell down. He felt as though he hadn't slept in weeks. "Now why don't you tell me about the patient you actually came here to see."

Sam shook his head and wandered over to the coffeepot. Grabbing down a cup from the cabinet, he filled the mug, took a sip and grimaced. "How can anybody screw up coffee this badly?"

"It's a gift," Cooper said, bracing one elbow on the table. "How's Kara?"

"She's fine. Probably better than you," Sam said, leaning back against the counter. "Did I mention that you look like hell?"

"Thanks." He took another gulp of coffee—not because he was getting used to the taste, but because the caffeine was the only thing keeping him awake. "She's okay? Really?"

"Yeah. I told you before, it was just the flu." Sam checked his wristwatch, took another sip of coffee, then choked it down before setting the almost full cup aside. "She's tired and weak, but she'll get better. Give her a couple more days to rest up. Keep her on light foods, a bland diet."

"Bland I can manage," Cooper muttered.

"Maggie would be happy to come over and help you out."

"No," he said. "I can take care of Kara. I want to."

"Hmm." Sam walked to the table, sat down opposite Cooper and stared at him thoughtfully.

"What?"

"Nothing. This is just interesting. I've never known you to have a domestic side."

"Cute." Cooper leaned back in his chair and said with a choked laugh, "Hell, Sam. I had no idea there was so much to do every day. I don't know how the hell Kara does it all. She never gets shook. Always has things organized. And never so much as has a nervous breakdown. Seriously, I haven't been paying her nearly enough money."

"I'm sure she'll be glad to hear that," Sam mused.

Cooper didn't even hear him. "I've spent so much time on the phone, dealing with my editor and agent and publicist, not to mention trying to get Kara to eat some soup and do laundry without flooding the place, I haven't written a word in two days."

"Or slept?"

Wryly, Cooper smiled. "Yeah. I've been sitting in a chair beside Kara in case she wakes up and needs something."

"Uh-huh." Sam shifted in his seat, threw one arm across the back of the chair and smiled to himself.

"Whatever you're thinking," Cooper told him, "forget it."

Sam drummed the fingers of his left hand against the tabletop. "Okay. If you don't want to talk about Kara, then why don't we talk about you?"

Cooper groaned inwardly. He was in no shape to be analyzed and Sam definitely had that "look" in his eyes. The look that said, *I know what your problem is and I have the solution.*

"Sam," Cooper said softly, "take pity on an exhausted man. Give me a break."

"You've been here for a few weeks now," Sam

said softly, completely ignoring Cooper's plea. "As far as I know, you still haven't been out to the lake."

Cooper's grip tightened on the handle of the mug until his knuckles went white. Fatigue pulled at him, but he stiffened despite the slump in his shoulders. "No, I haven't. Don't plan to, either."

Sam looked disappointed, somehow. "Damn it, Cooper. You can't keep hiding from that day."

Something squirmed in his guts and Cooper fought the urge to shift uncomfortably in his chair. "It's worked for me this long."

"You're here," Sam said quietly. "You came all the way to Coleville. Why not take it the rest of the way?"

"I came for Jeremiah's sake. I'm not here to relive the past." Deliberately, Cooper released his grip on the coffee mug and sat back in his chair. "I was in town the other day," he said, noting that Sam looked irritated by the change of subject. "I saw Donna."

"Barrett?" Surprised, Sam stared at him for a long minute. "I didn't know she was in town."

"Apparently, she's moved back."

"How's she look?"

"Good. But that's not my point," Cooper said, pushing his coffee cup away from him and leaning both forearms on the table as if he couldn't quite hold himself up straight in the chair without support. "I saw her and instantly, my mind went back to that summer. I could feel the sun. Smell the ocean." He sighed.

"Hell, Sam, I could have sworn I actually heard Mac laugh. It was all so close. Just by seeing Donna."

"Cooper…"

He looked into Sam's eyes and shook his head solemnly. "No. I buried the past, Sam. And I'm going to keep it buried."

Sam watched him for a few long seconds then sighed. "It's not buried, Cooper. It's with you every damn day. And until you face it—face *Mac*—you'll never really be free of it."

After Sam had gone, Cooper sat alone in the sun drenched kitchen and felt cold pressing in on him. Whether it was the ghost in the house or the ghosts in his own mind, Cooper acknowledged the truth. He didn't deserve to be free of the past.

He deserved to be haunted.

Kara pushed herself weakly into a sitting position against the pillows propped up on the headboard of the bed. She was finally starting to feel alive again. Barely. At least her stomach had stopped churning every few minutes. But she also felt like a slug. She hadn't even been able to work up the energy to crawl into the shower.

"How you feeling?"

She snapped a look at the doorway. Cooper stood there, leaning one shoulder against the doorjamb. Hands in his pockets, one foot crossed over the other, he looked tired. And impossibly good.

The last couple of days had been so hard. Not only feeling like death, but being so close to him. Having Cooper sit up at her side all through the night and knowing that he wasn't doing it because he loved her, but because he felt he owed her.

He pushed away from the door and walked toward her slowly. Kara grabbed at the quilt covering her and pulled it up higher, covering her chest, wanting to pull it up over her head. She knew what she must look like. She'd caught a brief glimpse of herself in the bathroom mirror earlier and had yelped in fright.

"Kara?" He waved one hand back and forth in front of her face. "You're zoning again."

"I didn't zone. I'm in a coma."

"Pretty chatty for a coma."

"Was there a reason for this visit?"

Twin black eyebrows lifted. "Should you still be this crabby now that you're getting better?"

"Cooper…"

"Relax. I only came to see if you felt well enough to try a shower."

She blinked at him, trying to dislodge a sudden, extremely clear image of the two of them, naked, wrapped together under a stream of hot water. His hands, slick with soap, sliding over her body, dipping between her legs, stroking, while his mouth…

"Kara?"

She came up out of the fantasy and gave herself a mental kick. Oh, sleeping with him had been a *big* mistake. Now she knew what she'd be missing for the rest of her life. And in her heart, she knew damn well there wasn't another man alive who would ever compare to Cooper Lonergan.

But the simple truth was, he wasn't hers and never would be. Might as well get used to that fact.

"I heard you," she said and threw the quilt back. Cool air hit her bare legs and she shivered. "And the answer is yes. I'm definitely willing to give it a try."

"Hey, not so fast," he cautioned, moving in to grab one of her arms as she jumped to her feet.

"I'm fine," she said, "I can do this myself—" She swayed unsteadily and leaned into his hard, muscled chest. The room did a nasty little tilt and she closed her eyes to steady herself. "Okay," she acknowledged a few seconds later, "maybe I could use a little help."

"You've been flat on your back for nearly three days, Kara." He wrapped one arm around her waist and Kara could have sworn she felt five separate stabs of heat from each of his fingers.

"You haven't had any food in your system," he reminded her. "So take it easy until you get your strength back, okay?"

His voice was tight, and she was pretty sure she heard his heart pounding out a frantic rhythm. Kara wasn't sure if it was worry or desire causing the jump in his blood pressure but decided to go with worry. Since that thought was less likely to break her heart.

Patting his chest, she straightened up, backing out of his embrace and then took a single step, wishing her legs didn't feel quite so wet-noodley. Her head spun crazily and her vision went a little fluffy at the edges.

"Whoa. Interesting sensation," she whispered just before Cooper scooped her up into his arms.

"Okay, we'll do this another way." He cradled her close and Kara indulged herself. Laying her head on his shoulder, she inhaled the scent of him—soap, shampoo and the spicy zing of his aftershave.

Her stomach wobbled, but it had nothing to do with the flu. It was simply the effect Cooper had on her. Only now, it was worse than ever before because she knew what it was to have him inside her. To feel his mouth on her skin, his hands on her body. She knew the shattering sensation of climaxes rippling through her system and the brush of his breath against her neck.

And oh, she wanted it all again.

Even knowing that it was going nowhere.

That he would never love her.

She wanted him so much, everything in her yearned.

"You okay?" he whispered, his breath dusting the top of her head.

"Yeah," she insisted firmly. "Just a little light-headed is all."

He left the bedroom, walked down the hall and stepped into the bathroom. The walls were a cool green and the old tile floor was laid in a pattern of green-and-white checks.

"You want me to help you?" he asked as he set her down onto her feet.

"No," she said, though her mind was screaming *yes!* No point in making this even harder on herself. Her shower fantasy burst once again into full bloom in her brain, and the images it produced left her nearly breathless with a hunger that shook her right down to her bones. But she steeled herself against it, and met his gaze squarely. "I'll be fine."

He didn't look as if he believed her. But still, he backed up toward the door. "I'll be close if you need me. I'm gonna change the sheets on the bed."

Kara blinked. "You are?"

Scowling, Cooper said, "You know, I wish you'd quit looking at me like that."

"Like what?"

"Like I'm performing a miracle or something whenever I do something around here. I *am* capable of a few things."

She smiled at his insulted tone and tried to smooth his ruffled feelings. "Of course you are, it's just—"

"I know." He held up one hand to stop the rest of her explanation and gave her a half smile. "I've never done it before. But then, never really had to, did I?"

"No," she mused, thinking about how she was usually the one taking care of him. She'd worked so hard for so long to make herself indispensable to him, it had never occurred to her that maybe she'd done too much. "I guess not."

He nodded and stuffed both hands into his jeans pockets. "Oh yeah, you didn't have another nightgown that I could find, so I put one of my T-shirts in there for you to wear while your nightgown gets washed."

She glanced down and saw his neatly folded white T-shirt. He'd even thought of this. She'd been in her nightgown for nearly three days now and she could hardly wait to get out of it. "More laundry?"

He shrugged and smiled. "Think I'm getting the hang of it."

"Thanks," she said, "for thinking of it."

"No problem," he said, backing the rest of the way out of the bathroom. "And if you get dizzy again, while you're taking a shower, for God's sake, sit down."

"I will."

He stopped. "Maybe I should just stay in the room with you, just in case…"

Oh, that's all she needed.

"Go away," she said, laying one hand on his chest and pushing him out of the room.

She closed the door and leaned back against it for a long minute or two, trying to keep from opening it again and inviting him inside. Then she heard his footsteps moving off down the hall and she sighed. In disappointment or relief…she wasn't sure.

Then shaking her head, she peeled off her night-gown and headed for the shower.

* * *

In the darkness, Cooper sat alongside the bed and watched Kara sleep. Moonlight spilled across the mattress illuminating her in a silvery light that made her already pale skin glow like fine porcelain. Her eyelashes were long and lay curved on her cheeks in a smudge of darkness that was vulnerable as well as tempting.

He sucked in a breath of air and blew it out again while leaning forward, forearms braced on his thighs. He couldn't seem to stop watching her and he wondered why he'd never noticed before just how beautiful she was. She sighed and shifted in her sleep, the quilt sliding down, baring her shoulder and the plain white T-shirt that covered her.

Damn, who would have thought a woman could look that good in a man's shirt? He could still see her, coming out of the bathroom. The hem of the T-shirt hit just beneath her bottom, baring her long, lean legs to his gaze. Her hair, freshly washed and dried, drifted around her shoulders in thick, tempting waves and her eyes, though still shadowed, looked clear for the first time in days.

His fingers itched to stroke her skin again as memory after memory rushed into his brain, crowding it with the images and sounds and scents of their lovemaking. Only a few nights ago, she'd opened herself to him and he'd discovered a depth and passion he hadn't expected.

His body stirred, tightening with a hunger that clawed at his insides until he wanted to howl with need. And he called himself all kinds of a bastard for wanting her when she was so clearly exhausted.

He leaned back in his chair and then jolted upright when an unearthly howl erupted from the bowels of the house. Jumping to his feet, he stared around the room, but it did no good. The wailing came from nowhere and everywhere. It seemed to seep from the walls as if even the house itself were keening in misery.

"Damn it," he muttered, swallowing past the knot lodged in his throat. It had been a couple of days since the ghost had made itself known. Cooper had almost begun to think that it had decided to leave them the hell alone.

Now though, it was back and louder than ever.

Another heartrending wail sobbed around him, sending a chill washing through him. Outside, a wind kicked up out of nowhere, rattling the window panes. Bits of dirt and pebbles were thrown high, pinging off the glass like eager fingers tapping, tapping, demanding entry.

The temperature in the room dropped suddenly and as the sobbing continued, cold gathered. Cooper moved closer to the bed, standing with his back to Kara, so that he stood as a sentry, between her and the growing cold.

Even as he did it though, he fought down a sharp laugh. What the hell could he do to a ghost? What he should do was grab up Kara and get her some-where...else. But he'd be damned if he was going to be chased out of his own house by the psychic energies of one long-dead woman and her erstwhile lover.

"Get out," he muttered thickly, and the sobbing throbbed in the air.

"Cooper?"

He spun around to find Kara sitting up in bed, pushing her hair back out of her eyes and looking around the empty room.

"She just started up," he muttered, glaring at the shadows as if trying to intimidate the spirit into silence.

Another howl was his answer. The sound rippled along his skin, and lifted the hair at the back of his neck.

"She's lonely," Kara whispered.

"She's *nuts*," Cooper countered.

A disembodied moan whined around them.

Kara reached for his hand and pulled him down onto the bed beside her. He sat down, back braced against the headboard and pulled her in close, if only to keep her warm in the bone numbing cold.

"She shouldn't have waited for him for so long," Kara said, her voice almost lost in the weeping.

Cooper shook his head, amazed that they were sitting in the dark, discussing the feelings of a woman long dead. "Hell, she'd waited two years. Maybe she should have waited a little longer. He *did* show up finally."

"Too late," Kara reminded.

"It didn't have to be too late," he said, raising his voice to be sure even the ghost heard him. "If she hadn't curled up and died, they could have been together. He's outside the house right now and she *still* won't let him in."

Kara looked up at his profile in the darkness and tried not to make too much of his words. The problem was, she wanted to believe that he was trying, subconsciously even, to tell her to not give up on him.

But if she started believing things like that, she'd only be setting herself up for the same kind of misery that haunted the woman trapped in this house.

Better if she did what that woman had not done.

Give up on the dream and move on.

Nine

Kara reluctantly woke up from the most erotic dream she'd ever experienced, to silent darkness. Apparently the ghost had given up for the night.

So what then had woken her?

An instant later, she knew. In her dream, Cooper's hands had moved over her body with smooth deliberation, caressing, stroking, driving her toward a climax she knew would be soul shattering.

Now that she was awake, she realized the dream was real. Cooper lay right behind her, spooned up along her back. At some point during the night, he'd undressed, because the heat from his naked body rushed into hers and she felt the hard, solid length of his erection pressing against her behind.

Yet even that delicious sensation was trumped by the feel of one of his hands cupped between her thighs. Damp heat pooled in her center and her breath staggered past a knot of need lodged in her throat.

Instinctively, she parted her thighs for him, silently asking that he touch her more surely, more deeply. Closing her eyes, she shifted against his hand, delighting in the frisson of sensations that swept through her in a rush. His fingers moved on her, dipping into her warmth, sliding over the tender, sensitive flesh.

She sighed and his name came out on a groan. "Cooper…"

"Right here," he whispered, bending his head to the curve of her neck, nibbling, licking.

"Yeah," she said breathlessly, "I got that…"

He smiled against her skin, then nibbled a little harder. "Sorry I woke you."

"No," she said, "you're not." Smiling, she gulped in another breath as his fingers continued their gentle invasion.

"Okay," he admitted, "I'm not."

She rolled over onto her back and stared up into his dark eyes. While she watched him, he dipped one finger and then two inside her and she swallowed hard, loving the feeling of him touching her so deeply. When her nerve endings stopped frying, she managed to ask, "What're you doing, Cooper?"

In the pale wash of moonlight, she saw one dark eyebrow lift. "I would have thought that was obvious."

She sucked in a breath as he shifted his grip on her and stroked a nearly electrically charged nubbin of flesh.

"Yes," Kara choked out a laugh that was just the tiniest bit hysterical. "I guess I meant, *why?* Why are you…we…" she lifted her hips, arching into his hand, "…oh, boy, that really feels so good."

"Yeah," he murmured, dusting a hard, brief kiss on her mouth. "It really does."

Fighting to maintain, to hold onto some semblance of her dignity—which Kara was beginning to think was way overrated—she shook her head on the pillow and demanded, "Is this some sort of sympathy thing?"

"What?"

"You know," she said, pausing as his fingers once again plumbed her depths, pressing, stroking. "Wow, you're good at this," she said even while her brain shrieked at her to think.

"It's a gift," he said, kissing her again, drawing the tip of his tongue along her bottom lip.

Deliberately, she focused her splintering concentration even while her hips rocked, setting a rhythm she ached to give herself up to. "But Cooper—I don't want a pity orgasm."

"Huh?"

"I've been sick and you want to make me feel better and—"

"You're crazy," he said, his voice filled with wonder. "I never knew that about you."

"I'm not crazy," she countered, trying not to notice that he was rubbing that sensitive spot again, "I'm just not interested in a 'poor little Kara, let's give her a ride' night."

His hand on her stilled, his palm pressed tight against her heat. "What're you talking about?"

"Come on, Cooper," she said, fighting to keep from begging him to rub her again. To stroke her inside and out. To push her over the edge into those fireworks she remembered so well from their one night together.

Her hips moved again, seemingly of their own accord. Apparently her body was smarter than she was. It didn't care why he was offering up an orgasm, it just wanted one.

But Kara ignored the tantalizing rush of sensation. Fought to keep her mind focused on what she knew to be true. To keep her from allowing him to do something that would mean nothing to him and, therefore, little to her.

Shaking her head, she met his gaze and said it, plain and simple. "You saw me sick as a dog, Cooper. You can't be feeling attracted to me after that disgusting display, so this has got to be some warped sense of a good deed—or—I don't know."

"You *are* nuts," Cooper said, spearing his fingers

up into her damp heat again, groaning as her head tipped back into the pillows.

"Cooper…"

"Look at me," he ordered thickly, his voice a raw scrape of sound. When her gaze was locked with his, he said, "I've been wanting you for days. I even wanted you when you were sick. Hell, there you were, bent over a toilet and all I could think about was what a cute behind you've got. How twisted is *that?*"

Kara ground her hips against his hand. "Really?"

"Really." He stroked her inner folds, driving her to the brink of desperation, only to pull her back from the edge and taunt her toward it again. "And," he said, dipping his head to claim a kiss, "I know you're still exhausted. Haven't had a good night's sleep in three nights, and am I letting you rest? Nope. I'm waking you up and hoping to hell you want me as badly as I want you."

"Really?"

"Will you stop saying that?" He dropped another kiss on her mouth, ran the tip of his tongue across her lips.

"Right," she murmured, expelling a long breath on a deep groan.

"So? Are you with me here, Kara? Or should I let you go to sleep?"

"Who needs sleep?" she asked breathlessly, opening her thighs for him, reaching up to wrap her arms around his neck.

"I was so hoping you'd say that," he admitted, dipping his head to nibble at the line of her throat as she tilted her head back, deeper into the pillow.

Kara finally stopped thinking.

Stopped questioning his motives.

And gave herself up to the pure pleasure swamping her.

Again and again, his clever fingers worked on her body even as he slid farther down and used his free hand to push up the hem of the T-shirt she wore. When her breasts were bared to the moonlight, he took first one hardened nipple into his mouth and then the other. Over and over, he suckled her, drawing on her skin as if trying to sip her being into his.

Dizzying sensations jolted through her and Kara could hardly keep up with them all. It felt as though her entire body were on fire and she encouraged the flames. She wanted them hotter, brighter. She wanted to be engulfed in the heat that was Cooper.

Shifting over her, he moved down her body, trailing damp kisses along her flesh. She grabbed at him, trying to pull him up for a kiss. To feel his mouth on her own. But he neatly avoided her grasping hands and settled himself between her thighs with an anticipatory sigh.

Opening her eyes, she looked at him and her breath caught. In the wash of moonlight pearling through the windows, his dark eyes gleamed with temptation and his tanned, hard body shone like marble.

"Cooper…"

"Shut up, Kara," he whispered with a smile. Then he lifted her hips off the mattress, slung her legs over his shoulders and covered her heat with his mouth.

She shrieked.

Kara heard her own voice ricocheting off the walls, but she couldn't care. Couldn't do anything but feel.

His lips, teeth and tongue took her higher, faster than anything ever had before. She fisted her hands in the sheet beneath her, trying desperately to keep that one little grip on sanity as her brain fractured in a wash of fiery sparks.

He suckled her here, too. And while his mouth did amazing things to her, he managed to slide one finger into her depths, doing to her from the inside what his mouth was accomplishing on the outside.

"Too much," she whispered brokenly. "All too much. I can't. Cooper, I can't—"

He chuckled and her eyes went wide even as her body stiffened at the approaching climax. She felt it build at a fever pitch and wondered absently if she'd survive. Then she knew she didn't care. She would risk anything to feel this. To have this man in this moment.

That one sensitive bud at her core felt as though it were electrified and when Cooper lapped at it with the tip of his tongue, Kara shrieked again. His big hands cupped her behind and held her steady as she shouted his name and rocked her hips wildly in his grasp.

Releasing her death grip on the sheets, she reached for him and as a raw, charging fury raced through her body, she held his head to her and watched him as he took her over the edge.

Her body still trembling, still humming with the incredible power of her orgasm, Cooper knew he couldn't wait another moment. He had to be inside her. Had to feel her body surrounding his, feel the internal tremors as her muscles fisted around his length, squeezing him dry.

Heart pounding erratically, Cooper laid her down onto the mattress and stretched out a hand to the bedside table. Blindly, desperately, he yanked the drawer open and didn't even blink when it fell free of the table and landed upside down on the floor. He couldn't care about anything. Not now. Not after tasting her surrender. Not after holding her while a storm crested within her.

Not after experiencing Kara's climax with a force stronger than anything he'd ever known.

His only thought now was to feel it again. To be inside her when it came, to push himself so high and so deep within her body that the climax they would share would be incredible.

"Cooper…?"

"Just a minute." He scrambled off the edge of the bed, tossed the drawer to one side and grabbed up one of the foil packets that had fallen out. Quickly, he unwrapped it, sheathed himself and was back on the bed. His only regret was that he had to wear the damn condom in the first place. He wanted, more than anything, to feel her slick warmth on his skin. To feel the matchstick heat of sensation that could only come from two bodies, sliding together, unprotected from each other.

But he was too smart and too concerned for Kara to take that kind of chance.

Her arms opened to him as he rejoined her on the bed and he kissed her, taking her mouth while the taste of her body was still with him. His tongue swept inside her mouth, exploring, stroking, silently demanding.

And she gave as good as she got.

Their tongues met in an erotic dance, twining together, twisting, caressing until neither of them could draw a breath without a struggle. Her hands dropped from his back and tugged at the fabric of the shirt she still wore.

Groaning, Cooper eased back up and in one quick movement, had the shirt up and over her head and tossed into a heap on the floor.

"Better," she said, lifting her head from the pillow to claim his mouth again. She nibbled at his bottom lip and he felt an answering tug of need deep in the core of him.

"Gotta have you," he whispered, his lips moving over hers hungrily. Not enough, his brain shouted.

Not nearly enough. He wanted to taste every square inch of her body. Wanted her beneath him, over him, under him. He wanted her every way a man could want a woman and when they were finished, he wanted to do it all again.

And again.

"Yes," she said, moving to accommodate him as he shifted, kneeling between her legs.

He entered her with one swift thrust and she gasped at the invasion. Cooper paused, throwing his head back, staring blindly at the ceiling, concentrating solely on the lush feel of his body embedded in hers. But in an instant, need crowded within him and pushed him onward.

Bracing his hands at either side of her head, he rocked his hips against hers. She lifted her legs high, helping him to go deeper. He bent his head, tasted her nipples, rolling his tongue across their pebbly tips, one after the other. His hips pistoned, her sighs and moans echoed his. She tossed her head from side to side on the pillow. Licked her lips.

The sight of her tongue, darting across her parted lips enflamed him and Cooper bent to meet it. Then, staring into her eyes, he watched as flames erupted within her. Watched as passion glazed the surface of her deep green eyes and sparkled with the rush of completion.

He felt the clawing, clamoring ache within and fought to hold it off. He wanted it to last. Wanted this moment to never end. And in fact, the only reason he finally gave into his own release was because the only way to do this over again was to allow the climax to happen.

Her body erupted beneath his.

She called his name, her voice breaking.

And an instant later, Cooper groaned and followed her into the abyss.

Hours passed as they found each other again and again. Every muscle in Kara's body ached—and yet, she'd never felt more complete. More satisfied. Cooper had taken her in every way possible, she mused and in return, she'd taken him a couple of times, too.

And now, with the first streaks of dawn blurring the sky into a slow blossom of rich color, she lay in the circle of Cooper's arms and fell into an exhausted sleep…and a shared dream.

Cooper held her hand and Kara felt the warm strength of his fingers curled around hers. They stood in the parlor of the old Victorian—not as it was now, but as it had once been.

A piano stood in one corner of the room, sunlight streaming through the window to dance across the ivory keys. A paisley shawl was draped across the gleaming top of the piano and atop it, were a dozen or more framed, sepia-toned photographs. A black-

and-white cat was curled up in an overstuffed chair and at the wide front window, a woman stood.

Outlined in gilded light, she stared out the window at the road beyond, as if watching for someone. One hand to her mouth, she wrapped her other arm around her waist as if trying to comfort herself, when there was no comfort to be found.

Her quiet grief echoed in the room, and her tears looked like diamonds in the light. She kept watch, waiting for the lover who had promised to return. She walked from window to window, hope and fear keeping pace, her steps muffled on the carpets beneath her feet. Somewhere, a clock chimed out the hour and the woman's shoulders hunched with every soft gong.

Kara felt the woman's misery as if it were her own. Even the house itself seemed to throb with the pangs of the woman's agony. Time stood still, in this one little bubble of memory. For decades, the woman had been trapped—by her own pain and desperation and there didn't seem to be an end coming.

Kara looked up at Cooper and saw his eyes flash with pity just before a shutter dropped over them, locking her out.

She felt, as well as sensed, his withdrawal.

And in her sleep, Kara clung to him, afraid somehow that he would slip away from her and she would be left—like the crying woman—waiting for a love that would never be.

* * *

Cooper woke up first, half surprised to find that the dream was gone. Kara lay curled against him, her small hand on his chest. He covered it with one of his own, then reluctantly, let her go.

How had they shared that dream?

How had they been pulled into the ghost's pain and made to feel it with her? And how could he have forgotten, even for a second, the lessons he'd learned so long ago? Seeing the ghost as she'd once been, a young, beautiful woman who'd lost everything because she'd ventured to love, had reminded Cooper love meant pain.

Frowning, he eased out of the bed, stubbed his toe on the drawer, still laying on the floor, and bit back an angry oath. Staring down at the naked woman lying in his bed, something inside him turned over and he almost wished things could be different. But he knew, better than most, that they couldn't.

As if she felt his gaze on her, Kara woke up. Stirring languidly, she opened her eyes to meet his and gave him a tentative smile.

"Did we just—"

"Dream?" he asked, then nodded tightly, uneasy with the reborn feelings crashing around inside him. "Yeah, we must have."

"But how?"

"I don't know," he muttered and grabbed up his jeans off a nearby chair. He had to get out of that room. Had to keep from looking at Kara, or he'd slip. He'd forget about lessons learned and ghosts and old pains and lose himself in the arms of the woman who was, he suddenly realized, *way* too important to him. He couldn't let that happen, he told himself sternly, because he'd learned at a very early age, that to love only invited disaster.

"I'm going downstairs. Make some coffee."

"Cooper?"

He shook his head and chanced a quick look at her. Instantly, he realized his mistake. Love shone in her eyes and that terrified him. His heart went hard and cold in his chest and his throat tightened until he wasn't sure he'd be able to breathe.

He turned his back on her, because he couldn't look at her and not want her. Heading for the door, he grabbed hold of the brass knob, turned it and paused, door partially opened. "I'll bring you some coffee and maybe some eggs. I think you're well enough now to have some solid food."

"Okay," she said, her voice filled with questions he couldn't—wouldn't—answer. "But Cooper, we have to talk about—"

He shook his head and stepped out of the room. "Nothing to talk about, Kara. Dream's over. Time to wake up."

Ten

Two days later, things were still strained between Kara and Cooper. But actually, she thought, *strained* wasn't the right word. After all, he'd only reverted to normal.

He was back to being the closed off boss she knew so well. Distracted, preoccupied, Cooper spent most of his time locked away in his makeshift office. She heard the tapping of his fingers at the keyboard, but rarely saw him all day.

They still had dinner together in the kitchen, but there was no lighthearted chitchat. No teasing, no laughter. Nor was there any hint that their night of lovemaking was still haunting him as it was her.

The long nights passed slowly, Kara's only company, a ghost with whom she was beginning to think she had far too much in common.

"Serious thoughts?"

Kara looked up as Maggie approached and found a half-hearted smile to offer. "Very," she admitted and shifted her gaze to Cooper, standing on the opposite side of his grandfather's yard, talking to Jeremiah and Sam.

If he felt her gaze on him, he didn't let her know. He stood slightly apart from the other two men, as if keeping a careful distance even from his family. It broke Kara's heart, but she didn't have a clue how to fight it.

Maggie eased down onto the chair beside Kara's and stretched her long tanned legs out in front of her. She cupped her right hand over her still flat abdomen as if stroking the tiny child nestled within. "Oh, the shade feels great. I swear it's at least ten degrees cooler under this tree."

"Mmm-hmm." Kara was only half listening. Most of her focus was on Cooper. The heat rippled the air and made his image waver slightly as if he were already no more substantial than a dream. She squelched a sigh as she realized she couldn't even imagine her life without Cooper in it. But she would have to find a way to move on. Still, she couldn't look away from him. She'd made up her mind to finally leave him and now, all she had left were these unguarded times when she could look at him and store up as many mental snapshots as she could.

"You haven't told him that you love him, have you?"

Kara shot Maggie a glance, then shook her head. "No. There's no point. Trust me, it's not something he wants to hear."

"Maybe it's something he *needs* to hear, though," Maggie insisted, lifting her hair off her neck and then twisting it into a ponytail with a rubber band she tore off her wrist.

Kara would like to think so, but even knowing that Maggie meant well, the other woman didn't know Cooper as well as Kara did.

"Sam was the same way," Maggie continued, her voice softening as she shifted her gaze to where the three men stood talking. Sam and his grandfather were laughing at something and Cooper, aloof and alone, stood watching.

"What do you mean?" Kara asked, more to be polite than from real interest.

"I think what happened to Mac affected all of the cousins," Maggie said. "I know it's haunted Sam all these years, so I'm sure Cooper and Jake feel the same way. I mean, if you think about it, they were all only kids. And to have your cousin die like that…right in front of you…it must have been terrible for all of them."

Something cold slithered through Kara as she slowly swiveled her head to look at the woman sitting beside her.

Maggie caught her expression and read it correctly. She winced. "You didn't know any of this, did you?"

"No." God, it hurt to admit that. She'd been closer to Cooper than anyone else in his life for the last five years and he'd never said a word. Never let her in. Never gave a hint that there was something so horribly traumatic in his past. Here then was the reason for his withdrawal from life. For his refusal to let anyone past the walls he'd erected around his heart.

"I'm so sorry." Maggie reached out and laid her hand on Kara's. "I never would have said anything, but I assumed you knew."

"It's not your fault," Kara said, fighting the swell of regret and disappointment rising inside her.

"God, I'm an idiot."

"Tell me," Kara urged quietly.

"I don't know..." Maggie shook her head and looked as though she wished she were anywhere but there at the moment.

"Maggie, I have to know."

The other woman sighed, glanced at the men across the yard, then back to Kara. "Yes, I think you do."

While she talked, Kara's heart sank further. With every word she heard, the connection she'd felt to Cooper unraveled just a bit more. Like an old tapestry being torn apart, the fragile threads of their years together disintegrated. Tears filled her eyes, not only for the boy Cooper had once been and the tragedy of that long-ago summer day…but for the man he was now because of it. For chances lost, dreams crushed.

And Kara finally admitted the hard truth that she'd resisted for so long.

Cooper would never allow himself to love her.

Cooper watched Maggie and Kara, sitting in the shade of the old oak tree and wondered what the two women were talking about. Meanwhile, Jeremiah's and Sam's voices rattled in his ears, but he wasn't really listening. It was as if he was standing behind a glass wall. He could see them, but he was apart from them.

Hell, he'd been apart from everything for days now. Since he and Kara had shared that dream. Memories clouded his brain all the time. Whenever he closed his eyes, he saw Mac's face. He remembered that summer day fifteen years ago and how he'd vowed that he would never lose someone he loved again.

And the secret to that was to never love.

Caring too much was simply an invitation to pain.

That was why he'd cut himself off from his grandfather and his cousins. Losing Mac had hit him hard. As a kid, you think yourself immortal. Invulnerable. Learning differently had cut him nearly in two. Then his parents had died not long after that summer, reinforcing his decision to keep himself separate from any kind of closeness.

All he cared about now were his books. The imaginary people he interacted with on a daily basis. When one of them died, it didn't tear him up. Didn't rip out his heart and soul and leave it battered and bloody on the ground.

But then there was Kara. The feelings she pulled from him terrified him, plain and simple. A humbling thing for a man to admit, but there it was. He didn't want to care, damn it. And he resented like hell that she'd awakened something in him that had been long—and safely—dead.

And as much as he wanted to stalk across the yard, pull Kara from her chair and drag her home to bed…he knew that road could only end in pain.

So he stayed where he was. On the outside, looking in. Every night, he lay awake in his bed, afraid to sleep for fear of seeing Mac die again. And he couldn't lose himself in Kara because he knew he couldn't give her what she wanted and this way, though it cost him, he was able to spare Kara any more pain than was necessary.

He wasn't a complete idiot. He'd seen that happy little glow in her eyes the morning after they'd loved each other half to death. The shine of joy and pleasure and the dream of tomorrow had all been written there in her expression.

And he knew damn well that ignoring her now was hurting her. But how much better to be hurt now than devastated later? If he let her believe that there could be a future for them only to back away? No. It was better this way.

Not easier.

Better.

"What do you think?" Sam asked, snapping his fingers in front of Cooper's face.

"What?" He scowled at his cousin.

"Jeremiah and I were talking about re-doing Gran's old sewing room as a nursery," Sam said, and the tone of his voice said that this wasn't the first time he'd said it. "I asked what you thought."

"I think it's none of my business," Cooper pointed out and looked away from the slow head shake of disapproval his grandfather sent him.

"You're a big help," Sam muttered. "What the hell's wrong with you, anyway?"

"Not a damn thing," he said, disgusted that he'd let his own feelings be seen so easily. Starting for the house, he asked, "I'm going for a beer. You two want one?"

"Yeah," Sam said.

"Not for me." Jeremiah lifted his still half-full bottle in explanation.

"Fine." Cooper stalked across the grassy yard and headed for the house as a dying man in the desert aimed for the only oasis for miles. He just needed a little space. Some time alone. Some time to get away from everyone who was watching him in either hope or disappointment.

He couldn't give any of them what they wanted. Didn't they see that?

As he hit the front step, he paused to listen. The low growl of a motorcycle engine cut through the air and halted Jeremiah and Sam's conversation. The deep rumble of power rolled toward them, heralding the approach of a man who could only be Jake, the last Lonergan cousin.

Beer forgotten for the moment, Cooper stood stock-still and waited.

Sheba, the puppy who thought of herself as a Great Dane, set up a barking, howling discord to alert everyone just in case they hadn't heard the same noise she had. Then the little dog ran to Jeremiah and cowered behind his overall-clad legs as a huge motorcycle, chrome gleaming, prowled into the yard.

Sam and Jeremiah were there in seconds, leaving Cooper to study the situation from a safe distance. Jake turned off the engine and climbed off the bike, one hand extended to Sam. Jake's long black hair fell down the middle of his back in a ponytail. He wore a white T-shirt, black jeans and scuffed black boots that looked as though they'd walked to hell and back. A United States Marine Corps tattoo colored Jake's right bicep and two days' worth of beard shadowed his jaws. He yanked off wraparound sunglasses as he grinned at Sam.

"Good to see you, man."

"You, too. Nice bike."

"It rides," Jake said with a shrug, then turned to grin at his grandfather. "Jeremiah. You're looking a lot less dead than I expected."

"Good to have you home, boy," the older man said and swept his last remaining grandson into a fierce embrace.

Maggie and Kara were headed across the yard toward the commotion when Jake turned to look at Cooper. "There's the World Famous Author," he said, his tone putting the words in capital letters. "Read the last one. Scared the hell outta me."

Cooper smiled and walked the few steps toward his cousin. "Thanks." Then he held out one hand and as his cousin grabbed it, he said, "It's good to see you, Jake."

The Lonergan boys were together again.

Was he the only one feeling Mac's absence so intensely?

"Same here." Then Jake's dark eyes lit up as he spotted the women. "And who are the gorgeous ladies?" he asked, a well-practiced smile on his face.

"Cut your engines," Sam said, laughing, as he grabbed Maggie into a tight hug. "This one's mine."

"Well then," Jake continued, not even missing a beat as he stepped up to Kara and gave her a wink, "That leaves you and me. Unless..." he turned to look at Cooper, a question in his eyes.

Everything in Cooper yearned to knock Jake back a step. To drape one arm around Kara's shoulder and announce that she was *his*. But he couldn't do it. Not to her. Not to himself.

Instead, he forced himself to shrug and said, "Jake, this is Kara. My…" Did she take a breath and hold it? Waiting to see how he would introduce her? Could anyone else in the yard feel that near tangible tension that suddenly sprang up between them? Or was he imagining more than was there? "…assistant," he finally finished and then he watched as the expectant light in Kara's eyes flickered out.

Coolly then, as if she and Cooper hadn't just shared a knowing look, she gave her hand to Jake and smiled up at him. "It's a pleasure to meet you. Cooper's told me nothing about you."

Jake took her hand and threaded it through the curve of his arm. "I can take care of that," he said and gave her another wink. "As soon as I get some food in me. It's been a long ride."

"Hell, yes," Jeremiah shouted enthusiastically, as if trying to fill the sudden, yawning void that had opened up in front of them. "We've got steaks in the fridge. Sam, fire up the grill and Maggie, how about you and Kara do up some potatoes?"

"No problem," Maggie retorted and slipped out of Sam's grasp with a quick kiss. Then as she passed Kara, she asked, "Mind helping me out?"

"Not a bit," Kara said smoothly and stepped away from Jake.

As she walked past Cooper, he caught her scent

on the air and inhaled deeply. He whispered her name, not sure what it was he wanted to say—or even if there was anything he could say that would make things less awkward between them. All he knew was, he had to try.

But if she heard, she paid no attention. She deliberately passed him by, as if he weren't even there.

And wasn't that what he wanted?

Kara wanted to cry, but damn it, she wasn't going to.

She'd done this to herself and she knew it. That knowledge though, didn't make this any easier to take. She'd set herself up. Let herself dream idle fantasies about Cooper and how it could be for them.

But the simple truth was, Cooper didn't want her. A couple of nights between the sheets—no matter how fabulous they'd been—didn't make a relationship. And she wasn't willing to settle for anything less.

Now, after talking to Maggie and spending the evening watching Cooper avoid being drawn into stories about the old days, she knew there was no more hope. He hadn't only pulled away from her, he'd also shut himself away from his own family.

"What're you doing?"

Cooper's voice came from behind her and though it startled her, she didn't turn around to look at him. Instead, she picked up her yellow blouse from the bed, folded it neatly and tucked it into the open suitcase in front of her.

"I'm leaving."

"What?" He stepped into the room, walked to her side and stared from the suitcase to her. "*Now?*"

"Yes, now." She swallowed hard, inhaled sharply and blinked furiously, to keep any tears at bay. She wouldn't cry in front of him. Wouldn't let him see that her heart was breaking.

"Were you even going to tell me?"

She glanced at him. His mouth was grim, lips pressed tightly together. "Of course I was, Cooper." She reached past him for the denim skirt she'd brought with her and never wore. Folding it neatly, she laid it into the case. "Besides, I already gave you my two weeks' notice, remember?"

"Yeah, but—" He stalked to the end of the bed, then came right back again. "I didn't think you meant it."

"Now you know."

"Damn it, Kara…" He shoved both hands through his hair then pushed them into the back pockets of his jeans. "What's this really about? I know you like your job, so—"

"Cooper," she said on a sigh, "you know darn well what it's about."

"It's about us, then." He nodded stiffly, pulled one hand free of his pocket to scrape it across his face. "It's about the other night and that dream and the damn ghost and—"

Kara shook her head, grabbed up the last of her blouses and tucked it away. "This has *nothing* to do with the ghost and *everything* to do with us. Well, me, really."

"Kara," he said softly, voice filled with regret, "I just can't give you what you want."

Oh, she knew that. Felt it. Deep in her bones. And she wanted to weep with the knowledge. But that wouldn't do the slightest bit of good.

"Cooper," she said softly, lifting her gaze to his. "Why didn't you tell me about Mac?"

He backed up a step and stared at her for a long minute. "Where did you—oh. Maggie."

"Yes, Maggie."

"She shouldn't have told you."

"You're right," Kara said quietly. "You should have."

He shook his head firmly, shutting out her statement and the remote chance that she might be right. "It was a long time ago."

"No," she argued. "For you, it was yesterday."

He sucked in a gulp of air. "I don't want to talk about this."

"I know that, too," she said and walked to him. Laying both hands on his arms, she felt the tension in his muscles. Felt the rigid self-control he was drawing on and her heart hurt for him. "It wasn't your fault, Cooper. It wasn't anyone's fault."

He blew out a breath. "You don't know."

"Maggie told me what happened."

"She wasn't there. Neither were you."

"You were a kid, Cooper."

He stepped out from under her touch and the shutters were back in his eyes, closing her out. "So was Mac."

The tips of her fingers still hummed with warmth as if she could still feel his skin beneath hers. But there was no point in pretending any longer. There would be no future with a man who couldn't see past his own pain to the promise of something beautiful.

Still, she had to try to help him. One last time. "There was nothing you could have done. Maggie told me that Mac broke his neck when he jumped in."

Cooper actually flinched at her words as if they were a physical blow. He swallowed hard and jerked a nod. "He did. He was trying to beat Jake and his jump did it. But he had to stay underwater longer, too."

Kara tried reaching out for him, but he shook his head firmly. "You wanted to know, well here's what Maggie couldn't tell you," he said tightly. "Sam wanted to go in after Mac. He was worried. Jake was pissed off about losing, but I was *glad*." He slapped one hand against his chest as a choked off, harsh laugh shot from his throat. "I was *happy* that Mac was staying under so long. Glad Jake was finally getting beaten. *I* talked Sam into waiting longer. If I hadn't..." his voice trailed off. "We'll never know

now. We might have saved him. If I'd just gone along with Sam and jumped in after Mac, he might still be alive. So don't tell me you understand. You couldn't."

"No," Kara said softly, empathetic pain rippling through her in response to the torment she read in Cooper's eyes—heard in his voice. "I can't know what you feel. What your regrets are. But I do know that Mac wouldn't want you torturing yourself forever over something that can't be changed."

His mouth worked as if he were grinding his teeth. "I loved him like a brother. And he died while we all stood there like morons."

"You didn't know."

"We *should* have known," Cooper countered quickly. "Should have felt it. And we didn't. And the misery of that day is still with me. I won't love somebody like that again, Kara. I won't risk it."

"I'm so sorry," she said as one stray tear escaped the corner of her eye and trickled down her cheek. "For Mac. For all of you." She inhaled sharply and added, "And I'm sorry for us."

Then she turned, walked back to the bed and closed her suitcase. She zipped it shut, the sound overly loud in the strained silence. Picking it up, she slung her purse over her shoulder and turned for one last look at Cooper.

"I'm going to your grandfather's. Maggie said I could stay in the guesthouse until my flight tomorrow night."

"You don't have to leave."

"Yes," she said, "I really do."

She walked to the open doorway and paused on the threshold to look back at him again. His gaze was locked on her and she wished desperately she could know what he was thinking, feeling. But Cooper had become too adept at hiding those feelings from everyone—including himself—to give anything away now.

"Be happy, Cooper," she said, then turned and walked away.

Eleven

Cooper was still standing where she'd left him, dumbfounded by the fact that Kara had actually gone, when he heard the front door open, then swing shut behind her. Silence pounded through the old house like hammer blows. He couldn't believe it. Kara. Gone.

Her image still fresh in his mind, he saw the hurt in her eyes and closed his own in a futile attempt to make that vision disappear. Instead, it became more clear.

"Damn it," he whispered into the empty room, feeling more alone than he ever had before. "I'd love you if I could, Kara. But it's too late for us."

Instantly, icy cold dropped onto the room as if an invisible blizzard was blowing through. Wind whistled around him, punching at him, driving him toward the doorway. His hair lifted in the swirling, chilly blast and he grabbed the doorjamb and hung on.

Throat tight, heart pounding, he looked around the bedroom in disbelief. A roar rose up with the wind and became a wild, frantic moan of pain. Framed pictures lifted off the walls and sailed in a wide, frigid circle. The overhead light flickered on and off in a frenzied flash like a strobe light in a nightclub. The mirror over the dresser shattered and reflective shards snapped into the room, landing on the floor in a tumble of jagged pieces.

Cooper let go of the doorjamb and braced his feet, leaning into the overpowering wind, determined to stand his own against the fury of the ghost. He stared at the mess and shouted to be heard above the wind, his breath misting in front of his face. "Knock it off! I don't owe you anything, you know!"

The wild keening became louder still and raised goose bumps on his flesh. His stomach dropped and he swallowed back a knot of pure adrenaline pumping through him. The painful, throbbing moan seemed to slice into his soul with an agony that was too deep for description.

And still the wind howled, pictures whirled in ever tightening circles and frost formed on the inside of the windows.

"She's gone and I can't stop her!"

More wailing, higher pitched, frantic.

The walls trembled and the wind screamed.

"I don't take orders from ghosts," he shouted, still trying to make himself heard. But even as those words sounded out in the room, a part of his brain argued with him.

Didn't he take orders from ghosts?

Wasn't everything he did because of Mac's ghost? Or at least the memory of him and what had happened so long ago?

Confusion rattled him and he staggered against the force of the cold battering at him. Was he really so different from the ghost trapped in this house?

Like him, hadn't she given up everything because of her own pain? Hadn't she spent the rest of her life, locked away in grief? Even in death, she stayed determined to shut out even the spirit of the man who was still trying to reach her.

She was so caught up in her own misery, she wasn't able to see a way out. Not then. Not now.

And suddenly, his own possible future stretched out in front of him and that, more than the ghostly cold, chilled Cooper to the bone.

"No," he muttered, shoving both hands through his hair and feeling the ice on his own fingertips. He wasn't like this trapped ghost. His situation was different.

But was it?

He'd cut himself off from love to protect himself from more pain. Kara had tried to get in, past the walls he'd put up around his heart and he'd shut her out. Hadn't this ghost done the same damn thing?

Wasn't she *still* doing it?

The wind abruptly died and the whirling pictures dropped to the floor with a clatter. The cold eased back and rivulets of water traced through the suddenly melting frost on the glass, as if the house were crying.

As the temperature in the room climbed back to normal Cooper stood stunned, like a survivor of a battle, and tried to make sense of his own thoughts.

Before it really was too late.

When a vehicle pulled into Jeremiah's yard an hour after she'd gone to bed, Kara sensed that it was Cooper. She lay awake, staring at the ceiling. She refused to get up and go to the window. Refused to look at him one more time, knowing that if she did, her resolve to leave would only weaken.

And she couldn't allow that.

Couldn't spend the rest of her life, waiting for Cooper to wake up and see that he had a right to live. To love.

So she burrowed under the quilt and willed herself into a restless sleep.

Cooper pounded on the back door of his grandfather's house. He glanced across the yard to the darkened guesthouse and fought the urge to go over there. To pound on the door and demand that Kara let him in.

Desperation ticked inside him like an over-wound clock. Turning back to the door in front of him, he pounded on it again, hard wood stinging his knuckles. He felt a tightly coiled spring inside him and wondered what would happen when it finally snapped.

When the door flew open, he staggered back a step and damn near fell off the back porch.

"Are you *nuts?*" Sam demanded, glaring at Cooper in the harsh glow of the porch light. "What the hell are you doing waking me up?"

"I need to talk to you." Cooper ignored his cousin's temper and pushed past Sam into the lamp lit kitchen. His sneakers squeaked on the linoleum as he paced a frantic route back and forth between the sink and the refrigerator. Stabbing his fingers through his hair repeatedly, he tried to shake loose the tumbling thoughts rolling through his brain, but he just couldn't make sense of them.

Which was why he'd come to Sam.

Sam had been there that day.

Sam knew what Cooper was living with because he had to live with it, too. But somehow, Sam had made it past the ugliness of that one day fifteen years ago. He'd made peace with Mac and Cooper desperately needed to know how he'd done it.

The door closed and Cooper looked at his cousin. Wearing only a pair of drawstring pajama bottoms,

Sam leaned back against the door, folded his arms across his bare chest and demanded, "What the hell is wrong with you, Cooper?"

"Nothing," he muttered, then corrected himself. "Everything."

"I'm gonna need more," Sam demanded, then headed to the fridge. Pulling out a jug of orange juice, he walked to a cupboard, took out two glasses and poured each of them a drink. Taking a sip, he said, "And keep it down, will you? Maggie spent most of the night heaving her guts up and she needs the rest."

"Sorry," Cooper said automatically, holding the small juice glass cupped in both palms. "But I had to see you."

"Okay," Sam said, picking up on the desperation wafting off Cooper in thick waves. He sat down at the table, pointed to a chair and said, "So here I am. Talk."

Cooper ignored the chair. He couldn't have sat still at the moment if his life had depended on it. Instead, he took a gulp of the OJ and said, "How'd you do it?"

"Do what?"

"Get past what happened to Mac." Cooper's gaze fixed on Sam in a steady stare. "I know you, Sam. You've spent the last fifteen years just like I have— just like Jake has. Avoiding family. Avoiding each other. All because of what happened that day."

Sam's gaze dropped to the glass of juice. "Yeah. I did."

"So what changed?"

He lifted his gaze again and shrugged. "I found Maggie."

"And just like that you could open up? You could change who you were?"

"Hell, no," Sam said, slumping back against the chair. "I didn't want to change. Didn't want to love her. Didn't want to stay here," he said, waving one hand to encompass the house, the ranch and all of Coleville. "But damn it, Cooper, I was tired of running from Mac."

"Is that what we're doing?" he asked thoughtfully. "Or are we running from what we didn't do that day?"

"A little of both, I think," Sam said. "Sit down, Cooper."

Slowly, Cooper sank onto the chair but kept his gaze fixed on his cousin. Quietly, he said, "Kara's leaving."

"I know."

"Of course you know," Cooper said with a strained chuckle. "She's *here*."

"And are you letting her go?"

"I can't stop her." It tore at him. Everything in him wanted to leave this house, march across the yard and pound on the door of the guesthouse until she let him in. He wanted to bury himself inside her and let her warmth wrap around him.

But how could he do that?

"You're an idiot."

Cooper's gaze snapped back to Sam's. "Thanks. I feel better."

Leaning forward, bracing both arms on the tabletop, Sam shook his head and said, "You shouldn't feel better. Kara's leaving and you're not doing anything to prevent it. You should feel horrible."

"I do," Cooper admitted. "But damn it, how can I love her? How the hell can I do that after Mac?"

"What's Mac got to do with it?"

"You're a great one to say that."

"Right. Okay. I get it. But I got past that," Sam said. "I almost lost Maggie. Almost lost the child we made together." He shook his head slowly, in disbelief, as if even *he* could hardly understand the man who'd made so many bad choices. "Do you really think Mac would have wanted that? Do you believe Mac wants us all to suffer for the rest of our lives?"

"No, I don't," Cooper said grudgingly. God, he could still see Mac so clearly in his mind. Forever sixteen years old, his eyes shining with mischief, his wild laugh punching the air as he challenged his cousins to one daredevil stunt after another.

Mac had loved life so much. Had squeezed every drop of fun out of every damn day he'd had. He'd hate knowing his cousins had pretty much resigned from life because of him.

"But how do you get past the fear?" Cooper asked quietly, studying the surface of the orange juice as if it had the secrets of the world etched on top. "How do you let yourself love somebody that freely again without being terrified of losing it?"

"You don't," Sam said, just as quietly. "The fear's always there. I can't even imagine losing Maggie. The thought of it terrifies me."

"Comforting."

"But the love's always there, too," Sam told him. "And without that, all you've got is the fear. That's an empty way to live, Cooper."

"Yeah."

"So, if you came here looking for advice…here it is." Sam stood up and looked down at him. "Make peace with Mac. Lay the past to rest so you can have a future."

"I don't know that I can."

"If you can't…" Sam said, "If you're willing to let Kara go out of your life because you're too scared to let her in—"

"Yeah?"

"—Then you don't deserve her anyway." He picked up his orange juice, drained it, then set the glass on the kitchen counter. "Turn off the light and lock the door when you go."

Cooper knew the way to the lake.

Could have found his way there blindfolded.

Time ticked past though as it took him more than twice as long to walk the distance as it should have. Every step felt as though he were dragging his feet free of mud. His brain knew he had to go back to the lake—face what had happened so long ago.

But his heart ached at the thought of it.

Fifteen years had passed, but the land hadn't changed much. He slowly climbed the ridge in the pale wash of moonlight and in the distance, heard the high-pitched howl of a coyote serenade. A soft, cool wind with the taste of the ocean on it, swept across the open fields and tugged at Cooper's hair. He turned his face into it and paused long enough to settle the frantic race of his heartbeat.

He'd never intended to come back here. To this place. Never thought he'd be able to.

And as he made it to the top of the ridge and looked out over the dark water, dappled in moonlight, he felt the years pass away. Once again, he was sixteen, standing with his cousins at the top of the world.

He felt the sun, hot on his bare shoulders. Heard Jake cussing a blue streak because Mac had out-jumped him. Listened to Sam chuckle as he carefully studied the stopwatch, timing Mac's underwater stretch. And heard himself saying *Give him another few seconds, Sam. He really wants to beat Jake. And I want him to. Mac's okay. Stop being an old woman.*

Wincing now, Cooper stared out at the spot where Mac had landed that last time. And he kept staring, as if he could see through the water to where they'd eventually found Mac, stretched out on the bottom of the lake—already dead.

They'd tried CPR. They'd tried pushing the water from Mac's lungs.

But they were too late.

And they'd lost not only Mac that afternoon, but their own innocence and sense of invincibility.

"Mac?" Cooper's whisper came low and strained, as if that single word had been squeezed out of his throat grudgingly. "You still here?"

The wind pushed at him playfully and in his mind, he heard laughter. Mac's laughter. Cooper spun around, half expecting to see the tall, lanky kid striding up the ridge to join him.

And the disappointment at finding himself all alone was staggering.

Still, remembering the furious temper of the ghost he'd left behind at the Victorian, Cooper wondered if Mac's spirit was trapped at the lake. Was he here, even now, waiting for his cousins to come back and—*what?*

"What could you be waiting for? To hear us say we're sorry?" he asked the wind. "What good would that do?"

Toward the east, the sky was beginning to lighten into a soft violet, heralding the coming dawn. Hours must have passed since he'd left the ranch house. Amazing that he'd been walking for so long.

He lifted his gaze from the rippled surface of the lake to the star-studded sky overhead. "We *are* sorry, you know. For all the good it does. You died too young, Mac. And we miss you. All of us do."

Shaking his head, he admitted, "God, I've relived that day a thousand times. Over and over again in my mind, I've replayed what happened. And every time, I save you." His voice broke and his gaze dropped, back to the lake, where his young life had shattered so completely.

"I want you to know that, Mac. Every time I remember that day, we save you." He choked out a laugh and rubbed his hand across his face. "Of course, we didn't when it really counted...God, I wish I could change it. Wish I could bring you back. Or hell, even talk to you. I've missed you so damn much."

A freshening wind slapped at him again, throwing his hair across his eyes and he found himself smiling in spite of the knife-like pain twisting inside him. Was the wind Mac's way of telling him to stop beating himself up over the past?

Or was that just wishful thinking?

Hell, up to a few weeks ago, Cooper had never really believed in ghosts. Now, he was convinced that something of who you were survived death. It wasn't a complete end. Maybe death really was just a bend in the road, beyond which we can't see. Maybe there's more out there than any of us have ever imagined.

God, he hoped so.

Hoped Mac was having a great time wherever he was. But could he move on, knowing that those he'd left behind were all still trapped in reruns of that summer day?

Cooper had never known pain like he'd experienced that day fifteen years before. Because he'd deliberately avoided it. By never allowing himself to love that freely, deeply, he'd kept himself free from pain—but he'd also hidden away from real joy. He'd lived a half life—safe but alone. Hell, Mac had lived more in sixteen years than Cooper had in thirty-one.

He'd locked himself away from life in some self-appointed penance for something he couldn't have changed. He'd felt guilty being alive when Mac was dead. And maybe, he thought, if something of Mac lingered in this place, maybe it was because none of his cousins had been able to let him go.

He'd hate to think that.

The three of them—Cooper, Sam and Jake—had all grieved in their own way, but they'd all shared at least one trait. They'd stayed away. From here.

From memories of Mac.

Yet, there'd been so much more to Mac than that one last day. And instead of focusing on those memories, they'd all chosen to relive the tragedy over and over again.

What a waste.

What a pitiful way to remember a boy they'd all loved.

Suddenly exhausted as emotions churned inside, Cooper dropped onto the grassy ground, drew his knees up and wrapped his arms around them. In the moonlight and the still chill of the night, Cooper felt the ice around his heart shatter and fall away. The cold he'd lived with for so long began to melt and he drew his first easy breath in fifteen long years.

Stretching out on the dewy grass, Cooper closed his eyes and felt the exhaustion of the complete release of tension seep through him like a rising tide. The aches and misery of years washed away, leaving him with only the memories of the good times they'd all had.

Of the summers that would live forever.

Of the boy who'd died too young, but had lived a lifetime in sixteen short years.

And in his mind, he saw Mac again. Young and laughing. Running up the ridge and leaping out into the lake—fearless, joyful.

Cooper smiled and whispered, "Thanks, Mac."

Twelve

Cooper woke with a jolt.

Sunlight streamed into his eyes and he squinted instantly in self-defense. A moment or two of complete confusion rattled through him. Where the hell was he and how did he—

The lake. He sat straight up and stared down from the ridge at the dark blue water below. Sunlight skittered off the surface, twinkling like downed stars.

He rubbed his eyes and stood up, stretching aching muscles. Not the most comfortable place to spend the night, he thought, but at the same time, it had been the best sleep he'd had in fifteen years. He'd finally come to terms with Mac.

Sorrow balled in the pit of his stomach, but this was a sweet sadness for something long missed. Not the lurch of guilt and pain that had so long been a part of his life.

"Kara was right," he said aloud, then shot a quick look at his watch. *Kara.*

She was leaving and he had to stop her. Had to try to make her see that he wasn't a complete loss. That he'd finally found a way to look ahead. To look into his own future and when he did, all he saw was her.

Then, as if Mac were standing right there beside him, he heard his cousin's voice say, *What're you waiting for? Go get her.*

Grinning, Cooper turned around and started running toward the ranch—toward Kara.

"Thanks for the ride," Kara said, reaching into the backseat to pull out her suitcase.

"Not a problem," Maggie told her and closed the door for her. "But are you sure about this? You've got a long day of just sitting at the airport waiting for your plane."

Kara inhaled sharply, deeply and glanced around at the people jostling for space at curb side check-in. Then she shifted her gaze back to Maggie. The woman stared at her with sympathy in her eyes, and though Kara appreciated the thought, she really didn't want to acknowledge it. And, if she'd spent the day at the ranch, she'd have been faced with that sympathy all day. Not only from Maggie, but from Sam and Jeremiah and even Jake.

And, there was always the chance that Cooper might drop by the ranch house. No. It was better this way. She'd rather spend the day at the airport than risk running into Cooper one more time.

"Don't worry about me," she chirped, putting a little too much cheer into her voice, "I've got a good book and a pile of magazines to read."

Maggie nodded as if she understood every thought that was racing through Kara's mind. "Okay. But if it's okay with you, when I get back to the ranch, I think I'll give Cooper a good hard kick."

Unexpectedly, a sheen of tears bristled at the backs of her eyes and Kara smiled tightly. "Thanks," she said and instinctively leaned in for a hug. Then before she could change her mind, she grabbed hold of the suitcase handle and headed for the terminal.

"Kara!" Cooper pounded on the door of the guesthouse, then moved to the front window. Stepping through the jungle of geraniums planted before it, he cupped his hands on the window glass and peered into the dark house. "Kara, damn it, open the door! I need to talk to you!"

Nothing.

"What the hell are you up to?" Sam called out from across the yard.

Cooper spun around. "I'm looking for Kara. Where is she?"

Sam leaned one shoulder against a porch post and lifted a cup of coffee for a sip. "She came here to get away from you, Cooper."

Pushing through the geraniums that fought him every inch of the way, Cooper stomped across the grassy dirt and stood at the bottom of the steps, glaring at his cousin. "Don't get in the middle of this, Sam."

"Get in?" Sam countered with a sneer, "You're the one who *dragged* me in, remember? Weren't you just here last night complaining to me?"

"Yeah," he admitted. "I was." Scraping one hand along the side of his head, he pushed his hair back then let his hand drop in disgust. "But things're different now. I—" He shut up suddenly and demanded, "Where is she?"

"She's gone."

"Gone?" Panic bubbled up in his throat but Cooper swallowed it. "What do you mean, *gone?*"

"What's all the shouting about?" Jeremiah demanded, stepping out onto the porch beside Sam. "Oh, Cooper. It's you."

"Yeah, it's me."

Sheba hurtled out the back door, squeezing through the legs of the two men to throw herself joyfully at Cooper. Bounding at his legs, she yapped and barked and ran in dizzying circles around him in a bid for attention. Cooper was too focused to notice.

"Man, can't a guy even get any sleep in the country?" Jake's grumble rolled over the puppy's gleeful barking in a growl of complaint. "I've slept in train stations quieter than this place."

"Great." Cooper threw his hands high, then let them fall again. "Everybody here now?" Narrowing a look at Sam, he demanded, "Where's Kara?"

"Why should I tell you?"

Jake grabbed Sam's coffee and took a long gulp.

"Hey, get your own."

Jake ignored him, only mumbling, "Tell him where she is, already, huh? And somebody shut that dog up."

"Still a prizewinner in the morning, aren't you?" Jeremiah snapped, then said, "Sheba! Cut it out."

The puppy immediately quieted and plopped her butt onto the ground beside Cooper, all the while managing to still wag her tail and squirm in place.

"Damn it Sam, tell me," Cooper said, ignoring the others. "Please."

Sam studied him for a long minute before making up his mind. Finally though, he nodded, took his cup back from Jake and looked at Cooper. "Maggie took her to the airport. She went early I think, to avoid seeing you again."

Cooper winced as the truth of that statement hit him like a slap. God, he'd been an idiot. The question was, was it too late to make up for it?

"Thanks," he said and headed for Jeremiah's beat-up ranch truck. "I'll bring the truck back later."

"Boy," Jeremiah shouted, taking the first couple of steps. "Wait up a minute there. I've got something I've got to say to the three of you and—"

Cooper never even looked back. "It'll have to wait, Jeremiah." He opened the truck door, climbed inside and fired up the engine. Slamming the door shut again, he threw the car into Drive, punched the gas pedal and muttered, "I've got something way more important to say. I only hope she'll listen."

"Hey!" A security guard shouted as Cooper parked the truck in front of the terminal and bailed out. "You can't leave that thing there!"

He didn't have time to move it. Didn't care enough to worry about it. His brain was focused on one thing. Kara. She was all that mattered now.

She was *all*.

"Have it towed," he shouted back and hit the automatic double doors in such a hurry they didn't have time to swing open for him. He'd worry about the truck later. Pay the fines, whatever.

Right now, he had to find her.

His gaze swept the crowd. People. Too many people. The noise level was immense. Kids cried, parents soothed, teenagers up against a wall, kissing goodbye as if facing Armageddon. Huge suitcases rolled across the gleaming linoleum, their steel wheels growling a warning at anyone in their way. A disembodied voice shimmied through the speaker system, but the words were garbled, as if the speaker was talking around a mouthful of marbles.

Cooper's gaze swung back and forth, searching every face. Stalking through the crowd, pushing through the congested terminal, he checked the television screens for arrival and departure times and located the gate that Kara's plane would be using.

He sprinted down the long, narrow passage, slipping in and out of the crowd, mumbling apologies, but never stopping. Never slowing. His heart raced and his brain moved even faster. One speech after another rose up in his mind, was considered, then rejected. He had to make her see. Understand.

Had to make her *believe*.

But how?

Just outside security, his gaze shifted quickly over the people standing in line until he found the one face he'd been searching for. Kara. She stood alone, staring into space.

His heart twisted in his chest and he swallowed hard. This was it. And if he blew it, he'd never forgive himself.

Hurrying to her, he stopped right in front of her and waited as she slowly lifted her gaze to his. He saw surprise and pleasure light up her eyes before those emotions were extinguished and buried under a sheen of regret.

He felt the solid punch of her pain as if it were a blow to his midsection, but he couldn't let it stop him. "I've been looking for you," he said inanely.

"I left the ranch early so I wouldn't have to see you again," she admitted.

"Yeah, I figured that out. And I don't blame you," he said. Reaching for her hands, he held them in both of his and tightened his grip when she would have pulled free. "Don't. Kara, please. You've gotta listen to me."

Hope lit up her eyes briefly, then was gone again in a wink. But the fact that it had been there at all, gave Cooper reason for a little hope himself.

"I really think we've said everything, Cooper."

"Not by a long shot," he argued, then fixed a steely stare on a businessman type who wandered up to take his place in line behind her. The man got the message and scuttled off quickly.

"Fine," she said. "Say what you came to say and then go, okay?"

"I'm an idiot."

Both of her eyebrows lifted. "Interesting start."

He gave her a half smile and squeezed her hands briefly. "There's more."

"I'm listening," she said and he could see her take a deep breath and hold it.

Shaking his head, Cooper searched for the right words but couldn't find them. "Damn it, I'm a writer.

I should be good at this. But now, when I need them the most, the words aren't there."

Hope was back in her eyes and just a hint of a smile was on her mouth. "Give it your best shot."

"Okay." Nodding, he said, "I'll say the most important part first and work back around to it again later."

She nodded, waiting.

"I love you."

She sucked in a gulp of air and tears began to glitter in her eyes. Panic jolted inside him.

"I don't want you to cry," he said desperately. "I wanted to make you happy. Make *us* happy."

"Then keep talking," she urged.

"You were right," he said, figuring every woman loved to hear that—especially when it was true. "I should have told you about Mac. Hell, I should have found a way to deal with that pain a long time ago. But I didn't. Because it was easier to hide from it. To hide from everything. Everyone."

She squeezed his hands. In support? Sympathy? He didn't know, so he kept talking.

"I hid from life for so long, Kara," he said, "I'd forgotten what real joy was. What life could be like. But the last week or so with you reminded me. I know we've been together for a long time, but here, it was different. In Coleville, we were really *together*, together. You know?"

"Yeah, I know what you mean."

"Good. Good." He nodded and fought for breath.

That voice over the loudspeaker came again and all over the airport, heads cocked to listen, to try to understand the garbled words. The security line moved forward.

Cooper and Kara ignored it.

"I went to the lake last night."

"You did?" Understanding lit up her eyes and highlighted the banked tears about to fall.

Cooper talked faster, hoping to forestall them.

"I did. I talked to Mac. Discovered something else you were right about. It wasn't our fault. And Mac doesn't blame us."

"Oh, Cooper…"

"I think he wants us to be happy," he was saying, feeling the truth of his words as they poured from him in a rush. "I think he expects us to live the kind of life he would have if he'd been given the chance. And Kara, I want that, too."

"I'm glad."

"Good," he said smiling, "because you're pretty much integral to my plan."

"I am?" Her fingers curled around his and he lifted their joined hands to kiss her knuckles.

"Oh, you really are. I love you, Kara. See? Told you I'd get back around to the most important part of this."

"I'm liking it so far."

He swallowed a knot of emotion so huge it threatened to choke him, but still he found a way to say,

"I never thought I could love this much. But I do. You're everything to me, Kara. And I want the chance to prove it to you."

"Cooper..."

He spoke fast, half afraid she'd shut him down before he could finish. "No, listen. I won't let you go without a fight, Kara. If you get on a plane, I'll follow you. If you move, I'll go wherever you do. I will spend the rest of my life proving to you just how much I love you. If you'll just give me that chance."

Kara's heart swelled in her chest so that she could hardly draw breath. This was everything and more than she'd ever hoped for. And oh, she wanted to believe. She looked into Cooper's eyes and read the very emotions she'd so hoped to see. But she had to have more.

She wasn't prepared to settle for less than everything.

"I love you, too, Cooper," she said.

"Thank God," he murmured, shoulders slumping in relief.

"But..."

"There's a but?"

She smiled at him. "I won't settle for being your assistant or live-in lover. I want it all, Cooper. I want to be married. I want kids. A family."

He gave her a grin that nearly knocked her off her feet. "Of course we'll get married. And we'll have dozens of kids!"

"Dozens?"

"That part's negotiable," he acknowledged, then added, "and you won't be my assistant anymore. We'll hire someone else."

Kara shook her head and leaned in for a long, lingering kiss. "Nobody butters your toast but me, Cooper."

He sighed and drew her into the circle of his arms. "Now that sounds like a plan." After a quick hug, though, he pulled back and said, "Come on. I'm taking you back to the house. We've got a lot of making up to do."

"Now *that's* a plan," she said, throwing his own words back at him.

They had to take a cab, since Jeremiah's truck had indeed been towed. But Cooper promised to ransom it… *later.*

He carried her up the short flight of steps to the front door, but before he could open it, the heavy wood door swung open in invitation. Tightening his grip on Kara, Cooper cautiously stepped into the foyer and stopped dead.

Warmth spilled through the old house and sunlight seemed to spear in directly through the walls, making the whole place brilliant with a hazy, golden glow as unearthly as it was beautiful.

"What?" Cooper whispered.

"Shh…" Kara urged, smiling. "Listen."

Cooper held his breath and waited. Then he heard the soft, musical sound that Kara had.

A young couple, laughing with unrestrained joy. Together at last.

Epilogue

The truck had been bailed out of the storage yard, Kara's already checked suitcase would be returned as soon as it reached New York and she and Cooper had already made quite an effort at starting their first child.

After dinner at Jeremiah's, the family sat around the kitchen table and waited for the older man to make the announcement he'd called them all together for.

At last, he stood up, and looked from one grandson to the other. "I can't tell you boys what it means to this old man to have you all home again." Then he smiled at Kara and Maggie in turn. "And to have you two in my family, makes me gladder than you'll ever know."

Kara reached for Cooper's hand and her heart skipped when he folded his fingers around it.

"But beyond missing you all," Jeremiah said, "there was another reason for getting you back here this summer."

"You're not going to try the 'I'm dying' thing again, are you?" Jake asked.

"Nope." Jeremiah had the grace to flush and in the overhead kitchen light, his eyes sparkled with something that looked a lot like expectation. "This is the God's truth. And I decided to wait until all three of you were here together to tell you."

"C'mon, Jeremiah," Sam urged, dropping one arm around Maggie's shoulders. "Spill it before you bust."

"Right then. Donna Barrett's back in town."

"I know," Cooper said. "I saw her at the drugstore. Hell, I'm the one who told you guys. So if that's your news, Jeremiah, it's a little late."

The old man scowled at him. "There's more. She didn't come back to town alone. She's got Mac's son with her."

* * * * *

BRENDA JACKSON

The
Durango Affair

Harlequin
Mills & Boon

Desire

DID YOU PURCHASE THIS BOOK WITHOUT A COVER?
If you did, you should be aware it is **stolen property** as it was
reported 'unsold and destroyed' by a retailer.
Neither the author nor the publisher has received any payment
for this book.

First Published 2006
First Australian Paperback Edition 2006
ISBN 0 733 56915 3

THE DURANGO AFFAIR © 2006 by Brenda Streater Jackson
Philippine Copyright 2006
Australian Copyright 2006
New Zealand Copyright 2006
Except for use in any review, the reproduction or utilisation of this work in
whole or in part in any form by any electronic, mechanical or other means,
now known or hereafter invented, including xerography, photocopying and
recording, or in any information storage or retrieval system, is forbidden
without the permission of the publisher, Harlequin Mills & Boon, Locked Bag
7002, Chatswood D.C. N.S.W., Australia 2067.

All the characters in this book have no existence outside the imagination of
the author, and have no relation whatsoever to anyone bearing the same
name or names. They are not even distantly inspired by any individual
known or unknown to the author, and all the incidents are pure invention.

This book is sold subject to the condition that it shall not, by way of trade or
otherwise, be lent, resold, hired out or otherwise circulated without the prior
consent of the publisher in any form of binding or cover other than that in
which it is published and without a similar condition including this condition
being imposed on the subsequent purchaser.

All rights reserved including the right of reproduction in whole or in part in
any form. This edition is published by arrangement with Harlequin
Enterprises II B.V.

Published by
Harlequin Mills & Boon
3 Gibbes Street
CHATSWOOD NSW 2067
AUSTRALIA

HARLEQUIN MILLS & BOON DESIRE and the Rose Device are trademarks
used under license and registered in Australia, New Zealand, Philippines,
United States Patent & Trademark Office and in other countries.

Printed and bound in Australia by
McPherson's Printing Group

BRENDA JACKSON

is a die "heart" romantic who married her childhood sweetheart and still proudly wears the "going steady" ring he gave her when she was fifteen. Because she's always believed in the power of love, Brenda's stories always have happy endings. In her real-life love story, Brenda and her husband of thirty-three years live in Jacksonville, Florida, and have two sons.

A *USA TODAY* bestselling author, Brenda divides her time between family, writing and working in management at a major insurance company. You may write Brenda at P.O. Box 28267, Jacksonville, Florida 32226; her e-mail address WriterBJackson@aol.com; or visit her Web site at www.brendajackson.net.

ACKNOWLEDGMENTS

To Gerald Jackson, Sr., my husband and hero.

To my Heavenly Father who gave me the gift to write.

Love does not delight in evil but rejoices
with the truth. It always protects, always trusts,
always hopes, always perseveres.
—*I Corinthians* 13:6–7

One

Durango Westmoreland stood at the window and focused his gaze on the mountains as a dark frown marred his handsome face. He had awakened that morning with an ache in his right knee, which could only mean one thing. A snowstorm was coming. The forecasters were reporting that it wouldn't hit Bozeman and would veer north toward Havre. But he knew differently. His knee didn't lie.

There was definitely nothing scientific about his prediction but still, even with a clear blue Montana sky, he knew he was right. A man didn't live in the mountains unless he was in sync with his environment. The mountains could hold you prisoner in the valley whenever a snowstorm hit, and their snowslides struck fear in the hearts of unsuspecting skiers.

These were the mountains that he loved and considered home even on their worst days.

Durango's thoughts shifted to another place he considered home: the city where he was born, Atlanta. He often missed the closeness of the family he had left behind there, and although he would be the first to admit that he liked his privacy—and his space—it was times like this when he missed his family most.

He did have an uncle who lived near, although definitely not a skip and a hop by any means. Corey Westmoreland's breathtaking monstrosity of a ranch was high in the mountains on a peak that everyone referred to as Corey's Mountain. However, now that Corey had gotten married, he didn't visit as often. So Durango had become somewhat of a loner who was satisfied with enjoying the memories of his occasional visits home.

One such visit was still vividly clear in his mind. It was the time he'd returned to Atlanta for his cousin Chase's wedding and had met Savannah Claiborne, the sister of the bride.

From the moment their eyes had connected there had been a startling attraction. He couldn't recall the last time he'd been so taken with a woman. In no time at all she had turned his world upside down. She had actually charmed her way past his tight guard and his common sense.

Later that evening, after seeing the bride and groom off, everyone, still in a festive mood, had remained in the hotel's ballroom and continued to party, intent on celebrating the night away.

Both he and Savannah were more than a little tipsy and pretty wired up when he had walked her to her hotel room at midnight. And at the time, accepting her offer of a nightcap had seemed like the right thing to do. But once alone, one thing led to another and they had ended up making love.

That night his total concentration had been on her. Even now the memories of their one night together were tucked away and reserved for times like this when the claws of loneliness clutched at him, and made him think about things that a devout bachelor had no business thinking about—like a woman in his life who would always be within arm's reach.

"Damn."

He shook such foolish thoughts away and blamed his uncle's recent marriage for such crazy notions. Durango quickly reminded himself that he had tried love once and it had earned him a scar on his heart. That wound was a constant reminder of the pain he had suffered. Now he much preferred the easy life with just him and his mountains. He kept women at arm's length, except for when he sought out their company to satisfy his physical needs. Emotional need was as foreign a concept to him as sunbathing in the snow-covered Rockies. He had risked his heart once and refused to do so ever again.

But still, thoughts of Savannah Claiborne clung to him, did things to him. And no matter how many times he told himself she was just another woman, some small thing would trigger memories of that night, and along with the memories came the startling realization that she wasn't just another woman. She was in a class all by herself. At those times he could almost feel her lying beside him, beneath him, while he touched her, stroked her and coaxed her to take him deeper while he satisfied the pulsing ache within him….

Needing to get a grip, he forced his breathing back

to normal and compelled his body to relax. He turned around and headed for the phone, deciding to call the rangers' station. They were down one park ranger due to Lonnie Berman being in the hospital for knee surgery, and if they needed an extra hand, Durango had no problem going in.

As he dialed the phone he felt his control sliding back into place. That was good. That was the way he wanted it and that was the way he intended to keep it.

Savannah Claiborne stood in front of the solid oak door, not believing that she had finally arrived in Montana and that in a few moments she would come face-to-face with Durango Westmoreland again. When she had made the decision to come and meet with him instead of making a phone call, she hadn't thought that delivering the news would be difficult.

Now that she was here she was discovering that it was.

She shook her head at her own stupidity, asking herself for the one hundredth time how such a thing could have happened to her. She wasn't a teenager who hadn't been educated on safe sex. She was a twenty-seven-year-old woman who knew the score about birth control. Too bad she had been too busy celebrating her sister's nuptials to remember to take her Pill, which had left her unprotected and was the main reason she would be having a baby in seven months.

And to make a sad song even sadder, she knew very little about her baby's daddy other than that he was a park ranger and that, in her opinion, he was an expert at making love...and, evidently, at making babies, whether he had intended to make this one or not.

She also knew from the discussions she'd had with her sister that Durango was a devout bachelor and intended to stay that way. She had no plans to change that status but was merely here to deliver the news. What he did with it was his business. Her goal was to return to Philly and become a single parent. Getting pregnant might not have been in her immediate plans, but she definitely wanted this baby.

She paused after lifting her hand to knock on the door and released a deep breath. She was actually nervous about seeing Durango again. The last time she had seen him was when he had walked out of her hotel room two months ago after spending the night with her.

A one-night stand was definitely not her style. She had never been one to indulge in a casual affair. But that night she had gotten a little tipsy and emotional after seeing just how happy her sister was. It really was pathetic. She could never handle alcohol and she knew it. And yet she had fallen into the partying spirit and had imbibed a little anyway.

Since that night, Durango had haunted her dreams and had been the cause of many sleepless nights…and now it appeared he was partly to blame for interrupting her mornings, as well. Recently she had begun to experience bouts of morning sickness.

The only other person who knew about her pregnancy was her sister Jessica. Jess had agreed with her that Durango had a right to know about the pregnancy and that Savannah should tell him in person.

Breathing in deeply, she inhaled and knocked on the door. His SUV was parked out front, which meant he was home.

Savannah swallowed against the thickness in her throat when she heard the sound of the doorknob turning. Then the door opened. She literally stopped breathing when she looked into Durango's face, beyond his toe-curling handsome features to see the surprise that lit his eyes.

Standing tall in the doorway, wearing a pair of jeans and a Western-style shirt that covered his broad shoulders and muscular chest, he looked just as gorgeous as before—bigger than life and sexier than sin. Her gaze studied all the features that had first captured her attention: the close-cropped curly black hair, his chestnut coloring, well-defined mouth and intense dark eyes.

"Savannah? This is a surprise. What are you doing here?"

Savannah's stomach tightened once again; she knew what she was experiencing was probably the same effect Durango had on countless other women. She took a deep breath and tried not to think about that. "I need to talk to you, Durango. May I come in?" she said in a quick rush.

He quirked an eyebrow and stared at her. Then he took a step back and said, "Sure. Come on in."

Durango was certain he didn't possess a sixth sense; however, he found it pretty damn eerie that the woman he had been thinking about just hours earlier had materialized on his doorstep at the worst possible time to be in Montana. Although January was the coldest month in the mountains, February wasn't much better. Whatever she wanted to talk to him about had to be mighty important to bring her all the way to his neck of the woods in the winter.

He studied her for a moment, watched as she removed her overcoat, knitted hat and gloves. "Would you care for something to drink? I just made a pot of hot chocolate," he said, still at a loss as to why she was there and finding it hard to believe that she really was.

"Yes, thanks. It would certainly warm me up some."

He nodded. Now that she had removed all the heavy outer garments and stood before him in a pair of designer slacks and a cashmere pullover sweater, he couldn't stop his gaze from wandering over her body. It was as perfect as he remembered. Her breasts were still full and firm, her waist was small and her hips were nicely curvy. His gaze then moved to her caramel-colored face. It was as beautiful as before, even more so, he thought. And those eyes…

He inhaled deeply. Those hazel eyes had been his downfall. He had been a goner from the moment he had first gazed into them at the rehearsal dinner. And the night when they had made love and he had held her gaze when she had reached a climax, locking into those eyes had sent him over the edge. He had experienced an orgasm that had been out of this world. Even now he couldn't help but swallow hard at the memory.

But then all it took was a look at her sleek designer attire for Durango to remember that Savannah was a city girl. She had the words dignified and refined stamped all over her, although he could clearly remember when she'd tossed gentility out the window and displayed a distinct streak of wildness that one night.

Suddenly the memory of all they had done that night made every ounce of blood in his body race to his groin. Jeez. He had to get a grip. What happened to that control he had gotten hold of earlier? He was behaving like a horny teenager instead of a thirty-five-year-old man.

"Make yourself comfortable," he managed to say after clearing his throat. "I'll be back in a second."

He walked off, wondering why he was handling her with kid gloves. Usually when a woman showed up at his house unannounced he told them in a nice or not-so-nice way, depending on his mood, to haul ass and not come back unless he issued an invitation. The only excuse he could come up with was that since she was Chase's sister-in-law, he was making her an exception to his rule. And yet he had an unsettling feeling that there was something different about her, something he couldn't put his finger on.

When he returned with the hot chocolate he intended to learn the real reason for Savannah's surprise visit.

Savannah watched Durango leave the room. What she was about to do wouldn't be easy, but she was determined to do the right thing. He deserved to know. Who knows? He might end up being a better father to his child than her father had been to her, Jessica and their brother, Rico.

She smiled when she thought of her brother. Although he wouldn't like the thought of her being a single parent, he would look forward to being an uncle. And if Durango didn't want to play a part in his child's life, Rico would readily step in as a father figure.

Savannah sighed and glanced around, taking a real good look at her surroundings through the eyes of the photographer she was, and noticing just how massive Durango's home was, the spaciousness spread over two levels. The downstairs interior walls were washed stone, a massive brick fireplace was to her right and a huge built-in bookcase adorned one single wall. The bookcase was completely lined with books. She couldn't help but smile, thinking that she certainly couldn't imagine Durango spending his free time reading.

In the center of the room were a comfy-looking sofa and love seat that were separated by a coffee table. There were also a couple of rocking chairs sitting in front of huge windows that provided a beautiful view of the mountains. Wooden stairs led up to what appeared to be a loft with additional bedrooms. All the furnishings looked comfortable yet personable at the same time.

"Here we go."

She turned when Durango reentered the room carrying a tray with two cups of steaming hot chocolate. Even doing something so domesticated, he oozed a masculine sensuality that was playing havoc on her body. Her hormone level was definitely at an all-time high today. Even her breasts felt more sensitive than usual.

"Thanks," she said, crossing the room to where he stood.

Durango set the tray down on the table. Savannah was standing next to him, so close he could smell her perfume. It was the same scent she had worn that night. He had liked it then and he liked it even more now. He handed her a cup, deciding that he had played the role of Mr. Nice Guy long enough. He needed to know what the hell she was doing here and why she needed to talk to him.

He glanced at her; their gazes met. The eyes staring back at him were anything but calm. "What's this about, Savannah?" he asked smoothly, deciding to cut to the chase. She had no reason to show up on his doorstep in the dead of winter to talk to him, two months after they had last seen each other, slept together, made love…unless…

His eyebrows furrowed at the same moment as he felt a jolt in the pit of his stomach. For a moment he couldn't breathe. He hoped to hell he was all wrong, but he had a feeling that he wasn't. He wasn't born yesterday and was experienced enough to know that one-night stands only showed up again if they were interested in a repeat performance—or if they had unwanted news to drop into your lap.

His heart began to pound when he saw the determined expression on her face. All of a sudden, the thought that she had tracked him to his mountain refuge to bear her unwanted news made him furious. "Let's have it, Savannah. What's the reason for your visit?"

Savannah slowly placed her cup back down on the tray, tilted her head and met Durango's accusing stare. There was razor-sharp intelligence in the dark depths of his gaze and she knew he had figured things out. So there was no reason to beat around the bush.

She momentarily looked away, inhaled deeply and then met his gaze once more. He had no reason to be angry. She was the one enduring bouts of morning sickness, and she definitely wasn't there to make any demands on him.

Lifting her chin, she met his glare with one of her own and said, "I'm pregnant."

Two

Durango inhaled sharply when he experienced what felt like a swift, hard kick in the gut. She didn't say the baby was his but he knew damn well that was what she was insinuating. He made love. He didn't make babies. However, with the memories of that night constantly on his mind, anything was possible. But still, he remembered what she had told him that morning before he'd left. And with that thought, he summoned up a tight smile. "That's not possible."

Savannah lifted an eyebrow. "If you want me to believe that you're sterile, forget it," she said through gritted teeth.

He leaned back against the table, casually crossing his arms over his chest. "No, I'm not sterile. But if I remember correctly, the morning after you told me not to worry about anything because you were on birth control."

Unconsciously mirroring his stance, Savannah also

crossed her arms over her chest. "I was. However, I forgot to take the Pill. Usually missing one pill wouldn't hurt, but in this case…I seem to be the exception and not the norm."

"You forgot to take the Pill?" Durango's heart continued to pound and he shook his head in disbelief. The one time she should have taken the Pill she had forgotten? How much sense did that make? Unless…

"Were you trying to get pregnant?" he asked in a quiet voice.

He watched her jaw drop in shock, and saw the stunned look in her eyes before anger thinned her lips. It was anger he felt, even with the distance that separated them. "How dare you ask me that!"

"Dammit, were you?" he asked angrily, ignoring her reaction to his question. He'd heard of women who slept with men just for that purpose, either to become a solo parent or to snare a husband. And the thought that she had used him, set him up, raised his anger to the boiling point.

"No, I was not trying to get pregnant, but the fact of the matter is that I did. You fathered my child whether you want to believe it or not. Trust me, if I had been trying to get pregnant, you would not have been a choice for my baby's daddy," she said, snarling the words.

Durango's jaw tightened. *What the hell did she mean by that? And why wouldn't he have been a choice for her baby's daddy?* He shook his head, not believing he was asking himself that question. It wasn't like he wanted to be a father to any woman's baby.

"I think it's best that I leave."

Her words snapped him out of his reverie. His glare

deepened. "Do you honestly think you can show up here and drop a bomb like that and then leave?"

She glared right back. "I don't see why not. The only reason I came here to tell you in person was because I thought you deserved to know and now you do. I've accomplished my goal. I didn't come here to ask you for anything. I'm capable of caring for my child without any help from you."

"So you plan to keep it?"

Fury raced through Savannah. "Yes, I plan to keep it, and if you're suggesting that I don't then you can—"

"No, dammit, that's not what I'm suggesting. I would never propose such a thing to any woman carrying my child. *If* the baby is mine, I take full responsibility."

Her stomach twisted, seeing the doubt in his eyes. "And that's the problem, isn't it, Durango?" she asked, shaking her head sadly. "You don't believe that the child I'm carrying is yours, do you?"

Durango studied her silently for a moment, remembering everything about the night of passion that they'd shared. He knew there was a very strong possibility, a high likelihood, that she had gotten pregnant if she hadn't been using birth control, but he was still too stunned to admit anything. "I believe there might be a chance," he told her.

That wasn't good enough for Savannah. Whether he knew it or not he was questioning her character. Did he think she would get pregnant from one guy and try pinning it on another?

Without saying another word she walked back over to where she had placed her coat, hat and gloves and began putting them on. "There is more than a chance. It doesn't matter whether you want to believe it or not, there is something wonderful growing inside me that you put there. Not knowing your child will be your loss. Have a nice life."

"Where the hell do you think you're going?" he asked in a growl of both anger and frustration.

"Back to the airport to catch the next flight out of here," she said, moving toward the door. "I've done what I came here to do."

"One moment, Savannah," he grated through clenched teeth when she reached the door and opened it.

She turned around and lifted her chin. "What?"

"If your claim is true then we need to talk."

"My claim *is* true, Durango, and considering your attitude, we have nothing more to say."

Before he could draw in his next breath she walked out and closed the door behind her.

Durango stood at the window and watched Savannah get in a rental car and pull away. He was still reeling from the shock of her announcement and waited a tense moment to make sure she was out of sight before moving away from the window.

He glanced across the room to the clock on the wall and saw it was just past noon. He wished he could turn back time to erase what had just happened in this very living room. Savannah Claiborne had come all the way from Philadelphia to tell him that he was going to be a father, and he had all but told her to go to hell.

No doubt Chase would have his ass when he heard how shabbily he had treated his sister-in-law. Crossing the room, he dropped down into a leather recliner. It was so hard to believe. He was going to be a father. No way. The mere thought sent him into a state of panic. It seemed that babies were sprouting up everywhere in the Westmoreland family. Storm and Jayla had had twins a few months back; Dare and Shelly had announced over the holidays that they were expecting a baby sometime this summer; and when he had talked to Thorn last week, he had mentioned that Delaney and Jamal were also having another child.

Durango was happy for everyone. But babies were things other people had—not him. It wasn't that he'd never wanted a child; he'd just never given thought to having one anytime soon. He enjoyed the carefree life of a bachelor too much. He was a man who loved his solitude, a man who took pride in being a loner.

However, the one thing a Westmoreland did was take responsibility for his actions, no matter what they were. His parents had taught him, relentlessly drilled it into him and his five brothers, that you could distinguish the men from the boys by how well they faced whatever challenges were put before them.

Another thing he had been taught was that a Westmoreland knew when to admit he was wrong. If Savannah Claiborne was pregnant—and he had no reason to believe that she wasn't—then the baby was his.

Admitting that he was going to be a daddy was the first step.

He inwardly cringed at what he knew should be his second step—take whatever action was needed to take care of his responsibility. He checked his watch as he stood up. He wasn't sure what time her plane would depart, but if he left now there was a chance he might be able to stop her.

The woman was having his baby and if she thought she could pop up and drop the news on him without any further discussion then she needed to think again. She was going to have to deal with him even if the very thought of getting involved with a city girl made his skin crawl.

It didn't take much for him to remember Tricia Carrington, the woman he had fallen in love with four years earlier. She had come to Yellowstone on a two-week vacation from New York with some of her high-society girlfriends. During those two weeks they had an affair, and he had fallen head over heels in love with her. His uncle Corey had seen through Tricia, had picked up on the manipulator and insincere person that she was and had warned him. But at the time, he had fallen too much in love with her to heed his uncle's warnings.

Durango hadn't known that he'd been the subject of a wager between Tricia and her friends. She had bet her friends that she could come to Yellowstone and do a park ranger before marrying the wealthy man her parents had picked out for her. After telling her of his undying love, she had laughed in his face and told him she had no intentions of marrying him, because he was merely a poor country bum who got dirt under his fingernails for a living. She was too refined for such a dead-end union and fully intended to return to New York to marry a wealthy man with connections. Her words had cut him to the core, and he had sworn that he would never give his heart to a woman again, especially to a stuck-up city girl.

And Savannah was definitely a city girl.

He had known it the moment he'd seen her. She had looked high-class, polished and refined. It had been noticeable in the way she'd been dressed, the way she had moved gracefully around the room. She was confident and looked as if she could be married to a member of the president's cabinet. She was exactly the type of woman that he had tried to avoid during the last four years.

However, he refused to let her being a city girl deter from what he needed to do. Now that the initial shock had worn off and he had accepted that he had unintentionally aided in increasing the Westmoreland line, he would take full responsibility and take charge of the situation.

Savannah had not been surprised by the way Durango had handled the news of her pregnancy. However, the one thing she had not expected and could not accept was his questioning if he was her baby's father.

"Do you want to return your rental car?"

The question from the woman standing behind the counter snatched Savannah's attention back to the present, making her focus on the business at hand. "Yes, please." She glanced at her watch, hoping that it wouldn't be difficult to get a return flight to Philadelphia. And once there, in the peaceful quiet of her condo, she would make decisions that would definitely change her life.

One thing was for certain—she would have to cut back her schedule at work. As a freelance photographer she could be called to go any place at any time. She realized she would miss the adventure of traveling both in this country and abroad.

But now she would need to settle down. After all, she had prenatal care and visits to the doctor to consider. She would talk to her boss about assigning her special projects. She appreciated the fact that over the years she had built a pretty hefty savings account and could afford to take time off both before and after her baby was born. She planned to take six months of family leave time when the baby came.

The one thing she didn't want to do was depend on anyone. Her mom would be overjoyed at the news of becoming a grandmother, but since Jennifer Claiborne had finally found real happiness with a man by the name of Brad Richman, and their relationship seemed to be turning serious—if their planned trip to Paris this week was any indication—the last thing Savannah wanted was for her mother to devote her time to her. Her sister, Jessica, was still enjoying the bliss of being a newlywed, and her brother, Rico, would be busy now that he had started as a private investigator.

As Savannah stepped aside to let the next customer be served, she placed her hand on her stomach, knowing whatever changes she made in her life would be worth it. She was having a baby and no matter how Durango Westmoreland felt, she was very happy about it.

Durango stood next to the water fountain and took in the woman standing across the semicrowded airport. Damn, she was beautiful…and she was carrying a baby in her shapely body.

His baby.

He shook his head. What the hell was he supposed to do with a baby? It was too late to ask the question now, since the deed was already done. He sighed when he saw her head over toward the ticket counter, knowing what he had to do. He quickly crossed the room to block her path.

"We need to talk, Savannah."

Durango's words startled Savannah to the point that she almost dropped her carry-on bag. She narrowed her gaze at him. "What are you doing here? We don't have anything to talk about. I think we said everything, so if you will excuse me—"

"Look, I'm sorry."

She blinked as she stared at him. "What did you say?"

"I said I'm sorry for acting like an ass earlier. My only excuse is that your news came as a shock."

Savannah's eye's shot fire at him. "And...?"

"And I believe that your baby is mine."

She crossed her arms over her chest and glared at him, refusing to let go of her emotions and start crying. Since becoming pregnant she had turned into a weeping willow. "And what has made you a believer all of a sudden?"

"Because of everything that happened between us that night and the fact that you said it is. I have no reason not to believe you." A slow smile played on his lips. "So that settles it."

If he believed that settled anything then he had another thought coming. "Nothing is settled, Durango. Fine, you've acknowledged that I'm having your baby. That means you'll be one of the first people on my list to get an announcement card with pictures when it's born."

She turned to walk away and he blocked her path again. "Like I said, Savannah, we need to talk. I won't let you deny me the right to be a part of my child's life."

Savannah raised her eyes to the ceiling. An hour ago

he had been humming a different tune. "If I had planned to do that, I wouldn't be here." After a deep, calming breath, she added, "I came because I felt you should know and to give you a choice. I didn't come to ask you for anything."

She suddenly felt her face flush from the way he was looking at her. Was her hair standing on end? Were her clothes wrinkled? The flight hadn't been kind to her and she'd almost gotten sick from all the turbulence they had encountered while flying over the mountains. Her hair was a tangled mess and her make-up had worn off hours ago. By the time the plane had landed and she had gotten a rental car to drive out to his ranch, she had been so shaken up she hadn't cared enough about her appearance to even put on lipstick.

"Whether you ask for anything or not, I have certain responsibilities toward my child and I want to talk about them," Durango said. "You've done what you came here to do and now that my head is back on straight, we need to sit down and discuss things like two mature adults."

Savannah lifted an eyebrow and gave him a speculative look. What did they have to talk about? She'd already told him she wouldn't be making any demands on him. She swallowed thickly when a thought suddenly popped into her head. What if he planned to make demands on her regarding their child? Just last week there was an article in the Philadelphia newspaper about a man who had sued his girlfriend for joint custody of their newborn child.

Maybe talking wasn't such a bad idea. It would be better if they got a few things straight in the beginning so there wouldn't be any misunderstanding later. "Okay, let's talk."

* * *

When they reached an empty table in the airport coffee shop, Durango pulled out a chair for Savannah to sit down on and she did so, on shaky legs. Her gaze drifted over his handsome face and latched on to his full lips. She couldn't help remembering those lips and some of the wicked— as well as satisfying—things they had once done to her.

She glanced away when his eyes met hers, finding it strange that the two of them were sitting down to talk. This was the first time they had shared a table. They had once shared a bed, yes, but never a table. Even the night of the rehearsal dinner he had sat at a different table with his brothers and cousins. But that hadn't stopped her from scrutinizing and appreciating every inch of him.

"Would you like something to drink, Savannah?"

"No, I don't want anything."

"So how have you been?" Durango asked after he had finished ordering.

She raised her eyebrows, wondering why he hadn't asked her that when he'd first seen her earlier that day. He had picked a hell of a time to try to be nice, but she would go along with him to see what he had to say.

She managed to be polite and responded, "I've been fine, and what about you?"

"Things are going okay, but this is usually the hardest time of year for rangers."

"And why is that?"

"Besides the icy cold weather conditions, we have to supervise hunters who won't abide by the rules and who want to hunt during the off season. And even worse are those who can't accept the restrictions that no hunting is allowed in Yellowstone's backcountry."

Savannah nodded. She could imagine that would certainly make his job difficult. Jessica had said he was a backcountry ranger. They were the ones who patrolled and maintained trails in the park, monitored wildlife and enforced rules and safety regulations within the areas of Yellowstone. She shuddered at the thought of him coming face-to-face with a real live bear, or some other wild animal.

"You okay, Savannah?"

He had leaned in after seeing her tremble. Surprise held her still at just how close he was to her. "Yes, I'm fine. I just had a thought of you coming into contact with a bear."

He pulled back, smiled and chuckled. "Hey, that has happened plenty of times. But I've been fortunate to never tangle with one."

She nodded and glanced around, wondering when he would forgo the small talk and get down to what was really on his mind.

"What do you need, Savannah?" he finally asked after a few moments of uncomfortable silence.

She met his gaze as emotions swirled within her. "I told you, Durango, that I don't want or need anything from you. The only reason I'm here is because I felt you should know. I've heard a lot of horror stories of kids growing up not knowing who fathered them or men not knowing they fathered a child. I felt it would not have been fair to you or my child for that to happen."

He raised an eyebrow. "Your child? You do mean *our* child, don't you?"

Savannah bit her lip. No, she meant *her child.* She had begun thinking of this baby as hers ever since she'd taken the at-home pregnancy test. She'd begun thinking of herself as a single mom even before her doctor had confirmed her condition. She had accepted Durango's role in the creation of her child, but that was as far as it went.

"Understand this, Savannah. I want to be a part in *our* child's life."

She felt a thickness in her throat and felt slightly alarmed. "What kind of a part?"

"Whatever part that belongs to me as its father."

"But you live here in Montana and I live in Philadelphia. We're miles apart."

He nodded and studied her for a moment then said, "Then I guess it will be up to us to close the distance."

Savannah sighed. "I don't see how that is possible."

Durango leaned back in his chair. "I do. There's only one thing that we can do in this situation."

Savannah raised an eyebrow. "What?"

Durango met her gaze, smiled confidently and said, "Get married."

Three

Savannah blinked, thinking she had heard Durango wrong. After she was certain she hadn't, she couldn't help but chuckle. When she glanced over at him she saw that his expression wasn't one of amusement. "You are joking, aren't you?"

"No, I'm not."

"Well, that's too bad, because marriage is definitely not an option."

He crossed his arms over his chest. "And why not? Don't you think I'm good enough for you?"

Savannah glared at him, wondering where that had come from. "It's not a matter of whether or not you're good enough for me, and I have no idea why you would believe I'd think otherwise. The main reason I won't marry you is that we don't know each other."

He leaned in closer, clearly agitated. "Maybe not. But

that didn't stop us from sleeping together that night, did it?"

Savannah's eyes narrowed. "Only because we'd had too much to drink. I don't make a habit out of indulging in one-night stands."

"But you did."

"Yes, everyone is entitled to at least one mistake. Besides, we just can't get married. People don't get married these days because of a baby."

His lips twitched in annoyance. "If you're a Westmoreland you do. I don't relish the idea of getting married any more than you, but the men in my family take our responsibilities seriously." In Durango's mind, it didn't matter that he wasn't the marrying kind; the situation dictated such action. Westmorelands didn't have children out of wedlock and he was a Westmoreland.

He thought about his cousin Dare, who'd found out about his son A.J. only after Shelly had returned to their hometown when the boy was ten years old. Dare had married Shelly. His uncle Corey, who hadn't known he'd fathered triplets over thirty years ago, was an exception to the rule. Corey Westmoreland could not have married the mother of his children because he hadn't known they existed. Durango's situation was different. He knew about Savannah's pregnancy. Knowing about it and not doing something about it was completely unacceptable.

He had knocked her up and had to do what he knew was the right thing. Given the implications of their situation, getting married—even for only a short period of time—was the best course of action. He and Savannah were adults. Surely they could handle the intimacies of a brief marriage without wanting more. It wouldn't be as if he was giving up being a bachelor forever.

"Well, consider yourself off the hook," Savannah said, reclaiming his attention. "The only person who knows you're my baby's father is Jessica, although I'm sure she's shared the news with Chase by now. If we ask them not to say anything to anyone I'm sure they won't."

"But *I'll* know, Savannah, and there's no way I'm going to walk away and not claim my child."

For a quick second she felt a softening around her heart and couldn't help appreciating him for declaring her child as his. But she would not marry him just because she was pregnant.

She gave him a brittle smile as she rose to her feet, clinging on to her carry-on bag and placing her camera pack on her shoulders. The sooner she left Montana and returned to Philadelphia, the better. "Thanks for the offer of marriage, Durango. It was sweet and I truly appreciate it, but I'm not marrying you or anyone just because I'm pregnant."

Durango stood, too. "Now, look, Savannah—"

"No, you look," she said, eyes narrowing, her back straight and stiff. "That's what happened with my parents. My mother got pregnant with my brother. Although my father did what some considered the decent thing and married her, he was never happy and ended up being unfaithful to her. It was a marriage based on duty rather than love. He met another woman and lived a double life with her and the child they had together."

She inhaled deeply before continuing. "Dad was a traveling salesman and my mother didn't know that he had another family, which included Jessica, on the West

Coast. His actions were unforgivable and the people who suffered most, besides his children, were the two women who loved him and believed in him. In the end one of them, Jessica's mother, committed suicide. And I watched the hurt and pain my mother went through when she found out the truth about him. So no matter what you say, I would never let a man use pregnancy as a reason to marry. I'm glad we had this little chat and I'll keep in touch."

Chin tilted, she turned and quickly walked away.

"I'm sorry, ma'am, due to the snowstorm headed our way, all flights out have been canceled until further notice."

Savannah stared at the man behind the counter. "All of them?"

"All of them. We have our hands full trying to find a place for everyone to stay so they won't have to bunk here for the night. It seems that all the hotels in the area are full."

The last thing she wanted to do was sleep sitting up in a hard chair.

"You're coming with me, Savannah."

She turned around upon hearing the firm voice behind her. "I'm not going anywhere with you."

Durango took a step forward. "Yes, you are. You heard what the man said. All flights out have been canceled."

"Is this man bothering you, miss? Do you want me to call security?"

Savannah smoothed the hair back from her face. This was just great. All she had to do was look at Durango's angry expression to see he did not appreciate the man's question. To avoid an unpleasant situation, she glanced over her shoulder at the ticket agent and smiled. "No, he isn't bothering me, but thanks for asking. Excuse me for a moment."

She then took Durango's arm and walked away from the counter. She was feeling frustrated and exhausted. "I think we need to get something straight."

Durango rubbed his neck, trying to work away the tension he felt building there. "What?"

She leaned over and got all into his face. "Nobody, and I mean nobody, bosses me around, Durango Westmoreland."

Durango stared at her for a long moment then forced back the thought that she was a cute spitfire. Okay, he would be the first to admit that for a moment he had been rather bossy, which was unlike him. He'd never bothered bossing a female around before. He then thought about his cousin Delaney, and remembered how overprotective the Westmoreland males had been before she'd gotten married, and figured she didn't count. But this particular woman was carrying his baby and he'd be damned if she would spend the night at the airport when he had a guest room back at his ranch that she could use. He decided to use another approach. It was well-known within his family that he could switch from being an ass to an angel in the blink of an eye.

He reached out and took her hand. "I do apologize if I came off rather bossy just now, Savannah. I was merely thinking of your and the baby's welfare. I'm sure sleeping here in one of those chairs wouldn't be comfortable. I have a perfectly good guest room at the ranch and you're welcome to use it. I'm sure you're tired. Will you come to the ranch with me?"

His words, spoken in a soft plea, as well as his

ensuing smile, only made Savannah's blood boil even more. She recognized the words for what they were—smooth-talking crap. Her father had been a master at using such bull whenever he needed to unruffle her mother's feathers. And she was close to telling Durango in an unladylike way to go to hell.

And yet, spending the night here at the airport wouldn't be the smartest thing to do. She would love to go someplace, soak in a tub then crawl into a bed. Alone.

She met his gaze, studied his features to see if perhaps there was some ulterior motive for getting her back to the ranch. She knew from her sister's wedding that Durango Westmoreland was full of suave sophistication and he was an expert at seduction. And although the damage had been done, the last thing she wanted was to lose her head and sleep with him again.

She pulled her hand from his. "You really have an extra guest room?"

He grinned and her breath caught at his sexy dimples. Those dimples had been another one of her downfalls that night. "Yes, and like I said, you're welcome to use it."

Savannah toyed with the strap on her camera pack as she considered his invitation. She then met his gaze again. "Okay, I'll go with you if you promise not to bring up the subject of marriage again. That subject is closed."

She saw a flash of defiance in his eyes and then just as quickly it was gone. After a brief span of tense silence he finally said, "Okay, Savannah, I'll adhere to your wishes."

Satisfied, Savannah nodded. "All right, then. I'll go with you."

"Good." He took the carry-on bag from her hand. "Come on, I'm parked right out front."

As Durango led her out of the terminal, he decided that what Savannah didn't know was that before she left to return home to Philadelphia, he and she would be man and wife.

"Here we are," Durango said, leading Savannah into a guest room a half hour later. "I have a couple of other rooms but I think you'll like this one the best."

Savannah nodded as she glanced around. The room was beautifully decorated with a king-size cherry-oak sleigh bed, with matching armoire, nightstands, mirror and dresser. Numerous paintings adorned the walls and several silk flower arrangements added a beautiful touch. It was basically a minisuite with a sitting area and large connecting bath.

"My mom fixed things up in here. She says the other guest rooms looked too manly for her."

Savannah turned and looked into Durango's eyes. Their gazes locked for the space of ten, maybe twelve heartbeats. "I like it and thank you. It's beautiful," she said, moments later breaking eye contact and glancing around the beautifully appointed room once again, attempting to get her control back intact.

Out of the corner of her eyes she saw him move closer into the room. She turned slightly and watched as he walked over to the window and pulled back the curtains. His concentration was on the view outside, but heaven help her, her concentration was on him. And what a view he was. How a man so tall, long-legged and muscular could move with such fluid grace was beyond her. But he managed to do so rather nicely.

She had noticed that about him from the first. There

was something inherently masculine about Durango Westmoreland and the single night they had made love, she had discovered that what you saw was what you got. He definitely could deliver. That night he had tilted her universe in such a way that she knew it would never be the same again. Even now, a warmth moved slowly through all parts of her body just thinking about all the things they had done that night. No second, minute or hour had been wasted.

Durango suddenly turned and his gaze rested on her, longer than she deemed necessary, before he said, "It looks simply beautiful out of this window. Nothing but mountains all around. And this time of year when the snow falls, I think it's the most gorgeous sight that you'd ever want to see." He then turned back around and looked out the window again.

Mildly interested and deciding not to pretend otherwise, Savannah crossed the room to stand beside him and her breath caught. He was absolutely right. The panoramic view outside the window was beautiful. She hoped she had the chance to capture a lot of it on film before she left. "Have you lived here long?" curiosity pushed her to ask.

He met her gaze and smiled. "Almost five years now. After I finished college and got a job with the park ranger service, I lived with my uncle Corey on his mountain for a couple of years, until I saved enough money to buy this land. It was originally part of a homestead, but after the elderly couple who owned it passed on, their offspring split up the property and put individual parcels up for sale. My ranch sits on over a hundred acres."

"Wow! That's a lot of land."

He smiled. "Yes, but most of it is mountains, which is one of the things that drew me to it. And a good portion of it is a natural hot springs. The first thing I did after building the ranch house was to erect my own private hot tub out back. If the weather wasn't so bad, I'd let you try it out. A good soak it in would definitely guarantee you a good night's sleep."

Savannah couldn't help but smile at the thought of that. "A good night's sleep sounds wonderful. The flight out here was awful."

Durango chuckled. "Unfortunately it usually is." He then checked his watch. "How about I put dinner on the table? Earlier I smothered pieces of chicken in gravy, and made cabbage and mashed potatoes. You're welcome to join me after you settle in."

Savannah felt her stomach growl at the mention of food. Dinner was her favorite mealtime since she could never keep any breakfast down for too long. The only thing she had risked eating that day had been saltines. "Thanks, and I'd like that. Do you need any help?"

"No, I have everything under control." He turned to leave the room then stopped before walking out the door. "You're a city girl, but your name isn't."

Savannah arched a brow. She remembered what Jessica had shared with her once regarding Durango's aversion to city women. "It's my mom's favorite Southern city and she thought the name suited me."

He nodded, thinking the name suited her very feminine and genteel charm, as well.

A short while later Savannah followed the aroma of food as she walked down the stairs to the kitchen. She stopped and glanced around, getting a good look at the wood-grain kitchen counters and the shiny stainless-steel appliances. The kitchen was a cook's dream. From one side of the ceiling hung an assortment of copper pots. Unlike most men, Durango evidently enjoyed spending time in his kitchen.

He must have heard her sigh of admiration because he then turned, looked at her and smiled. "All settled in?"

Forcing her nervousness away, she nodded. "Yes. I didn't bring much since I hadn't planned on staying."

"You might as well get comfortable. I wouldn't be surprised if you're stuck here for a couple of days."

Savannah frowned. "Why would you think that?"

Durango leaned back against the counter and gestured toward the window. "Take a look outside."

Savannah walked quickly over to the window. There was a full-scale blizzard going on. She could barely see anything. She turned around. "What happened?"

Durango chuckled. "Welcome to Montana. Didn't you know this was the worst time of year to come visiting?"

No, she hadn't known. The only thing that had been on her mind, once she'd made her decision, was to get to him and tell him about the baby as soon as she could.

She glanced back out the window. "And you think this will last a couple of days?"

"More than likely. The only thing we can do is to make the most of it."

Savannah turned and met his gaze, taking in what he'd just said. It was simply a play on words, she presumed. She hoped. Being cooped up in the house with Durango for a couple of days and *making the most of it* wasn't what she'd planned on happening. It didn't take much to recall just how quickly she had succumbed to his sexiness. All it had taken was a little eye contact and she'd been a goner.

"Come on, Savannah. Let's eat."

Savannah regarded him for a moment before crossing the room to the table where he'd placed the food. "Aren't you concerned about losing power?"

Durango shook his head. "Nope. I have my own generator. It's capable of supplying all the energy I need to keep this place running awhile. Then there are the fireplaces. I had one built for every bedroom as well as the living room. No matter how cold or nasty the weather gets outside, you can believe we'll stay warm and cozy inside."

Staying warm and cozy was another thing she was afraid of, Savannah thought, taking a seat at the table. There was no doubt in her mind that she and Durango could supply enough sensuous fire to actually torch the place.

"Everything looks delicious. I didn't know you could cook," she said, helping herself to some of the food he had prepared, and trying not to lick her lips in the process. She was so hungry.

Durango smiled as he watched her dig in, glad she had a good appetite. A lot of the women he'd dated acted as if it was a sin to eat more than a thimbleful of food. "I'm a bachelor who believes in knowing how to fend for myself. On top of that I'm Sarah Westmoreland's son. She taught me Survival 101 well."

Savannah tasted the mashed potatoes and thought they were delicious. "Mmm, these are good."

"Thanks."

After a few moments of silence Durango said, "I noticed you aren't showing yet."

Savannah met his eyes. She had felt the heat of his gaze on her, checking out her body, when she'd crossed the room to stand at the window. "I'm only two months, Durango. The baby is probably smaller than a peanut now. Most women don't start showing until their fourth month."

He nodded. "How has the pregnancy been for you so far?"

She shrugged. "The usual, I guess. What I'm battling now more than anything is the morning sickness. Usually I don't dare eat anything but saltines before two o'clock every day, which is why I'm so hungry now."

Durango's eyes widened. "You're sick every day?"

He looked so darn surprised at the thought of such a thing that she couldn't help but chuckle. "Yes, just about. But according to the doctor, it will only last for another month or so."

She tilted her head and looked at him. "Haven't you ever been around a pregnant woman?"

"No, not for any length of time. When I went home for Easter last year, Jayla was pregnant and boy, was she huge. Of course, she was having twins." He grinned. "Twins run in my family and there's even a set of triplets."

Savannah raised her eyes heavenward. "Thanks for telling me."

Catching her off guard, Durango reached across the table and captured a lock of her hair in his hand, gently twining the soft, silky strands in his fingers. "I think triplets would be nice, and all with beautiful hazel eyes like yours."

Savannah swallowed tightly as her grip on sanity

weakened. The way he was looking at her wasn't helping matters. She sensed his intense reaction to her was just as potent as hers to him. It was just as strong as it had been that night, and at that moment the desire to have his hands on her again, touching her breasts, her thighs, the area between her legs, was strong and unexpected. If he were to try anything right now, anything at all, it would take all her willpower to resist him.

"I want to be around and see how your body changes with my baby growing inside you, Savannah," he whispered huskily.

His words flowed over Savannah, caressing her in places she didn't want to be touched, and making a slow ache seep through her bones. "I don't know how that will be possible, Durango," she whispered softly.

"It would be possible if we got married."

She frowned and pulled back from him, breaking their contact. "You agreed not to bring that up again."

A smile touched the corners of his lips. "I know, but I want to make you an offer that I hope you can't refuse."

She lifted her eyebrows. "What kind of offer?"

"That we marry and set a limit on the amount of time we'll stay together. We could remain married during the entire length of your pregnancy and for a short while afterward—say six to nine months. After that, we could file for a divorce."

She was stunned by his proposal. "What would doing something like that accomplish?" she asked, feeling the weight of his gaze on her and wishing she could ignore it.

"First, it would satisfy my need and desire to be with you during your pregnancy. Second, it would eliminate the stigma of my child being born illegitimate, which is something that is unacceptable to me. And third, because you believe I'll end up doing to you what your father did to your mother, at least this way you'll know up front that the marriage will be short-term and you won't lose any sleepless nights."

Savannah's frown deepened. "I never said I thought you would do me the way my father did my mother."

"Not in so many words, but it's clear you believe if I married you just for the baby that things wouldn't work out between us. And in a way I have to agree. You're probably right. Our marriage would be based on a sense of obligation on my part. There has to be more to hold a marriage together than just a baby. And to be quite honest with you, I'm not looking for a long-term marriage. But a short-term union, for our baby's sake, would be acceptable to me. I believe it would be accept-able to you, as well, because we'd know what to expect and not to expect from the relationship."

It seemed like a million questions were flashing in Savannah's mind, but she knew the main one that she needed to ask. "Are you saying you'd want a marriage in name only? A marriage of convenience?"

"Yes."

She swallowed and continued to meet his gaze. "And that means we won't be sharing a bed?"

He studied her for a moment and knew what she was getting at. His desire for her was as natural as it could get, and he didn't see it lessening any. If he wanted her at such a high degree now, he could just imagine how things would be once they were living together as man and wife under the same roof. Yes, he would definitely want to sleep with her.

Leaning back in his chair, he said, "No, not exactly. I have other ideas on the matter."

She could just imagine those ideas. "Then keep whatever ideas you have to yourself. *If,* and I said *if,* I go along with what you're proposing, we will *not* share a bed."

"Are you saying that you didn't enjoy sleeping with me?"

Savannah huffed an agitated sigh. Who had slept that night? Neither of them had until the wee hours of the morning. From what she remembered—and she was remembering it quite well—it was round-the-clock sex. And she had to admit, it was the best she'd ever had. The year she'd spent with Thomas couldn't even compare. "That's not the point."

"Then what *is* the point?" Durango countered.

"The point is," Savannah said, narrowing her eyes at him, "regardless of the fact that I did sleep with you that night, I usually don't jump into any man's bed unless I'm serious about him." She decided not to tell him that she'd only been serious with two other guys in her entire love-life history.

He leaned forward. "Trust me, Savannah, once we're married, we'll be as serious as any couple can get, even if we plan for our marriage to last a short while. Frankly I see no reason why we shouldn't sleep together. We're adults with basic needs who know what we want, and I think we need to start being honest with ourselves. We're attracted to each other, and have been from the first, which is why we're in this predicament. Things got as hot as it gets.

"And," he continued with an impatient wave of his

hand to stop her from saying whatever it was that she was about to say, "we might not have been in our right minds that night, since we might have overindulged in the champagne, but we did enjoy making love. So why pretend otherwise?"

Savannah scowled. She wasn't pretending; she just didn't want a repeat performance, regardless of how enjoyable it had been. "You're missing the point."

"No, I think that you are. You're pregnant and I want to be a part of this pregnancy. It's important that I be there with you during the time you're carrying our baby, to bond with him or her while he or she's still in your womb and for some months following that."

"And just how long are you talking about?"

"Whatever period of time we agree on, but I prefer nothing less than six months. I'd even go into another year if I had to."

She frowned. "I wouldn't want you to do me any favors."

"It's not about doing you any favors, Savannah. I intend to always be a part of my child's life regardless of whether you and I are together. But I think six months afterward should be sufficient, unless you want longer."

When hell freezes over. For a few moments Savannah didn't say anything. What could she say when he was right? They had been attracted to each other from the first.

But what happened that night was in the past and she refused to willingly tumble back into bed with him again, and he had another thought coming if he assumed that she would. Evidently he was used to getting what he wanted, but in this case he wouldn't be so lucky.

She then thought about the other thing he'd said, about wanting to connect to their child while it was still in her womb. She remembered reading in one of her baby books how such a thing was possible and important to the baby's well-being. Some couples even played music and read books to their child while it was still growing inside the mother. Never in her wildest dreams would she have thought that Durango would know, much less care, about such things.

She pushed her plate back, glad she had eaten everything since it would probably be the last meal she'd be able to consume until this time tomorrow. "I need to think about what you're suggesting, Durango."

At the lift of his brow she decided to clarify. "I'm talking about the marriage of convenience *without* you having any bedroom rights. If your offer hinges on the opposite then there's nothing for me to think about. I won't be sleeping with you, marriage or no marriage." She then thought of something.

"And where would we live if I went along with what you're proposing?" she asked.

He shrugged broad shoulders. "I prefer here, but if you want I can move to Philly."

Savannah knew that Durango was a man of the mountains. Here he was in his element and she couldn't imagine him living in Philadelphia of all places. "What about your job?"

"I'll take a leave."

She lifted an eyebrow. "You'd be willing to do that?"

"For our child, yes."

She searched his face and saw the sincerity in his words, and they overwhelmed her as well as frightened her. He was letting her know up front that although he didn't want a long-term commitment, he was willing to engage in a short-term one for the sake of her child.

Their child.

She stood. "Like I said, I need to think about this, Durango."

"And I want you to think about it and think about it good. If you're dead set against us sharing a bed then that's fine. My offer of marriage still stands."

He stood and came around the table to stand in front of her. "There are bath towels, a robe and whatever else you might need in the private bath adjoining your room. If you need anything else let me know. Otherwise, I'll see you in the morning."

"I'll help you with the dishes and—"

"No, leave them," he said quickly, releasing a frustrated breath. There was only so much temptation that he could handle and at that moment he wanted nothing more than to kiss her, taste her. But he knew that now was not the time. She needed a chance to think about his offer.

"I'll take care of the dishes later after checking out a few things around my property," he added.

"You sure?"

"Yes."

"All right."

Durango watched as Savannah quickly walked off. He couldn't help but shake his head. Nothing had changed. The attraction between them was still as hot as it got.

Four

The next morning Savannah awoke more confused than ever. She had barely gotten any sleep for thinking about Durango's proposal. In a way it could make their mistake even bigger. On the other hand, he seemed sincere in wanting to help her through her pregnancy, and she wouldn't deny him the chance to bond with his child, especially when very few men would care to do so.

Deciding she didn't want to think about Durango's proposal any longer, she sat up in bed and glanced out the window. The weather was worse than it had been the day before, which meant she couldn't leave today unless the conditions miraculously cleared up.

At least the fireplace was blazing, providing warmth to the room. She settled back in bed, and remembered opening her eyes some point during the night and seeing Durango in front of the fireplace, squatting on his heels and leaning forward, trying to get the fire going. At the time she had been too tired and sleepy to acknowledge his presence.

With the aid of the moon's glow streaming through the window, she had lain there and watched him. A different kind of heat had engulfed her as she watched him working to bring warmth to the room. His shirt had stretched tight to accommodate broad shoulders and the hands that had held the wrought-iron poker had been strong and capable...just as they'd been the night he had used them on her. And later, when he had pushed himself to his feet, she had admired his physique—especially his backside—through heavy-lidded eyes, thinking that he had the best-looking butt to ever grace a pair of jeans.

She startled when there was a knock on her door. Knowing it could only be Durango, she swallowed hard and said, "Come in."

He walked in, bringing enough heat into the room to make the fireplace unnecessary, and his smile made Savannah's insides curl, making her feel even hotter there. How would she ever be able to remain immune to his lethal charm?

"Good morning, Savannah. I hope you rested well."

"Good morning, Durango, and I did. Thanks. I see the weather hasn't improved," she said, sitting up in bed and tucking the covers modestly around her chest. Because she hadn't figured this would be an extended trip, besides her camera pack, which she was rarely without, she'd only brought a book to read on the plane, her makeup and one change of clothing. She'd been forced to sleep in an oversize Atlanta Braves T-shirt that she had found in one of the dresser drawers.

"No, the weather has gotten worse and I need to leave for a while and—"

"You're going out in that?" she asked.

His eyebrows raised a half inch and the smile on his face deepened. "This is nothing compared to a storm that blew through last month. I'm a member of the Search and Rescue Squad so I'm used to going out and working in these conditions. I just got a call from the station. A couple of hikers are missing so we have to go out and find them. There're a number of isolated cabins around these parts and I'm hoping they sought shelter in one of them."

She nodded and moved her gaze from his to glance out the window again. She couldn't imagine anyone being caught out in the weather and hoped the hikers were safe.

"Will you be all right until I get back?" he asked.

She met his gaze again. "I'll be fine." She watched as he turned to leave and quickly said, "Be careful."

Pausing to glance back at her, he said, "I will." He smiled again and added, "I don't intend for you to give birth to our child without me."

Savannah had hoped this morning would be different, but as soon as her feet touched the floor she began experiencing her usual bout of morning sickness and quickly rushed to the bathroom.

A short while later, after brushing her teeth, rinsing out her mouth and soaking her body in a hot tub of water, she wrapped herself in a thick white velour robe that was hanging in the closet and padded barefoot to the kitchen, hoping Durango kept saltine crackers on hand.

A sigh of gratitude escaped her lips when she found a box in his pantry and opened the pack and began consuming a few to settle her stomach. She walked over to the window and glanced out at the abundance of twirling snowflakes. If it kept snowing at this rate there was no telling when she would get a flight out.

Durango stomped the snow off his shoes before stepping inside his home. The thought of Savannah being there when he returned was what had gotten him through the blinding cold while the search party had looked for the hikers. Luckily they had found them in fairly good condition in an old, abandoned cabin.

Quietly closing the door behind him, he slid out of his coat and glanced across the room. Savannah was curled up on the sofa, asleep. Her dark, curly hair framed her face, making her even more beautiful. She looked so peaceful, as if she didn't have a care in the world, and he could have stood there indefinitely and watched her sleep.

When she stirred slightly it hit him that even now something was taking place inside her body. His seed had taken root and was forming, shaping and growing into another human being. For a brief moment a smile touched his lips as he envisioned a little girl with her mother's black curly locks, caramel-colored skin and beautiful hazel eyes.

Females born into the Westmoreland family had been a rarity and for almost thirty years his cousin Delaney had been the only one, having the unenviable task of trying to handle a dozen very protective Westmorelands—her father, five brothers and six male cousins.

Then, just eighteen months ago, it was discovered that his uncle Corey had fathered triplets that included a girl—Casey. Mercifully, this discovery had taken some of the attention off Delaney.

Now Storm and Jayla had daughters and he heard that Dare and Shelly, as well as Delaney and Jamal, who had sons already, were hoping for girls this time around. Just the thought of a future generation of female Westmorelands made him shudder. But still, he liked the idea of having a daughter to pamper, a daughter who was a miniature version of Savannah.

He had to admit there were a number of things about the woman asleep on his couch that stirred feelings inside him. One was the fact that she hadn't used her pregnancy to force his hand. He could name a number of women who definitely would have shown up demanding that they marry by the end of the day. Savannah, on the other hand, hadn't been thrilled by the suggestion and even now hadn't agreed to go along with him on it. For some reason Durango liked the thought of having her tied to him legally, even for a short while.

He gazed down at her. She was wearing the oversize T-shirt and jogging pants that he had left out for her. Both were his and fit rather large on her. Even so, he couldn't help but notice the curve of her breasts beneath the cotton shirt. They seemed larger than he'd remembered. It was going to be interesting, as well as fascinating, to watch her body go through the changes it would endure during the coming months. And more than anything, he wanted to be around to see it.

He shook his head, thinking that if anyone had told him last week he would be feeling this way about a pregnant woman, he would not have believed them. He knew he would have a hard time convincing his best friend, McKinnon Quinn, that he'd not only accepted Savannah's pregnancy but was looking forward to the day she gave birth. He and McKinnon were known to be the die-hard bachelors around these parts and had always made it a point to steer clear of any type of binding relationship.

When Savannah made a soft, nearly soundless sigh in her sleep and shifted her body, making the T-shirt rise a little to uncover her stomach, Durango stifled a groan and was tempted to go over and kiss the part of her body where his child was nestled. He closed his eyes as his imagination took over when he knew he wouldn't want to stop at just her stomach. Even now her seductive scent filled the room and tantalized his senses. He felt tired, exhausted, yet at the same time he felt his body stirring when he remembered the heated passion the two of them had once shared. A passion he was looking forward to them sharing again one day.

Savannah awoke with a start, immediately aware that she was no longer alone. The smell of food cooking was a dead giveaway.

Her memory returned in a rush and she recalled her bout with morning sickness and how she had decided to lie on the sofa when a moment of dizziness had assailed her. She must have fallen asleep. She couldn't help wondering when Durango had returned. Why hadn't he awakened her? Had they found the missing hikers?

"Did you eat anything?"

The sound of Durango's deep voice nearly made her jump. She met his gaze and instantly, her body was filled with a deep, throbbing heat. He had removed the pullover sweater he'd been wearing over his jeans earlier and was dressed in a casual shirt that was open at the throat, giving him a downright sexy appeal, not that he needed it.

There was something about him that just turned her on. It would be hard to be married to him—even on a short-term basis—without there ever being a chance of them sharing a bed. But she was determined to do just that.

Knowing she hadn't answered him, she said, "No, but thanks for leaving breakfast warming for me in the oven. My stomach wasn't cooperating and I wouldn't have been able to keep anything down. I found some saltines in your pantry and decided to munch on those."

Durango nodded, recalling her mentioning the previous day that she'd been unable to eat most mornings. "Have you seen a doctor?"

"Yes, although I'm going to have to find another one soon. Dr. Wilson is the same doctor who delivered me and Rico and he's retiring next month."

"Isn't he concerned with you being sick every day? Are you and the baby getting all the nutrients you need?"

Savannah shrugged as she sat up. "Healthwise Dr. Wilson says that both the baby and I are fine."

He leaned back against the wall. "When you go to the doctor again I'd like to be there."

"In Philadelphia?"

"Wherever you decide to go doesn't matter. And since your doctor is retiring, just so you'll know, there's a good obstetrician here in Bozeman and she's female."

She tipped her head back and looked at him and wished she could stop her pulse from racing at the sight of his lean, hard body. "Really? That's good to know."

He smiled. "I thought it would be."

He came into the room and sat in the chair across from her, stretching his long legs out and crossing them at a booted ankle. "Have you thought about what I proposed last night?"

"Yes, I thought about it."

"And?" he asked gently, knowing she was a woman who couldn't be rushed.

"And I need more time to make up my mind," she said, fixing her gaze on his boots.

"I wish I could tell you to take all the time you need, but time isn't on our side, Savannah. If we do decide to get married there needs to be a wedding."

Her head snapped up. "A wedding?"

He smiled at her surprised expression. "Yes. I don't anticipate one as elaborate as Chase's, but as you know, we Westmorelands are a large family with plenty of friends and acquaintances and—"

"It's not as if it would be a real marriage, Durango, so why bother?"

"Because my parents, specifically my mother, who won't know why we're getting married, would expect it."

"Well, personally I can't see the need for a lot of hoopla over something that won't last. If I decide to accept your proposal, I prefer that we go off somewhere like Vegas and not tell anyone about it until it's over. They will eventually know the real reason we got married in a few months anyway."

Durango nodded, knowing she was right. His family,

who knew how he felt about marriage, would know it wasn't the real thing no matter what he told them. "What about your mother?"

"She's leaving tomorrow for Paris and won't be back for a couple of weeks. If I do decide to marry you, she'll be okay with my decision and it won't bother me that she won't be at the ceremony since she knows I don't believe in happily-ever-after."

Durango rubbed the back of his neck with an irritated frown. It wasn't that he didn't believe in fairy-tale romances, but after Tricia he figured it would be more fantasy than reality for him. "Fine. If you agree, we can elope and then if our parents want to do something in the way of a reception later, that will be fine. All right?"

She sighed. "All right."

"So when will you let me know your decision?"

"Before I leave here. Do you think the weather will have improved by tomorrow?"

"I'm not sure. Usually these types of snowstorms can last for a week."

"A week? I didn't bring enough clothes with me."

He thought now was not a good time to tell her he wouldn't mind if she walked around naked. "The last time Delaney was here she left a few of her things behind. The two of you are around the same size so you should be able to fit into them if you want to try."

"You don't think she'd mind?"

"No."

"All right then, if you're sure it's okay."

He stood. "Do you think your stomach has settled enough for dinner? I cooked a pot of beef stew."

"Yes, I think it will be able to handle it. Would you like some help in the kitchen?"

"If you're up to it you can set the table."

She stood. "I'm up to it. Did you find the hikers?"

"Yes, we found them and they're fine. Luckily one was a former Boy Scout and knew exactly what to do."

She smiled, relieved, as she followed him into the kitchen. "I'm glad."

Savannah was amazed at the degree of her appetite and flushed with embarrassment when she noted that Durango had stopped to watch her, with amusement dancing in his eyes, as she devoured one bowl of stew and was working on her second.

She licked her lips. "I was hungry."

"Apparently."

When she pushed the empty bowl aside, he chuckled and said, "Hey, you were on a roll. Don't stop on my account."

Her brows came together in a frown. "I've had enough, thank you."

"You're welcome. I've got to keep the ballerina on her toes."

"What ballerina?"

"Our daughter."

Savannah raised a glass of milk to her lips, took a sip and then asked, "You think I'm having a girl?"

"Yes."

She tipped her head, curious. "Why?"

He leaned forward to wipe the milk from around her lips with his napkin, wondering when the last time he had given so much time and attention to a woman was.

"Because that's what I want and I'm arrogant enough to think I'll get whatever I want."

Savannah didn't doubt that—not that she thought he got anything and everything he wanted, but that he was arrogant enough to think so. "Why would you want a girl?"

"Why wouldn't I want one?" he asked. There was no way he would tell her the reason he wanted a little girl was that he wanted a daughter who looked just like her. He couldn't explain the reasoning behind it and at the moment he didn't want to dwell on the significance of it.

"There are more males in your family, and considering that, I'd think for you a son would be easier to manage," she said.

He chuckled, amused. "I think we managed my cousin Delaney just fine. With five brothers and six older male cousins we were able to put the fear of God into any guy who showed interest in her. I see no problem with us getting the same point across with the next generation of Westmoreland females."

His smile deepened. "Besides, don't you know that girls are the apples of their fathers' eyes?"

"Not in all cases," she said, thinking of the relationship she and Jessica never had with their father.

"But let me set the record straight," Durango said, breaking into her reverie. "I would love either a boy or girl, but having a daughter would be extra, extra special."

Savannah smiled, thinking his words pleased her, probably because she was hoping for a girl, as well. In some ways it surprised her that a man who was such a confirmed bachelor would want children or be interested in fatherhood at all.

At that moment an adorable image floated into her mind of Durango and a little girl who looked just like him sitting on his lap while he read her a story.

"So what do you think?" Durango asked.

Savannah glanced up after going through the items of clothing that Durango had placed on the bed. "I think they'll work. I don't wear jeans often so the change will be nice, and the sweaters look comfy. They will be good for this weather."

"So what do you plan to do tonight?"

The low-pitch murmur of his voice had her lifting her head and meeting his gaze. She wished there was some way she didn't get turned on whenever she looked into their dark depths. "I thought I'd try and finish a book that I brought with me."

"Oh, and what type book is it?"

She shrugged. "One of those baby books that tells you what to expect during pregnancy and at childbirth."

"Sounds interesting."

"It is." She tried ignoring the sensations that were moving around in her stomach. Having Durango in her bedroom wasn't a good idea and the sooner she got him out, the better, but there was something that she needed to find out first.

"There's something I'd like to ask you, Durango. It's something I need to know before I can make a decision about marrying you."

He lifted an eyebrow. "And what is it you need to know?"

She moved away from the bed and sank down on the love seat. She would have preferred having any conversation with him someplace else other than here, in the coziness of the bedroom with a fireplace burning with its yellow glow illuminating Durango's handsome features even more. At least she wasn't standing next to the bed any longer.

Knowing he was waiting for her to speak, she met his gaze and asked, "I want to know what you have against *city women*."

Five

Some questions weren't meant to be asked.

Savannah quickly reached that conclusion when she saw Durango's jaw clench, his hands tighten into a fist by his side and an angry flare darken his eyes. Another thing that was a dead giveaway was the sudden chill in the air, not to mention the force of his stare, which caused her to draw a quick breath.

Her question, which had evidently caught him off guard, was calling for every bit of his self-control and she began feeling uneasy. Still, she needed to know the reason for his aversion since it was something that obviously quite a few people knew, at least those who were close to him.

She watched his lips move and knew he was muttering something under his breath. That only increased her curiosity, her need to know. "Durango?"

When he finally spoke his voice was low with an edginess that hinted she had waded into forbidden waters. "I'd rather not talk about it."

Savannah knew she should probably let the matter drop, but she couldn't let the question die because a part of her really wanted to know.

Evidently he saw that determined look in her features and he said, "It doesn't concern you, Savannah. You're having my baby. I've asked you to marry me so there's no need for us to start spilling our guts on every little thing that happened in our pasts. I'll respect your right to privacy and I hope that you will respect mine."

Savannah couldn't help wondering about what he didn't want to tell her. What pain was he still hiding in his heart? God knew she had plenty of skeletons she'd kept hidden in her mental closet. Secrets she'd only shared with Jessica. His request for privacy was a reasonable one. She shouldn't be digging into his past, but she needed assurance that whatever his problem was, she wouldn't be affected by it, and until she had that certainty, she wouldn't back off.

"All that's well and good, Durango, but if I am to marry you, even if it's only for a short while, I need to know I won't be mistreated because of someone else's transgressions."

"You won't."

The words had been spoken so quickly that Savannah hadn't had a chance to blink. She heard both regret and anger in his voice.

"This is only about you and me, Savannah, and no one else. Don't let anything that happened before sway your decision now."

Savannah's gaze wandered over his muscular form. He was leaning with a shoulder pressed up against a bedpost, his booted feet crossed at the ankles and his arms folded over his chest. He was watching her with as much intensity as she was watching him.

Seconds ticked by and with the passing of time something heated and all-consuming was passing between them. And she knew if it continued that she couldn't be responsible for her actions…and neither could he.

Even now he was spiking heat inside her just standing there, saying nothing. She continued to feel an overpowering need. Desire was inching its way up her spine and then she remembered his taste and how she couldn't get enough of him the last time.

He continued to hold her gaze and he was having a hypnotic effect on her. And then he moved toward her, with his slow, graceful stride. Crossing the room, he reached out and gently tugged her up off the sofa.

She knew at that moment what he wanted, what he needed. They were the same things she desired. Lowering his face, bending to cup the back of her head with his hand, he kissed her. The moment their lips touched, her hands automatically slipped inside the back pockets of his jeans. It was that or remain free and be tempted to squeeze his butt like Mr. Whipple used to squeeze the Charmin.

And when their lips locked and he inserted his tongue inside her mouth, the contact was so intimate, heated and passionate that she knew there was nothing she could do but stand there and enjoy it.

And she did.

They were consenting adults and a little kiss never

hurt anyone, she convinced herself when her tongue joined in with his. But this was no little kiss, she discovered moments later. The tongue stroking hers was strong and capable, arousing her to a pitch higher than he'd done that night in her hotel room.

It was the usual Durango kiss—long, hot, sexy. The kind of kiss that made your toes curl, your breasts feel full and your stomach tingle. She closed her eyes to feel more deeply the sensations that crowded her mind and the electrical charges that were burning all over her body. She breathed in his scent, glorying in the slow, methodical way he was making love to her mouth.

Too soon, he reluctantly broke off the kiss. She slowly opened her eyes, met the deep intensity of his gaze, expelled a deep breath, then dragged in an unsteady one, feeling satisfied. And even now she saw his gaze was still locked on to her lips.

"I enjoy kissing you," he said softly, throatily, as if that explained everything, especially every tantalizing stroke of his tongue.

She watched those dark, intense eyes that were focused on her mouth get even darker. "Um, I can tell."

She had to admit that nothing about her visit to his home had turned out like she'd planned. She had come to tell her news and leave. It was too bad she hadn't stuck to her plans. But then, if she had, she wouldn't be standing here discovering once again what true passion was like. Before meeting him, she hadn't had a clue.

"I think I'd better go. I'll see you in the morning," he whispered low against her moist lips.

And before she could blink or catch her next breath, he was gone.

* * *

The moment the door closed behind Durango, Savannah could feel her stomach muscles tightening. She swayed slightly when the floor beneath her feet felt shaky. Talk about a kiss!

Muttering darkly—probably some of those same words Durango had said earlier, but hadn't wanted her to hear—she crossed the room and dropped down on the bed. His kiss was one of the reasons she was in this predicament. She had invited him into her room for the two of them to indulge in some more champagne. She hadn't gotten to completely filling his glass before he had taken both the bottle and glass from her hand and had filled her mouth with his instead. He hadn't kissed her silly—he had kissed her crazy. The taste of him had been hot, delicious and incredibly pleasurable. She had lusted for him, after him, with him and by the time they had made it to the bed, they had stripped naked.

They were extremely attracted to each other. Deep down inside she knew that Durango didn't like their explosive chemistry any more than she did. She had seen the way his eyes had flashed when he had lifted his mouth from hers, as well as the way his jaw muscles had tightened. Also, there was the way he always looked after kissing her senseless, like he needed divine intervention to help him deal with her and the sexual response they stirred up in each other.

"And to think that he's proposing marriage," she mumbled in a low voice that rattled with frustration. "So okay, it will only be for a short while, as he's quick to remind me every chance he gets," she said, shifting to her back and folding her arms over her chest. "What will I get out of this arrangement?"

More kisses, her mind immediately responded. *And if you stop being so dang stubborn, you'd also get a temporary bed partner. What do you have to lose? You'll be entering into a relationship with your eyes open and no expectations. You'll know up front that love has nothing to do with it. Besides, you'll be giving your child a chance to develop a relationship with a father who cares.*

Because of her experience with her father, that meant everything to Savannah. She believed that even when their marriage ended, Durango would remain a major part of his child's life.

Savannah also needed to think about the other reasons why marrying Durango was a good idea.

Pulling her body up, she shifted to her side. First was the issue of having a temporary bed partner if she decided to go that route. She'd dated but had never been into casual sex so she hadn't been involved with anyone since Thomas Crawford. She had dated Thomas exclusively for a year and things between them had been going well until he'd gotten jealous about an assignment she'd gotten that he had wanted. He'd even tried convincing her to turn the job down so he could have it— talk about someone being selfish and self-centered. It had been over a year, close to two since she'd broken up with Thomas or slept with anyone. The night she had shared a bed with Durango hadn't just been a night of want for her; it had been a night of need, a strictly hormonal affair in which she really hadn't acted like herself.

She tipped her head to the side and moved on to the

other reason for marrying Durango. *Expectations*. Their expectations would be set and neither of them would be wearing blinders. She knew their marriage would not be the real thing. He didn't love her and she didn't love him. Having reasonable expectations would definitely make things easier emotionally when the time came for them to split.

The more she thought about it, the more she knew that accepting his offer of marriage was the best thing. Her child would be getting the type of father that she never had; a father her baby would be able to depend on.

And then there were all the other Westmorelands who would be her child's extended family. She had seen firsthand at Chase and Jessica's wedding just what a close-knit group they were. Being part of a large family was another thing she'd missed growing up, but it was something her child could have.

Her brain began spinning with all the positives, but she forced herself to think about the negatives, as well. At the moment she could only imagine one. *The possibility of her falling in love with him.*

She couldn't even envision such a thing happening, but she knew there was that possibility. Durango would not be a hard man to love. A woman could definitely lose her heart to him if she wasn't careful. He was so strong and assertive and yet, he was also a giving and a caring person. She noticed his sensitivity in the ways that he saw to her needs: making sure he'd left breakfast for her; coming into her room in the dead of night to make sure she was warm enough; inquiring about her and their baby's health.

But still, there was no way she could ever fall in

love. She doubted that she could give him or any man a slice of her soul or a piece of her heart.

She knew that no matter how much she enjoyed the time she would spend with Durango during her pregnancy, she could not lose her heart to him. Ever.

Several hours had passed since Durango and Savannah had shared that heated kiss, and the residual effects were so strong that he couldn't think straight enough to balance his accounting records. Instead of concentrating on debits and credits he was way too focused on the incredible sensations he was still feeling, the electrical jolts that were still flowing through his body.

He had kissed women, plenty of times, but none had left a mark on him like Savannah Claiborne had. There was something about her taste, a succulent blend of sweetness, innocence and lusciousness, all rolled into one tangy, overpowering flavor that sent all kinds of crazy, out-of-control feelings slithering all through his body. She made his temperature rise, clogged his senses and forced his pulse to race.

"Dammit."

He slapped the accounting books shut and turned away from the computer screen. The last thing he needed was to make a miscalculation on the ledger for the horse-breeding business he co-owned with his good friend McKinnon Quinn.

He leaned back in his chair and his thoughts returned to Savannah. He just hoped her decision would be the one he wanted. He simply refused to consider any other possibility.

Six

"What the hell! Savannah? Are you all right?"

Savannah heard the footsteps behind her. She also heard the concern as well as the panic in Durango's voice, but she was too weak to lift her head and turn around. She didn't want him to see her like this. How humiliating was it to be on your knees on the floor of a bathroom, holding your head over a commode?

"Savannah, what's wrong?"

The moment she could, she expelled a breath and said the two words she hoped would explain everything. It appeared that he hadn't gotten the picture yet. "Morning sickness."

"Morning sickness? Is this what morning sickness is all about?"

Savannah suppressed a groan. What had he thought it was about? She was about to give him a snappy answer when her stomach clenched warningly. It was just as well since at that moment her body quickly reminded her of her condition and without any control, she closed her eyes, lowered her head and continued to bring up portions of yesterday's dinner.

"What can I do?"

It was on the tip of her tongue to tell him what he could do was go away. She didn't need an audience. "Nothing," she managed to say moments later. "Please, just leave me alone."

"Not even if your life depended on it, sweetheart," he said softly. Crouching down on the floor beside her, he wrapped his arms gently around her and whispered, "We're in this thing together, remember? Let me help you."

Before she could tell him that she didn't need his help and there wasn't anything he could do, he proved her wrong when she felt another spasm of nausea. He took a damp washcloth and began tenderly wiping her face and mouth.

Then he held her while her stomach began settling down. She was so touched by this generous display of caring, she leaned against his supporting body, while his huge hand gently stroked her belly into calmness. And as if with a will of its own, her head fell within the curve of his shoulder. No man had ever shown her so much tenderness. Okay, she confessed silently, Rico had always been there for her when she needed him, but since he was her brother he didn't count.

"That's right, baby, just relax for a moment. Everything is going to be fine. I'm going to take care of you," he murmured softly, brushing his lips against her temple and placing a kiss on her forehead.

Then she heard the toilet flushing at the same time as she was scooped up in Durango's strong arms. And after closing down the toilet lid, he sat down on it with her cradled in his arms as he continued to gently stroke her stomach. A short while later, as if she weighed nothing, he stood and sat her on the countertop next to the sink.

"Do you think a soda will help settle your stomach?" he asked, staring down in her eyes.

With the intensity of his gaze, her breath nearly got clogged in her throat but she managed to say, "Yes."

"Will you be okay while I go and get you one?"

"Yes, I'll be fine."

He nodded. "I'll be right back."

As soon as he left, Savannah inhaled a deep breath. As usual, her bout with nausea was going away just as quickly as it had come. Deciding to take advantage of the time Durango was gone, she gently lowered her body off the counter and immediately began brushing her teeth. She had just finished rinsing out her mouth when Durango returned.

"Here you go."

She took the cold can of ginger ale he offered and after quickly pulling the tab, she took a sip, immediately feeling better. After finishing the rest she lowered the can from her mouth, licked her lips and said, "Thanks, I needed that."

She quickly began studying the can. Durango was staring at her and she felt embarrassed. She knew she looked a mess. One of the things she had learned at the all-girl school her grandparents had sent her to was that a lady never showed signs of weakness in front of a man.

She'd also been taught that a man was not supposed to see a woman at her worst. Unfortunately some things couldn't be helped. Besides, it wasn't as if she had invited him to join her in the bathroom this morning. Why had he come, anyway?

As if reading her mind, he said, "I know you said you usually don't eat anything in the morning, but I was about to have breakfast and wanted to check to make sure you didn't want to join me."

"I would not have been able to eat anything."

"Yeah, I can see why. And you go through this every morning?" he asked, and once again she heard the deep concern in his voice.

"Yes, but it's not always this bad. I guess eating all that stew at dinner last night wasn't such a good idea."

"Evidently. What did your doctor say about it?"

She sighed deeply. "There's not a lot he could say, Durango. During the early months of pregnancy, morning sickness happens."

"That's not good enough."

She held up both hands to stop him. She knew he was about to urge her to see a local doctor. "Look, not now, okay? More than anything I need to get myself together. Just give me a few minutes."

"And you're sure you're okay?"

"I'm sure."

"Is there anything else I can get you?"

She shifted uneasily, not used to this amount of attention. "No, thanks. I don't need anything."

He nodded. "Okay then, I'll leave you alone to get dressed."

He turned to leave then slowly turned back around

and surprised her when his mouth brushed over hers. "Sorry my kid is causing you so much trouble," he said after the light caress.

And before she could gather her wits and say anything, he had walked out of the bathroom, leaving her alone.

Durango paced the living room, glad he hadn't gone out. He winced at the thought of how things would have been for Savannah if she'd been alone. Then it struck him that she *had* gone through it alone before. She lived by herself and there had to have been times when she'd been sick and no one had been there with her. When she'd first mentioned this morning sickness thing, he'd thought she just experienced a queasy stomach in the morning and preferred not eating until later. He had no idea she spent part of each morning practically retching her guts out.

He paused and rubbed his hand down his face. It was easy to see he wasn't used to being around a pregnant woman. There hadn't been any babies in his family until Delaney had given birth a few years ago, and then she'd spent most of the time during her pregnancy in her husband's homeland in the Middle East.

Although he had only been around Jayla a few times while she was pregnant, the only thing he'd been aware of was that she was huge. Because she had been carrying twins she always looked as if she was about to deliver at any moment. He didn't recall Storm ever mentioning anything about Jayla being sick and throwing up every morning. It seemed that he needed to be the one reading a baby book.

Shoving his hands into the pockets of his jeans, he

began pacing again. Okay, so maybe he was getting freaked out and carried away. Savannah had claimed what she was going through was normal, but even so, that didn't mean he had to like it.

He turned when he heard the sound of her entering the room. As he studied her he found it hard to believe she was the same woman who just moments ago had looked as if she were on the brink of death. Talk about a stunning transformation. She had changed into a pair of jeans and a top and both looked great on her. Immediately the thought came to his mind that she looked good in anything she put on her body, whether it was an expensive gown, slacks and a top, jeans or an oversize T-shirt.

She had added a touch of makeup to her features, but mainly her natural beauty was shining through, and it was shining so brightly that it made the room glow... which wasn't hard to do considering the weather outside. The storm was still at its worst, although the recent weather reports indicated things would start clearing up at some point that day.

"You okay?" he asked, quickly crossing the room to her.

She smiled faintly up at him. "Yes, I'm fine and I want to apologize for—"

"Don't. There's nothing to apologize for. I'm glad I was here."

She hated to admit it, but she was glad he'd been there, too. Although she had gone through the same ordeal alone countless times, it had felt good to have a shoulder to lean on. And it had been extremely nice knowing that that particular shoulder belonged to the man who had a vested interest in her condition.

She also didn't want to admit that she was fully aware of how handsome he looked this morning. Though to be honest, he always looked good in jeans and the Western shirts he liked to wear. Deciding she needed to think about other things, she walked over to the window and glanced out. She noticed the weather was still stormy. "Will you have to go out today?"

He moved to stand beside her and glanced out the window, as well. "Maybe later. The reports indicate the weather will begin clearing up soon."

"It will?" she asked, surprised, turning to face him.

"Yes."

She smiled brightly. "That means there's a possibility I'll be able to leave today."

"Yes, there is that possibility," he said. "I know you can't eat a heavy breakfast but is there something I can get for you that might agree with your stomach?"

"Um, a couple of saltines and a cup of herbal tea might work."

"Then saltines and herbal tea it is," he said, turning and walking toward the kitchen.

"And Durango?"

He turned back to her. "Yes?"

With her heart pounding she said, "I've made a decision about your proposal. I think we should talk about it."

He nodded. "All right. We can sit and talk at the kitchen table if you'd like."

"Okay," she said, and followed him into the kitchen.

"So, what have you decided?"

Savannah lifted her head from studying the saltines on the plate in front of her. She had thought things through most of the night but his actions that morning had only solidified her decision.

She set down her cup of tea and met his gaze. "I'm going to take you up on your offer and marry you."

She watched as he sat back in the chair and looked at her with something akin to relief. "But I'd like to explain the reasons for my decision and why I still won't sleep with you," she added.

"All right."

She paused after taking another sip of her tea, and then said, "I think I told you I didn't want to get married just because I was pregnant."

He nodded. "Because of that ordeal with your father, right?"

"Yes."

"How did your parents meet?"

"In college. When Mom showed up at her parents' house with my father over spring break in her senior year of college and announced that she planned to marry him after she graduated and that she was pregnant, my grandparents hit the roof. You see, my maternal grandparents never approved of interracial romances, so they weren't too happy about my parents' relationship."

"I can imagine they weren't."

"Those were certainly not the future plans that Roger and Melissa Billingslea had for their daughter. But nothing would change my mother's mind. She thought Jeff Claiborne was the best thing since raisin bread and when they couldn't convince her that he wasn't, my grandparents threatened to disown my mother."

"Did that work?"

"No. Mom and Dad were married a few months later.

According to Mom things were great at first, but then he lost his job with this big corporation and had to take a job as a traveling salesman. That's when things started going downhill. Dad began changing. However, it took almost fifteen years for her to find out that he'd been living a double life and that he had a mistress as well as another daughter living out west."

Durango took a sip of coffee. Chase had pretty much told him the story one night over a can of beer.

"It wasn't easy for me and Rico growing up," she said, reclaiming his attention. "Some people view children from mixed marriages as if they are from another planet. But with Mom's help we got past all of that, and eventually my grandparents came around. And it didn't take long for them to try to take over our lives. My grandmother even paid for me to go to an all-girl high school. But when it came time for college, I decided to attend one of my own choosing and selected Tennessee State. I'm glad I did."

Durango took another sip of his coffee. He appreciated her sharing that bit of history with him but felt compelled to ask, "So what does any of that has to do with my asking you to marry me...or why you won't sleep with me once we're married?"

Savannah leaned back in her own chair. "More than anything I want my child to be a part of a large, loving family. I also want my child to know that its father is a part of its life because he wants to be, and not because he was forced to be."

A part of Durango reached out to her, feeling her pain caused by a father who hadn't cared. He was not that kind of man and he was glad she knew it. "I will be a good father to our child, Savannah."

She smiled wryly. "I believe that you will, Durango. Now the issue is whether I believe you will be good to me, as well."

He lifted his brow. "You think I'll mistreat you?"

She shook her head. "No, that's not it. I think you are a man who likes women but I don't want to be just another available body to you, Durango. Not to you or to any man."

Durango placed his teacup down, thinking that if she expected an apology from him for all the women he'd enjoyed before meeting her, she could forget it. Like he'd told her before, what was in the past should stay in the past, unless...

His stomach tightened at the thought that she might assume he would mess around on her. He met her gaze. "Are you worried about me being unfaithful during the time we're married?"

She met his gaze. "That has never crossed my mind. Should it have?"

"No."

He was glad it hadn't crossed her mind because even if she did deny him bedroom rights, he would never give her a reason to question his fidelity. He shook his head. If nothing else, since that night they'd spent together, Savannah had shown him that was definitely a difference between women. Some were only made to bed and some were meant to wed. Savannah, whether she knew it or not, was one of the marrying kind.

She deserved more than a short-term marriage. She deserved a husband who would love and pamper her, for better or for worse and for the rest of her life. A smart man would be good to her and treat her right. Someone who would treat her like a woman of her caliber should be treated. And more importantly, he should be a man who could introduce her to the pleasures men and women shared, pleasures she was denying herself.

He would never forget that night when she had gotten an orgasm. She had acted as if it had been her first one and she hadn't expected the magnitude of the explosion that had ripped through her body. And now he was glad he had shared that with her. But he wanted to share other things with her, as well. And she was wrong if she thought them sleeping together would just be for his benefit. Somehow he had to convince her it would be for her benefit, as well. She needed to understand that a woman has needs just like a man. If nothing else, he needed to prove that to her.

But now was not the time to make waves. He was fairly certain there would be opportunities for what he had in mind before and after their wedding, and he planned to take advantage of both.

"I think of you as more than an available body, Savannah," he said truthfully. "And I'm sorry that you see things that way. In my book, there's nothing wrong with men and women who like and respect each other satisfying their needs, needs they might not be able to control…especially when they're alone together."

He sighed. She was listening to everything he said yet he could tell his discussion of needs was foreign to her. She might have experienced wanting and desire in her lifetime, but she hadn't had to tackle the full-fledged need that sent some women out to shop for certain types of sex toys.

He studied her, watched how her fingertips softly stroked the side of her cup. Her light touch made him wish that she would stroke him the same way. He realized that although she had no idea what the gesture was doing to him, he was excruciatingly aware of her. She looked beautiful just sitting there, absorbing his words yet not fully understanding what he meant.

But eventually she would understand.

"However, if you prefer that we don't share a bed at any time during our marriage, then I will abide by your wishes." Even as he said those words, in his heart he intended that in time her wishes would become the same as his.

She smiled, appearing at ease with what he had said. "So I guess the only other thing we need to agree on is when the marriage will take place and where we'll live afterward."

He nodded. "Like I told you, I'm flexible as far as living arrangements but I think we should get married right away, considering you're already almost two months along."

Savannah did agree with the need to move forward with their marriage but she didn't want him to have to take a leave of absence from his job because of her. It would be easier for her to move to Montana. She could do freelance work anywhere. He could only do his work as a ranger here.

"I think I'd rather live out here, if you don't mind."

That surprised him. A city girl in the mountains? "What about your job? I thought as a freelance photographer you traveled a lot, all over the country."

"Yes, but being pregnant will slow my travels down a bit. Besides, I think I'll be able to work something out with my boss, if my moving out here won't be a problem with you."

Durango shook his head, still bemused but pleased. "No, it won't be and I think you'll be able to adjust to the weather."

"I think so, too."

A feeling of happiness—one he wasn't ready to analyze—coiled through him as he thought of getting married to the mother of his child. "So, when can we marry?"

Savannah shrugged. "I'll let you make all the arrangements. Just tell me when and where you want me to show up."

"And then afterward you'll move in here with me?"

"Yes, and we'll remain married until the baby is at least six months old, which is probably the time I'll be going back to work. Is that time period okay with you?"

"Yes, that's okay. And you still prefer a small wedding?"

"Yes, the smaller the better. Like I said, I don't have a problem eloping to Vegas. A lot of hoopla isn't necessary," she said.

Durango smiled at her. "All right. Considering everything, omitting the hoopla is the least I can do."

Later that day, while Savannah was taking a nap, Durango had a chance to sit down, unwind and think about her decision to marry him.

She understood, as he did, that short-term was short-term. They weren't talking about "until death do us part" or any nonsense like that. They were talking about him being there during the months of her pregnancy, the delivery and the crucial bonding period with his son or daughter.

Hearing about his marriage would be a shocker to

everyone since the family all knew he'd never intended to ever settle down. But the one thing he did know was that his mother would be elated. She had initiated a campaign to marry her sons off. Jared had been the first to go down in defeat and ever since she'd been eyeing him with gleaming hope in her eyes. It didn't bother him that Sarah Westmoreland would enjoy the taste of victory, at least for a short while.

No matter how brief it would be, Durango wanted to make his marriage to Savannah special. He thought of a place they could elope to rather than Vegas. His brother Ian had recently sold his riverboat and was now the proud owner of a casino resort on Lake Tahoe. Durango hadn't had a chance to check things out for himself, but he'd heard from his brothers and cousins that Ian's place was pretty nice. Perhaps Lake Tahoe would be a classier destination for his and Savannah's quickie wedding.

A smile touched the corners of his lips. He planned on sharing an elopement with Savannah that she wouldn't forget.

Now that her decision had been made, Savannah had to tell someone about it. She would tell the one person with whom she shared all her secrets, her sister, Jessica.

She reached for her cell phone off the nightstand and quickly punched in her sister's number in Atlanta. Jessica answered on the second ring.

"Hello."

"Jess, it's me, Savannah."

"Savannah, how did things go in Montana? What did Durango say when you told him? What are you going to do now that he knows?"

Savannah smiled. She'd known Jessica would be full of questions. "I'm still in Montana. I can't fly out due to a severe snowstorm."

"Where are you staying?"

"With Durango. He offered me a place to stay and I accepted."

"That was nice of him."

"Yes, it was. Besides, we had a lot to talk about. And as for your second question, I think I shocked him when I told him I was pregnant. At first he was in denial but then he came to his senses, and…"

"And?"

"And he asked me to marry him."

"Oh, and what was your answer?"

Savannah knew Jessica's point in asking that question. Jessica knew better than anyone how she felt about marrying as the result of an unexpected pregnancy. Her parents had been a prime example that a marriage based on responsibility rather than love didn't work out. "At first I told him no, and—"

"At first?" Jessica cut in abruptly and asked, "Does that mean you eventually told him yes?"

A slight smile touched Savannah's lips. "Yes, I've decided to marry him, but it's going to be to my baby's advantage and it's only going to be on a temporary basis."

"I don't understand. What's going to be on a temporary basis?"

"Our marriage."

There was a pause and then Jessica said, "Let me get this straight. You and Durango have agreed to marry in name only for just a short while?"

Savannah sighed. "Yes, we've agreed to marry and

stay married until our child is at least six months old. That's about the time I'll be ready to return to work full-time."

"And what about you and Durango during this marriage of convenience?"

"What about us?"

"Will the two of you share a bed?"

"No. Our marriage will only be temporary."

"But the two of you will live together? Under the same roof? In the same house? Breathe the same air?"

Savannah frowned, wondering what Jessica was getting at. "Yes. Is there a problem with that?"

"Savannah, the man is a Westmoreland."

Savannah rolled her eyes upward. "And? Am I missing some point here?"

"Think about it, sis. You've slept with him before."

"Yes, and I wasn't fully in my right mind when I did so."

"And you think you won't desire him without being tipsy?"

"Honestly, Jess, of course I'll desire him! Durango is a sexy man. I might not be as sexually active as some women, but I'm not dead, either. A woman would have to be dead or comatose not to notice Durango. I'll admit that I'm attracted to him but that's as far as things are going to go. I can control my urges. I don't have to be intimate with a man, no matter how sexy he is."

"But we're not talking about any man, Savannah, we're talking about a Westmoreland. Trust me, I know the difference. Once you become involved with one, it won't be easy to deny yourself or to walk away later."

"For crying out loud, no matter what you might

think, Jessica, he's just a regular man," Savannah said, intent on making Jessica understand.

"If he was a regular man you wouldn't be in the situation you're in now. Okay, you did overindulge in champagne that night, but you can't convince me that you weren't hot for him already. You asked me about him just moments before the wedding, remember? You *were* interested. I even saw the heat in your eyes. Durango had gotten inside your head before you'd taken your first sip of champagne. That should tell you something."

Savannah expelled a breath. "It does tell me something. It tells me that I'm attracted to him. I've already admitted that. But what you don't realize is that now I'm immune to him."

"And what about falling in love?"

"Falling in love? Lord, Jessica, you know I'm immune to that, as well, doubly so thanks to our poor excuse for a father. Besides, if I even thought about falling in love with Durango, which I won't, all it will take is for me to remember that the only thing connecting us is the baby. The only reason I'm even considering marrying him is to give my child the things I never had, exposure to a warm and loving large family, which I believe the Westmorelands are, and to give Durango a chance to bond with our child. He really wants that and I feel good that he does. Our father didn't care. He was too busy playing two women to give us the time of day."

"At some point you have to let all that go, Savannah," Jessica said softly. "You can't let what Jeff Claiborne did or didn't do dictate your life or your future."

Savannah swallowed a lump in her throat. Some things were easier to get past than others. Her father's mistreatment of his three kids as well as two good women was one of them. "I can't, Jess, and I honestly don't understand how you can. You lost your mother because of him."

"Yes, but I never thought all men were like him, and neither should you."

When Savannah didn't say anything for a long time, Jessica said, "Savannah?"

"Yes," Savannah answered and then sighed.

"Be careful."

"Be careful of what?"

"Of being surprised by the magnitude of a Westmoreland's charm and appeal. When they decide to lay it on thick, watch out. Whether you want to believe it or not, it's easy to fall in love with a Westmoreland man. Trust me, I know. I never intended to fall in love with Chase, remember? He was supposed to be the enemy. And now I can't imagine living my life without him. I love him so much."

"And I'm happy for you, Jess. But you and I are different people. I never believed in happy endings—you did. Just accept my decision and know that for me it's the right one. When I walk away, that will be it. No love lost because there isn't any. Durango doesn't love me and I don't love him, but we're willing to come together and formulate a relationship for our child."

There was a lengthy pause and Savannah wasn't sure she had convinced her sister she had nothing to worry about, but she hoped that she had.

"So, when will the wedding take place?"

"I told Durango that considering the circumstances, I don't want a lot of fuss. So we're eloping to Vegas or someplace and then we'll tell everyone afterward. In a few months, when I begin looking like a blimp, they'll figure out why we married, anyway."

"And you're okay with that?"

"Sure, I'm okay with it. And for the time being, be happy for me, Jess."

"I am happy for you. Have you told Jennifer and Rico yet?"

"No, not yet. I'm not telling either of them until after the marriage takes place. I don't want anyone to try to talk me out of it. You're the only one I've told. I don't know if Durango will tell anyone in his family."

"And when is the trip to Vegas?"

"I don't know, but I'm sure it will be soon. Probably in the next couple of weeks. Durango wants us to get married right away. But he's warned me that once his family hears about our marriage that his mother will probably want to do a huge reception. I'm okay with that."

"And knowing Jennifer, she'll want to do one, as well."

"And I'll be fine with that, too. It will be simpler if they combine their efforts and host one party together. Mom met Mrs. Westmoreland at your wedding and they hit it off so I can see them getting together and planning a nice celebration."

"Yes, I can see them doing that. I'm getting excited just thinking about it."

Savannah smiled. "Get as excited as you want, as long as you remember the marriage won't last. I'll come out of this the same way I'm going into it."

"And what way is that?"

"With realistic expectations."

Seven

As soon as Savannah walked out of the bedroom and saw Durango, their gazes met. The instant attraction that was always there between them began sizzling toward a slow burn.

She would love to photograph him, would definitely appreciate the image she would capture through the lens of her camera and would tuck the developed pictures away to pull out whenever her wild fantasies kicked into gear.

"How was your nap?"

His question snapped her out of her naughty thoughts. Because she'd gone to sleep right after talking with Jessica, she had closed her eyes with Durango on her mind. She had thought about him, dreamed about him, relived the night they had made love….

"Savannah?"

She quickly realized she hadn't answered him. "The

nap was good. How about if I make dinner tonight? While hunting for saltines the other day I came across all the ingredients I'd need to make spaghetti."

He lifted a concerned eyebrow. "Will that agree with your stomach?"

She chuckled as she dropped down on the sofa, trying to ignore just how sexy he looked with his shoulder leaning against a doorway that separated the living room from the dining area. He was standing with his thumbs hooked in the front pocket of his jeans, and the chambray shirt he was wearing was straining across his muscular chest.

"In the afternoon everything agrees with my stomach, Durango. It's the mornings that I have to worry about. So how does spaghetti sound?" she asked, hoping her voice didn't contain the sizzle that she felt.

He lifted one shoulder in a shrug. "Great, if you're up to it. That will give me a chance to take a shower. And I need to talk to you about a few things."

Savannah's dark brow lifted, which helped to downplay the fluttering she felt in her stomach. "Talk to me about what?"

"While you were resting I took the liberty to make a few calls and check on some things. You did say you were leaving all the arrangements to me and would be fine with everything as long as I left out the hoopla."

"Yes, I did."

"Well, I've made wedding plans and want to discuss them with you, to make sure they meet your approval."

She blinked in surprise. While she'd been napping, he'd evidently been busy. "Wedding plans? Then we definitely need to talk after your shower."

"All right, I'll be back in a minute." Before turning

to leave, he asked, "Are you sure you don't need my help with dinner?"

"No, I can handle things."

"Yes, I'm sure you can," he countered, smiling.

And when he walked out the room she had a feeling that he'd been hinting at more than just her spaghetti.

"Everything tastes good, Savannah."

"Thank you." She tried looking at anything and everything other than the man sitting across the table from her. Doing so was simply too tempting. After glancing out the window and seeing it was still snowing, she scanned the room and took in the beauty of his kitchen and again mentally admired the setup of everything, including the pots that…

"Are you okay?"

His question forced her to do something she hadn't wanted to do. Look directly at him. The moment she did so she felt fiery tingles move down her spine. "Yes, I'm okay. Why do you ask?"

"No particular reason."

Sitting this close to him she could actually smell his scent, one that was all man. But that didn't compare to how he'd looked when he had entered the kitchen after his shower wearing jeans that hung low on his hips and a shirt he hadn't bothered to button.

"Are you ready to talk about the plans I've made?"

His question pulled her mind back from lurking into a territory where it had no business going. "Sure."

He stood and began gathering the dishes off the table. "Instead of going to Vegas I thought it would be nice if we went to Lake Tahoe instead."

She raised an eyebrow. "Lake Tahoe?"

"Yes, my brother Ian recently bought a casino resort there. I heard it's truly spectacular and I would like to take you there."

"Lake Tahoe," she said again, savoring the idea. She had visited the area a few years ago and had thought it was beautiful. She smiled across the table at Durango. "All right. That sounds like a winner to me, so when do you want to do it?"

"Day after tomorrow."

"What!"

He chuckled at her startled expression. "I think Friday would be a perfect day for us to leave for Lake Tahoe. Starting today the weather will begin improving and tomorrow you can—"

"Hold up. Time out. Cut." She caught her breath for a moment and then said, "Durango, there's no way I can marry you on Friday. I have to go back home and take care of a few things. I have to plan for the wedding. I have to—"

"We're eloping, remember? And besides, I thought you didn't want a lot of hoopla."

He had her there. "I don't, but I hadn't thought about getting married *this* soon."

"The sooner the better, don't you think? You're a couple of months already. Jayla began really sticking out there by the fourth month. I remember when I went home for my father's birthday during Easter and she was huge, almost as big as a house."

Savannah raised her eyes to the ceiling, hoping he had the good sense not to mention such a thing to Jayla. Even pregnant, women were sensitive when it came to their weight. "She was carrying twins, Durango, for heaven's sake."

"And how do you know you aren't? Multiple births run in my family. My father is the twin to Chase's father and both of them had twins. Then Uncle Corey had triplets, so anything is possible."

That wasn't what Savannah wanted to hear. She much preferred having one healthy baby, but of course she would gladly accept whatever she got. "I couldn't possibly get ready for Lake Tahoe by Friday. I didn't bring any clothes here with me and I would need to purchase some things."

"There're several stores in Bozeman that will have everything you need. Tomorrow can be a shopping day."

Savannah felt rushed and decided to let him know it. "I feel like you're rushing me," she said briskly.

A smile touched his lips. "In a way I am. Now that we've decided to do it, why wait? I want us to marry as soon as possible."

She couldn't help wondering why. Did he think she would change her mind or something? She was carrying his baby, and until she'd shown up and announced that fact, he hadn't been interested in marriage. She had thought she would have at least a couple of weeks, maybe even a month before they actually did anything. She'd assumed she would leave tomorrow to return to Philadelphia and they would make plans for the wedding over the phone. This was definitely not what she had expected.

"Savannah, why are you hesitating? We should move forward and get things over with."

Get things over with? Well, he certainly didn't have to make it sound like marrying her was something being forced upon him. No one had asked him to do it. Getting married was his idea and not hers. She was about to tell him just that when he did something she hadn't expected. He tugged her hand and pulled her out of her chair, wrapping his arms around her and pulling her against him.

Startled, her head came up the moment her body pressed against his. Very little space separated them. A smile touched the corners of his mouth for a few seconds before he said softly, "You're trying to be difficult, aren't you?"

She swallowed. It wasn't easy to gaze into the dark eyes holding hers captive. "Not intentionally."

"Then why the cold feet? I've already checked the airlines and there are plenty of flights available, and I've talked to my brother Ian."

At her frown he said, "And yes, I told him we decided to get married, but I didn't tell him why. He said that he would love to have us as his guests for the weekend. He's making all the necessary arrangements."

He studied her features for a moment then asked, "Are you having second thoughts about eloping, Savannah? Do you prefer having a small wedding here so that we could invite our families?"

"No," she said quickly. "I still prefer keeping things simple. I guess I'm hesitating because it never dawned on me that I might be returning to Philadelphia a married woman."

"Then I guess you aren't prepared to return to Philadelphia with a husband in tow, either."

His words were a shocker. "You're going back with me?"

"Yes. You'll have to introduce me to your family sometime."

Her head was reeling from the thought of him returning to Philadelphia with her. "You've already met my family at Chase and Jessica's wedding."

"Yes, but I met them as Chase's cousin, not as your husband. Besides, we'll be newlyweds and it will seem strange for us not to be together."

"Yes, but—"

"And I want to take you home to Atlanta, as well, to meet my family. Not as Jessica's sister but as my wife. Although everyone will probably reach their own conclusions as to why we eloped and got married, it's really none of their business. We'll tell them that we met at the wedding, fell madly in love and decided to get married."

Savannah couldn't help but smile at Durango's ridiculous statement. There was no way anyone would believe such a thing, and from the mischievous grin touching his lips, he knew that, as well.

"Let's keep them guessing," Durango said, chuckling. "Our decision doesn't concern anyone but us."

Savannah couldn't help but agree with that, especially after her conversation with Jessica. Everything he was saying made sense. Now that they had decided to marry, why prolong things? "Fine, if you think we can pull it off, then Friday is fine."

"Good. And there's something else you'll need to do tomorrow."

"What?"

"Visit the doctor in town. I've already made you an appointment for tomorrow morning."

Savannah pulled back slightly and frowned. "Why?

Don't you believe I'm pregnant? Or do you want to have it verified before going through with the marriage ceremony?"

"No, that's not it," he said tightly. "I just want the doctor to check you out to make sure you're okay. You gave me a scare this morning and I just want to make sure you and the baby are fine."

Savannah met his gaze and saw the sincerity in his eyes and knew he had spoken the truth. "Okay," she finally said. "I'll go to the doctor for a checkup if it will make you happy."

"It will," he said. "And thank you."

Savannah drew in a deep breath. She needed space from Durango and took a step back. "I'll get started on the dishes and—"

"No, you did the cooking so it's only fair that I clean up the kitchen."

"Durango, I can manage to—"

"Savannah, that's the way it's going to be. Just relax. You'll have more than enough to do over the next couple of days, and it seems the weather is going to cooperate."

She glanced out the window and saw it had stopped snowing. This was the break in the weather she'd been waiting for. But now, instead of packing to return home to Philly, she'd be preparing for a wedding.

"If you're sure that you can handle the dishes by yourself, then I need to call and talk with my boss. I had told him I would be back in the office on Monday."

"Okay." When she turned to leave he said, "And Savannah?"

She turned back around. "Yes?"

"I planned for us to stay in the same suite but it has two bedrooms. Will that be a problem?"

She swallowed deeply as her gaze held his. "No, that won't be a problem as long as there will be two bedrooms."

The smile that suddenly touched his lips made her stomach flutter and made heat flow all over her. "Then we're all set. I'll call the airlines and book us a flight."

They were eloping to Lake Tahoe.

Durango's announcement of last night was the main reason for Savannah's sleepless night. And the magnitude of it must have shocked her system because she had awakened the next morning without any feelings of nausea.

However, it seemed that Durango intended to be prepared because when she opened her eyes, she found him sitting in the chair beside her bed with a plate of saltines and a cup of tea all ready for her.

"Good morning."

The sensuous sound of his voice so early in the morning sent shivers all through her, and the concerned smile that touched his lips wasn't helping matters, either.

"Good morning," she said, pulling herself up in bed. Although she appreciated his kindness and thoughtfulness, she would have much preferred if he had given her a minute or two to freshen up. She would have liked to comb her hair and wash the sleep from her eyes.

"Are you feeling okay this morning?"

"Yes, thanks for asking. For some reason I'm not feeling nauseated." She decided not to tell him her suspicions on the reason why.

"I'm glad to hear that." He then nodded his head toward the fireplace. "I tried keeping it warm in here during the night."

Her gaze followed his to the roaring flame. "Thank you." Because she hadn't been able to sleep, she had been aware of each and every time he had come into her room and checked the heat.

"This is going to be a busy day for us since we'll be flying out first thing in the morning."

Savannah's gaze returned to his. "I imagine that it will be."

"After our doctor visit, I'll take you to the mall. I figured you would probably want to shop alone, so I'll use that time to pay McKinnon a visit and then come back later for you. You do remember my best friend McKinnon, don't you?"

"Yes, I remember him." She definitely remembered McKinnon Quinn, just like she was sure a number of other women would. With his beautiful golden-brown complexion and thick ponytail, she had admired his handsome features that reflected his mixed-race ancestry. She had actually blinked twice when she'd first seen him because the man had been simply gorgeous. But even with McKinnon's striking good looks, it had been Durango who had caught her eye and held it.

"I guess I'll leave you alone so you can get dressed now," Durango said, standing and placing the tea and saltines on the nightstand.

It took fierce concentration to keep Savannah's mind on their conversation and not on Durango as he got out of the chair. He was dressed in a pair of jeans, a pullover sweater and a pair of black leather boots. She didn't care how many times she saw him dressed that way, but each time his appearance grabbed her attention. "Thanks for the crackers and tea," she said.

Durango smiled. "Don't mention it."

Savannah's breath caught in her throat from that one smile, and when he turned his head to glance out the window, she grabbed that opportunity to study him some more. His eyes were focused on the mountains as if weighing a problem of some kind, and she wondered if perhaps he thought the good weather wouldn't last. When he turned his head he caught her staring at him and for a brief breath of a moment she felt the sizzle that always seemed to hang in the air between them.

"I'd better be going. There's a couple of things I need to check on outside before we leave," he said and, as if tearing his gaze from hers, he glanced over at the fireplace. "That thing keeps this room pretty hot, doesn't it?"

She followed his gaze. It was on the tip of her tongue to say that at the moment she thought it was him, and not the fireplace, that made the room pretty hot. Instead she said, "Yes, it does."

Savannah had to admit, however, that she did enjoy sleeping in a room with a fireplace. She had gotten used to the stark smell of burning wood, the sound of loose pieces crackling as they caught fire, and more than anything, she liked the comforting warmth the fire provided.

"Do you think you'll be able to eat any food this morning?" Durango asked, interrupting her thoughts.

She frowned, deciding not to chance it. "I'd better not try it. Those saltines and tea will do just fine. Thanks."

Moments after Durango had left the room, Savannah

sat on the edge of her bed thinking about all the things she had to do to get ready for tomorrow. Just thinking about everything made her feel exhausted. But she was determined to get through the day and in a way, she was looking forward to her visit to the doctor.

A quiver raced through her stomach at the thought that Durango would be there, too, sharing the experience with her.

Eight

"So how's the baby?" Durango asked the doctor nervously.

Lying flat on her back on the examination table, Savannah shifted her gaze to Durango, who was standing beside her. She heard the deep concern in his voice and saw how his eyebrows came together in a tense expression.

She then switched her gaze to Dr. Patrina Foreman. Dr. Foreman was a lot younger than Savannah had expected. She was a very attractive woman and she appeared to be about twenty-eight. Within minutes of talking to her, Savannah was convinced that even though she might be young, she was definitely competent. Dr. Foreman had explained that her mother, grandmother and great-grandmother had been midwives, but that she had decided to complete medical school to offer her patients the best of both worlds. She could provide modern medical treatments as well as the type of care and personal attention that midwives were known to give.

Dr. Foreman lifted her gaze from applying the gel on Savannah's stomach and smiled before saying, "Listen to this for a moment and then tell me what you think."

And then they heard it, the soft thumping sound of their child's heartbeat, for the first time. Hearing the steady little drumbeat did something to Savannah, touched her in a way she hadn't expected and made her realize that she really and truly was going to have a baby.

Tears, something else she hadn't expected, came into her eyes and she glanced up at Durango and knew he was just as moved by the sound as she was. He reached out and firmly touched her shoulder, and at that moment she knew that no matter how they did or didn't feel about each other, her pregnancy was real and they were listening to valid proof of just how real it was. There was no doubt that hearing the sound was a life-altering experience for both of them.

"You hadn't heard it before?" Durango asked softly.

"No. This is my first time."

"There's nothing like parents hearing the fetal heartbeat for the first time," Dr. Foreman said quietly. "There's always something special and exciting about it. The baby's heartbeat is strong and sounds healthy to me."

Durango chuckled. "Yes, it does, doesn't it? This is all rather new to me and I was kind of worried."

"And you have every right to be concerned, but it seems mother and baby are doing just fine," Dr. Foreman replied, removing the instrument from Savannah's stomach. "Make sure that you continue to take your prenatal vitamins, Savannah."

"And what about all that vomiting she's been doing?" Durango asked, wanting to know.

Dr. Foreman glanced at him. "Morning sickness is caused by the sudden increase of hormones during pregnancy and is very common early in the pregnancy, but it's usually gone by the fourth month." She smiled at Savannah and said, "So, hopefully you won't have to suffer too much longer."

"I prefer she didn't suffer at all. And what about the baby? Will it be hurt by it?" Durango asked, in a tone that said he really needed Dr. Foreman's assurance.

"It shouldn't, but of course it can become a problem if Savannah can't keep any foods or fluids down or if she begins to lose weight. Otherwise, morning sickness is a positive sign that the pregnancy is progressing."

Dr. Foreman then opened a drawer and pulled out a package and handed it to Savannah. "This might help. It's the same type of acupressure wristbands that doctors give out on cruise ships to prevent seasickness. A lot of my patients swear that wearing it helps to reduce the morning sickness."

For the next ten to fifteen minutes, Dr. Foreman answered all of Savannah and Durango's questions. Then she congratulated them when Durango mentioned they were getting married.

"I really like her," Savannah told Durango when they left the doctor's office. "And I hadn't expected her to be so young."

Durango smiled as he ushered Savannah out the building to where he had parked his truck. "Yes, Trina is young but I've heard that she is one of the best. She was born and raised around these parts and her husband Perry was the sheriff. He was killed a few years ago in the line of duty while trying to arrest an escaped convict."

"Oh, how awful."

Durango nodded. "Yes, it was. Perry was a good person and everyone liked and respected him. He and Trina had been childhood sweethearts."

Durango opened the door to his truck and assisted Savannah in settling in and buckling her seat belt. "Was it a coincidence or did you deliberately buy this particular SUV?" she asked grinning. It was ironic that his name was Durango and that was also the model of the vehicle that he drove.

He chuckled as he snapped her seat belt in place. "Not a coincidence. I thought I'd milk it for all it's worth since Dodge decided to name a vehicle after me," he said arrogantly, giving her that smile that made her stomach spin. "Besides, we're both known to give smooth and unforgettable rides," he added softly while gazing into her eyes.

For a moment Savannah couldn't speak since she of all people knew about the smoothness, as well as the intensity, of Durango's ride. The very thought was generating earth-shattering memories of the time he had pleasured her in bed.

She watched as he walked around the front of the truck to get into the driver's seat. "You're taking me to the mall now?" she asked, trying to get her heartbeat back on track. If she was having trouble keeping her thoughts off him now, she didn't want to think how things would be once they were married.

"Yes, I'm taking you to the Gallatin Valley Mall," Durango said, pulling out of the parking lot and returning her attention. "You should be able to find everything you need there. Do you want me to stay and shop with you?"

"No, I'll be fine," she quickly said, knowing she needed her space for a while. "If there's one thing a woman knows how to do on her own it's shop."

Stealing a glance at him she couldn't help wondering how he really felt about marrying her and suddenly needed to know that he was still okay with their plans.

"Durango?"

"Yes?"

The truck had come to a stop at a traffic light and she knew his gaze was on her but she refused to look at him. Instead she looked straight ahead. "Are you sure getting married is what you really want to do?" she asked as calmly as she could.

"Yes, I'm sure," he said in a voice so low and husky, Savannah couldn't help but turn to meet his gaze. Then in a way she wished she hadn't when she saw the deep, dark intensity in his eyes. He then smiled and that smile touched her, and she couldn't help but return it.

"If I wasn't before, Savannah, I am now, especially after listening to our baby's heartbeat. God, that was an awesome experience. And according to Trina, it has all the vital organs it will need already. It's not just a cluster of cells but a real human being. A being that we created and I want to connect to it more so than ever."

Savannah sighed in relief. The last thing she wanted was for him to ever regret marrying her. She was satisfied that he wouldn't.

* * *

Bozeman, one of the most diverse small towns in the Rocky Mountains, was known for its hospitality and was proud of its numerous ski resorts. It was a city that attracted not only tourists, but also families wanting to plant their roots in a place that offered good quality of life.

Durango drove straight to the mall and parked the truck. He even took the time to walk Savannah inside, saying there were a couple of things he needed to purchase for himself. He gave her his cell phone number in case she finished shopping early so she could reach him.

Once they parted ways, Savannah became a woman on a mission as she went from store to store. Within a few hours she had purchased everything she needed and had indulged herself by getting a few things she really hadn't needed, like a few sexy nightgowns she had purchased from Victoria's Secret. It wasn't as if Durango would ever see her in any of them, but still, she couldn't help herself. She liked buying sexy things.

A few hours later Savannah had made all of her purchases, and contacted Durango on his cell phone. He told her he had just pulled into the parking lot and would meet her at the food court in the center of the mall. He suggested that they grab dinner at a really good restaurant there.

She had been in the food court for only a few minutes when she glanced across the way and saw him. Her pulse quickened. There was no way she could discount the fact that he was a devastatingly handsome man, and she wasn't the only female who noticed. As he crossed the mall in long, confident strides, several heads turned to watch him, and for a moment Savannah felt both pride and a tinge of jealousy.

She quickly dismissed the latter emotion. He wasn't hers and she wasn't his. But still, as he continued to walk toward her, closing the distance separating them, she saw the look in his eyes, deciphered the way he was looking at her with that steady dark gaze of his. It was the same way he had looked at her the night of Chase and Jessica's wedding.

And as if it was the most natural thing to do, when he reached her he leaned down and kissed her. Surprised, she returned the brief, but thorough kiss while her heart thumped ominously in her chest.

"Did you get a lot accomplished today?" he asked softly against her moist lips.

Not able to speak at first, she nodded. Then she said breathlessly, "Yes, I think I have everything I'm going to need. And I think I found an appropriate dress for tomorrow."

Durango chuckled as he took her hand in his and led her toward the restaurant where they would dine. "I'm sure it's more than appropriate. I bet it's perfect and I can't wait to see you in it."

Later that night while packing, Savannah had to admit that it had been a simply wonderful day. First the visit to the doctor and then her shopping trip to the mall and last, having dinner with Durango at that restaurant. The food had been delicious and Durango's company had been excellent. Over a candlelight dinner he had told her about his partnership with McKinnon's horse farm and how well it was doing.

Closing her luggage, Savannah smiled when she recalled the message Jessica had left on Durango's answering machine, telling them to expect her and Chase at Lake Tahoe tomorrow. A part of Savannah had been both elated and relieved that elopement or not, a stubborn Jessica would not let her get married without her sister being there. Durango also seemed pleased that his cousin was coming, as well.

She looked up when she heard the knock on her bedroom door. "Come in."

Durango entered, dressed in a pair of jogging pants and a T-shirt with a towel wrapped around his neck. "I was about to get into the hot tub and was wondering if you would like to join me."

"But it's cold outside."

He smiled ruefully. "Yes, but once you get into the tub you'll forget how cold it is. It's the best thing to stimulate sore, aching muscles. Try it. I guarantee that you'll like it."

Savannah thought of all the walking she had done earlier that day at the mall and decided a soak in the hot tub sounded good. But still…

"Is it large enough for the both of us to fit comfortably?" The thought of being crammed into a hot tub with Durango was too much to think about.

"Yes, it can hold five to six people without any problems."

She nodded. Good. He could stay on his side of the tub and she could stay on hers. "All right, then let me change into a swimming suit." She had bought one that day at the mall and had to dig it out from the suitcase.

After Durango left Savannah changed her clothes, thankful that the swimming suit she had purchased was a one-piece and wasn't overly provocative. The attraction between her and Durango was bad enough without adding fuel to an already hot fire.

"For a moment I thought I was going to have to come back inside to get you."

She chuckled and quickly padded on bare feet across the deck to the hot tub. "Sorry. My mom called right when I was about to come outside."

His eyebrows lifted. "Did you tell her about our plans for tomorrow?"

"Yes," Savannah said as she quickly dispensed with her robe and eased inside the tub, deliberately sinking as far down as she could and letting a sound of "ahh" ease from between her lips. Once she got settled in a comfortable position she added, "I didn't give her a lot of details and told her we can have a long discussion when she returns from Paris. But she is very astute in reading between the lines, so I'm sure she has an idea why we're having a quick wedding."

Durango studied her eyes since her face was the only part of her he could see. She had water covering her entire body, from her shoulders to her toes. She was almost completely submerged.

"Did your mom know we'd been involved?" he asked, wishing he had X-ray vision that would enable him to see her body through the water. But he had caught a glimpse of her curves when she had removed her robe. Although she had tried to be quick about it and to not draw any attention to herself, she had failed miserably. Her swimsuit was sexy, and the cut was a snug fit that showed off her shapely thighs and bottom.

"If she does it's not because I've told her anything,"

Savannah said, cutting into his thoughts. "However, she did mention when we met for lunch last month that she couldn't help noticing that we were having a hard time keeping our eyes off each other at the wedding." She decided not to add that her mother had also noticed when the two of them had left the reception together.

"Hey, this feels nice," she said, liking how the hot water seemed to penetrate the tired muscles of her body. "And you were right. I don't feel how cold the temperature is."

"I'm glad. And by the way, you can come from hiding under the water. I promise not to jump your bones if you do," he said slowly, grinning.

She met his gaze and smiled sheepishly. "I didn't think that you would. I was merely making sure I wouldn't freeze to death."

"And now that you know that you won't?"

She took a deep breath and eased more of her body out of the water. When the hot, bubbling, swirling water came to her waist like it did his, she felt a sizzling sensation flow down her spine and settle in the pit of her stomach. He was staring at her. Her bathing suit was decent, but it was fashioned in a style that made anyone aware of the fullness of her breasts.

"I like your swimming suit. At least what I've seen of it so far," he said. His voice was low, intimate.

"Thanks." She then glanced around. "So what made you decide to put this hot tub in?"

He gave her an intent look, knowing she was trying to change the subject. "It was an easy decision since I was taking advantage of one of the natural hot springs located on my property."

"Oh, you have others?"

He grinned, knowing he had told her that already. "Yes, but don't expect me to show them to you tonight," he said, leaning back against the wall of the tub and deliberately stretching out one of his legs. He made it seem like an accident, an innocent mistake when his thigh touched her thigh. She gasped and slowly eased back to give him more space.

"Going someplace?" he asked with a totally innocent look on his face.

"No, I'm just trying to give you more room."

"I don't need more room."

"Could have fooled me," she muttered under her breath.

"You say something?"

She glanced over at him. "No, just thinking out loud."

Before she could blink he had pushed away from the wall and had glided over to her, putting his face inches from hers. "Now what did you say, Savannah?"

Savannah pulled in a sharp intake of breath. Not only was Durango's face near hers, but she could feel the heat from his entire body. He was within touching distance. He was making the already hot water that much hotter.

"Did I ever tell you how much I like kissing you, Savannah?" he asked.

A shudder of desire ran through her, first starting at her toes and easing its way to the top of her head. "I don't recall if you have or not," she said silkily, watching his lips inch even closer.

"Well, let me go on record and say that I do. You have a unique taste," he said in a deep, husky tone.

"I do?"

"Yes. It's so tantalizingly sweet that I can feast on it for hours."

Another shudder ran through her. "No man has ever told me that before."

He smiled. "Then maybe you haven't kissed the right man."

"Maybe."

"And although you haven't given me any bedroom rights while we're married, you haven't denied me kissing rights, have you?" he asked in a sensual tone.

"Ahh, no." *But maybe I should,* she quickly thought.

"Good, because I'm going to enjoy kissing you whenever I can."

She held her breath when he leaned forward, wrapped his arms around her waist and took the tip of his tongue and began slowly, sensuously, passionately tracing the outline of her mouth.

She moaned deep and eased his name from between her lips just moments before he slipped his tongue inside her mouth. Moaning more, she returned his kiss as their tongues met, mingled and stroked. The signals they were exchanging were intimately familiar, and all it took was the shift of their legs to bring their bodies right smack together, making her feel the very essence of his heat. She knew exactly what that huge, hot engorged body part pressed against her midsection meant.

Savannah wanted to pull back, stop playing with fire, cease indulging in temptation, but she couldn't. Her legs felt weak, her thighs were becoming a quivering mass and her mouth was definitely getting branded the Durango way. And when he reached up and touched the tip of her breasts through the soft and clingy material of her swimsuit, she almost lost her bearing. She would have done so if his hands weren't still around her waist, holding her close.

He pulled back slightly and whispered hotly against her moist lips, "I also like touching you. You feel hot all over."

It was on the tip of her tongue to say that thanks to him she *was* hot all over, but at that moment he leaned forward and took that same tongue into his mouth again, ending further conversation. Her heartbeat kicked up a notch when his hand moved from her waist and slid lower and when he shifted their bodies so he could sufficiently caress the area between her legs, through the soft material of her swimsuit, she almost cried out at the sensations he elicited.

"I know this part of you is off-limits," he said in a deep, throaty voice that sent even more heat running through her. "But I can tell it wants me. It wants how I can make it feel, Savannah. It's hot for me, the same way I'm hot for you. For two months I've lain in my bed at night and thought about us, how we were that night, how good we were together and how good we could be again."

While he was talking, drumming up memories, his thumb continued to caress her, driving her mad, insane with desire and her head fell forward to his chest, her breathing became choppy and her mind was overtaken by passion.

"It's going to be hard for us to share space being such passionate individuals and not want to do something about it, don't you think?" he asked hotly against her ear.

"Yes, I'm sure it will be," she agreed, easing the words from between her lips.

"But I'm honor bound to abide by your wishes and I will…unless you change your mind and give me the word to do otherwise. And then there won't be any stopping me, Savannah."

Savannah didn't know what to say. And when she thought of what would happen if she ever changed her mind as well as the movement of his fingers on her, a needy ache flamed to life between her legs. And when a shudder began passing through her again, igniting every cell in her body, sending sensations rushing through her, she called out his name. Just with the use of his fingers he had pushed her over the edge, giving her the big "O" without fully penetrating the barriers of her clothing.

Durango gently pulled on her hair to bring her face back to his and he kissed her, literally drank his name from her lips, as his hungry and demanding mouth devoured her, giving her a taste of what she would be missing, and giving him a thorough taste of her.

Savannah forced her mouth away from his when breathing became a necessity. The first thing she noticed was that sometime during their kiss she had wrapped her legs around him. She didn't remember doing it but Durango *had* been kissing her senseless and the only thing she did remember was the magnitude of that kiss, the explosiveness of it.

She inhaled deeply. Jessica was right. This wasn't a regular man. This was a Westmoreland and they didn't do anything halfway. She had a pregnancy to prove it. What other man could make a woman scream his name in ecstasy while still wearing clothes?

She looked up at him to say something and he leaned forward and kissed her again. This kiss was slow, lingering and just as hot as the kisses that he'd lavished on her before.

When he pulled back his dark eyes held her with deep intensity. And his voice was strained when he said, "I meant what I said, Savannah. I want to make love to you again, but unless you give me the word, kissing is as far as it will go between us."

She nodded and closed her eyes, knowing he would respect the boundaries she had set. But she also knew that he intended to use his kisses to break down her defenses. When she felt him easing away, she opened her eyes and watched him get out of the hot tub. His wet swimming trunks clung to his body like a second layer of skin, and the evidence of his desire for her was still evident.

He was silent while he toweled off, watching her watch him. He smiled knowingly. "Tomorrow is our wedding day and regardless of the reason that brought us to this point, Savannah, I intend to make it a special day for you. For the both of us."

Moments later when the patio door closed behind him, Savannah sank deeper into the water, already feeling the loss of Durango's heat. Whether she wanted to or not, a part of her couldn't help but look forward to tomorrow, the day when—even though it would be temporary—she would become Mrs. Durango Westmoreland.

Nine

The following day when they pulled up to the entrance of the Rolling Cascade Casino and Resort, Savannah was at a loss for words. As a photographer she had traveled to many picturesque sites, but she thought nothing could have prepared her for the car ride from Reno to Ian Westmoreland's exclusive resort on Lake Tahoe.

She and Durango had flown into Reno and had rented a car for the drive to Lake Tahoe. They decided to take what he declared to be the scenic route; the panoramic view was spectacular and more than once she had asked Durango to stop the car so she could take pictures of the snowcapped mountains, the enormous boulders and the clusters of shrubs and pine trees that grew almost down to the lake.

Just minutes from Stateline, Nevada, the Rolling Cascade looked different from the other sprawling casinos they had passed. Ian's resort was a beautifully designed building that overlooked Lake Tahoe and was surrounded by a number of specialty shops, clothing stores and a myriad of restaurants.

Durango had explained that the Cascade had been vacant for almost a year after it was discovered that the previous owner had been using the casino as a front for an illegal operation. When it had gone up for sale, Ian and his investors had been ready to bring their casino business on land. Hurricane Katrina had made it impossible to continue his riverboat's route along the Mississippi from New Orleans to Memphis.

Ian had remodeled the establishment to be a small community within itself. Having been open for six months, the resort had already shown amazing profits and was giving plenty of stiff competition to the likes of the Las Vegas–style casinos situated close by.

"This place is simply beautiful," Savannah said when Durango brought the car to a stop. Within seconds, members of the resort's staff were there to greet them and to assist with their bags.

Durango smiled as he placed a muscled arm around her shoulders as they walked inside the building. The Cascade's inside was just as impressive as its outside. Durango stopped and glanced around, letting out a low whistle. Moments later he said, "Ian really did it up this time. I think he's found his calling."

"I think so, too, brother."

Both Durango and Savannah turned to find a smiling Ian standing directly behind them. He gave Durango an affectionate bear hug and leaned over and brushed a kiss on Savannah's cheek. "I'm glad you like what you see," Ian said and smiled.

"We do," Savannah replied, returning his smile and thinking that all the Westmoreland brothers and cousins resembled each other. They were all tall, dark and handsome; however, Ian's neatly trimmed short beard added a rakish look to his features. "And I appreciate you having us here," she added.

Ian grinned. "No reason to thank me. It's about time Durango came down from the mountains and went someplace other than Atlanta. Besides, it's not every day that a Westmoreland gets married. Come on and let me get the both of you checked in. I have the wedding chapel reserved for five o'clock. That will give you time to rest and relax a bit before the ceremony."

"Have Chase and Jessica arrived yet?" Durango asked as he and Savannah followed Ian over to the check-in counter.

"Yes, they got in a few hours ago and last time I checked they were getting ready to take a stroll around the shops."

A huge smile then touched Ian's lips. "And I have a surprise for you, Durango."

"What?"

"I got a call from McKinnon. That appointment he had scheduled for today got canceled and he was able to get a flight out and will be arriving just in time for the wedding."

Durango smiled, pleased his best friend would make the wedding after all.

Less than ten minutes later Durango and Savannah were stepping inside what Ian had told them was a vacant owner's suite, which to Savannah's way of thinking looked more like an exclusive condo with its three bedrooms, two full baths, gigantic fireplace, kitchen area and beautiful balcony that overlooked Lake Tahoe.

Savannah gave an inward sigh of relief at seeing the three bedrooms, although one of them she assumed due to its size was intended to be a master suite. She didn't want a repeat of the temptation she had faced the previous night while in the hot tub with Durango, and was grateful for the spaciousness of the place.

"I'll let you choose whichever bedroom you prefer," Durango said, closing the door behind him.

She turned around and smiled sheepishly. "Because of all the stuff I brought along with me, I'll take the biggest of the three bedrooms, if you don't mind."

He chuckled. "No, I don't mind." He glanced at his watch. "We have a few hours to kill. Do you want to take a walk around the lake?"

"I'd love to, and it was nice of Ian to let us use this suite, wasn't it?"

Durango grinned. "Yes, he can be a nice enough guy when he wants to be. But there are times when he's known to be a pain in the ass."

Savannah knew he was kidding. Anyone who hung around the Westmorelands for any length of time could tell they were a close-knit group. "Give me a few minutes to freshen up, okay?"

"Sure."

When she reached her bedroom, Durango called out to her.

"Ian mentioned there's a private hot tub on the twelfth floor if we wanted to try it out," he said.

Images of the two of them in the hot tub last night and the heated kiss they had shared floated into Savannah's mind. Just the thoughts made a tingly feeling settle in the pit of her stomach. "I think I'll pass on that."

"You sure?" he asked, grinning, making her remember in blatant details their hot-tub antics of the night before.

"I'm positive."

"If I didn't know the score I'd think you and Durango were excited about getting married."

Savannah glanced at her sister as she slipped into her wedding dress. She and Durango had run into Chase and Jessica while touring the grounds around the lake. Jessica had suggested that Savannah get dressed for the ceremony in the suite she and Durango shared. Durango would dress in Chase and Jessica's room. That way the bride and groom wouldn't see each other in their wedding attire before they were married.

"You're imagining things. Durango and I came to an agreement to do what's in the best interest of our child. That's the only reason we're getting married."

Jessica Claiborne Westmoreland laughed, reached out and hugged her sister and said, "Hey, whatever, I still think the two of you look good together."

Savannah looked at Jessica in mild exasperation. "And I told you not to get any ideas, Jess."

"If you don't want me to get any ideas, then how about explaining these?" she said, gesturing to all the sexy sleepwear Savannah had unpacked earlier. "If these aren't for Durango's enjoyment then who are they for?" she asked, picking up one of the negligees.

"For me. You know how much I like wearing sexy things to bed," Savannah said, reaching out and taking the item from Jessica and tossing it back on the bed. "Since Durango and I won't be sharing a bed, what I sleep in is no business of his."

Jessica tipped her head, regarded Savannah thoughtfully and said, "You still haven't gotten it yet, have you?"

"Gotten what?"

"The fact that a Westmoreland man isn't anyone to play with. How long do you think the two of you will be able to fight this intense attraction? Even today he was looking at you when he thought you weren't looking and you were looking at him when you thought he wasn't looking. The two of you were doing the same thing at my wedding."

"And your point?"

"The point is that you know what happened as soon as the two of you were alone and behind closed doors."

"We indulged in too much champagne that night, Jess. That won't happen this time because I don't plan to consume any alcohol while I'm pregnant."

"There's another way a woman can get tipsy, Savannah. There is such a thing as being overtaken by sexual chemistry and losing your head," she said, letting her gaze stray to the nightgowns once again.

"I don't plan to lose my head."

"What about your heart?"

"That, either. Now tell me how I look."

Jessica glanced up and fell silent. She had seen the short, white lace dress on the hanger and thought it looked okay, but on Savannah the dress looked like it had been made just for her, and just for this special occasion. Savannah looked so beautiful it almost brought tears to Jessica's eyes.

"Well, what do you think?" Savannah asked when Jessica didn't say anything.

"I think that you look simply beautiful and I'm sorry that Jennifer isn't here to see you," Jessica said, almost choking with emotion.

"Hey, knock it off, Jess. This wedding is no big deal. The only reason we're getting married is because I'm pregnant...remember?"

Jessica reached out to pick up another skimpy piece of lingerie only to have Savannah shoo her hand away. She chuckled and then asked, "So when are you going to let Rico know you're a married woman?"

Savannah closed her luggage with a firm click. "Durango and I will be calling and telling everybody the news when we get back. We had hoped to take off for Philly and Atlanta next week to drop the bomb in person, but because one of the park rangers is out on medical leave, it will be another month before Durango can take time off work. Maybe that's just as well since it will give everyone a chance to get used to the idea."

"I can't wait to see the Westmorelands' reaction when they hear the news. Durango is the last person anyone would have thought would marry."

"Yes, but let me remind you again that the only reason he's doing so now is because I'm pregnant, and don't you forget it."

Jessica laughed. "After seeing all those sexy things, the big question is whether after this weekend you'll forget it."

* * *

Durango turned around the moment he felt Savannah's presence in the wedding chapel. Immediately his breath caught at the sight of how strikingly beautiful she looked in her dress. It was perfect. Typically you couldn't improve on perfection, but in Savannah's case she had by adding the string of pearls around her neck, as well as with the way her hair shimmered like a silk curtain around her face, making her hazel eyes that much more profound. She was a vision straight out of any man's fantasy.

"Your bride is a beautiful woman, Rango. I'm not sure that's a good sign."

Durango arched an eyebrow and switched his gaze from Savannah to the man standing by his side, who'd leaned closer to whisper in his ear. McKinnon Quinn was the only person to whom he had told the real reason he was getting married, although he was sure Chase knew, as well. "Somehow I'll deal with it, McKinnon."

McKinnon chuckled. "I'm glad it's you who'll be doing the dealing and not me. A woman that beautiful might cause me to have a few weak moments."

Durango hoped like hell that he would be a stronger man than McKinnon when and if those moments occurred. He glanced over at Chase and Ian, wondering if they had the same thoughts as McKinnon since they had shifted their gazes from Savannah to stare at him.

A few moments later Durango was standing beside Savannah as they faced the older man who was employed by the Cascade to perform wedding ceremonies. Durango had no problem saying *I do* to any of the things the man asked him since he planned to adhere to his marriage vows for the brief time the marriage lasted.

Although he had been fully aware of each and every question he'd been asked, he'd also been fully aware of the woman standing beside him. The subtle scent of her perfume was zapping his senses. She could arouse feelings in him that were better left alone. And today of all days, the flesh beneath his suit was burning with memories of the time they had spent in the hot tub together.

"I now pronounce you man and wife. You may kiss your bride."

The man's words intruded on Durango's thoughts, giving him a mental start at the realization that the ceremony was over. He was now a married man and it was time to seal his vows with the traditional kiss. He turned to Savannah and saw her tense although she gave him a small smile.

At that moment he wanted to assure her that everything was going to be all right and they had done the right thing for their child. He reached out and touched her, gently ran the backs of his knuckles down her cheek while looking deeply into her eyes. And within seconds he felt her relax.

When a sigh of contentment eased from her lips he leaned forward. The kiss he'd intended was to be brief and light. But the moment his mouth touched hers, a strong sense of desire overtook him and he kissed her with a force that surprised even him.

His common sense told him that now was not the time for such a strong display of passion, but slipping his tongue into her mouth, wrapping his arms around her small waist and hungrily mating his mouth with hers seemed as natural as breathing. And the feel of her palms gliding over his shoulders wasn't helping one iota.

It was only when McKinnon touched his shoulder

and jokingly said aloud, "I see these two are off to a good start," that Durango pulled back.

"I'd rather the two of you not mention anything to the family about my marriage just yet," Durango said to Ian and Chase a few minutes after the ceremony had ended and he could speak with them privately. "I want to be the one to tell them."

Both men nodded. Then Ian said, "Mom isn't going to be happy about not being here at your wedding."

"Yes, but this is the way Savannah and I wanted to do things."

"When are you going to tell everyone?" Chase inquired. It wasn't easy keeping secrets in the Westmoreland family.

"I'm going to call the folks when we get back. Once I tell Mom, the news will spread like wildfire. But it will be another month before we'll be able to travel home. One of the rangers is out on medical leave and we're shorthanded."

"When you do come home expect Aunt Sarah to have one hell of a wedding reception planned," Chase said, grinning. "She might be upset at first about your elopement, but she'll be ecstatic that another one of her sons has gotten married."

Durango nodded, knowing that was the truth. "I don't have a problem with her planning a reception," he said, thinking his mother was going to be surprised when she did see Savannah because she'd be showing a little by then. Then Sarah Westmoreland would be happy for two reasons. Another one of her sons would have married and she would have her first grandchild on the way.

"Your bride is on her way over here to claim you for more pictures," Ian said, grinning since he had been the one to hire a private photographer for the occasion. He wanted to have lots of pictures for his mother once she found out about the quickie wedding. Although Durango hadn't told him why he and Savannah had eloped, Ian thought he knew his brother well enough to know there was only one reason why a devout bachelor like Durango would have gotten married. Time would tell if his assumption was true.

"Savannah is a beautiful woman," Ian said, pretty sure his brother already knew it.

"She is, isn't she?" Durango agreed as he watched Savannah cross the room.

"You're a lucky man," Ian decided to add for good measure.

Durango continued to watch as Savannah came closer and at that moment he couldn't help but think the very same.

An hour or so later Savannah was stepping out of the shower. She glanced around the bathroom and noticed that the spa-style bathtub was large enough to accommodate at least four people.

She couldn't help wondering what Durango was doing. After sharing a wedding dinner with Ian, Chase and Jessica, they had returned to their suite, said goodnight and gone to separate bedrooms.

A part of her was disappointed that he hadn't kissed her goodnight. But she knew the reason why he hadn't. One kiss would lead to another, then another and eventually to something neither of them could handle. Durango was intent on keeping his word to keep his distance and she appreciated him for doing so.

He had looked so darn good at the ceremony that for one tantalizing moment she had wished that their wedding was real. But she knew that wasn't possible. In about a year or so, he would be going his way and she would be going hers. After all, they were sharing an in-name-only marriage.

But still...

Would having Durango for a temporary lover be so bad? It was amazing how you could develop an all-consuming craving for something you were perfectly fine doing without only months before. Prior to her one night with Durango she'd dated, but had never been into casual sex. She hadn't been involved with anyone since she'd broken up with Thomas Crawford and she hadn't felt as if she was missing out. But all of that changed the night she and Durango had conceived their baby. From that night on she had been acutely aware of her body and its needs.

And then there were the memories that wouldn't go away. Durango and their night together had definitely left her with some lasting, vivid ones and a particularly special little moment, she thought, affectionately rubbing her tummy.

She glanced over at the bed and looked at the gown she intended to sleep in tonight. Alone. If she decided to share an intimate relationship with Durango, she had to remember that it would be with no strings attached. He didn't love her and she didn't love him. Remembering that would definitely make things easier emotionally when the time came for them to part ways.

She crossed the room and picked up the low-cut, short, barely there, flesh-tone nightgown and thought about the kiss they had shared after the man had announced them man and wife. She could still feel the heat from his lips on hers and just thinking about that kiss and the one they had shared last night in the hot tub sent shudders racing through her body. There was something about Durango Westmoreland that just kept her blood heated. Jessica had been right. Westmorelands weren't ordinary men.

Durango had been right, as well. There was no way they could entertain the thought of being married— even on a short-term basis—without there ever being a chance of them sharing a bed. She could see that now. Some marriages could truly be in *name* only, but she realized now that theirs would have to be in *bed* and *name* only. And she could handle that because once the marriage ended, she would begin living a solitary life. Her total concentration would be on raising her child. She wouldn't have time to become involved with a man. To be perfectly honest, it wouldn't matter to her if she never had another lover. Her affair with Durango would be enough to sustain her.

She knew what he said about abiding by her decision until she indicated she wanted things to be different between them. Well, now she had decided. She wanted things to be different.

Savannah saw Durango the moment she stepped out of the bedroom. He was standing on the balcony, gazing out at the lake. His chest was bare and he was wearing a pair of black silk pajama bottoms. His broad muscled

chest and shoulders seemed to catch the remnants of the
fading sunlight and it gave his dark skin an even richer
glow. She wished she had time to get her camera and
capture him on film so she could always have the breathtaking image at her fingertips.

As she continued to watch him her heartbeat quickened and the heat he had deliberately turned up earlier
with his kiss was inching its way into a flame as she felt
her body respond to his mere existence. And then, as if
he'd sensed her presence, he turned slowly, capturing
her eyes with his.

They stood there for a moment, separated by a few
feet while sexual tension flowed between them the same
way it had that night in Atlanta, and Savannah could feel
herself slowly melting beneath the heat of Durango's
intense stare.

And then he moved, slowly closing the distance
separating them, soundless as his bare feet touched
the carpeted floor. She wondered if he knew the effect
he was having on her, or if he knew just how beautiful he was.

Usually one didn't think of a man as beautiful, but
in this case she had to disagree. Durango Westmoreland
was handsome, good-looking and devastating. But he
was also beautiful in a manly sort of way. It was there
in the shape of his face, the intensity of his dark eyes,
the build of his high cheekbones and the fullness of his
lips. The closer he got to her, the more her body responded and she braced herself for the full impact when
he came to a stop in front of her. He glanced down at
her outfit and then met her gaze. She saw the questions
in his eyes and felt the heat in them, as well.

"I've changed my mind about a couple of things," she said softly, thinking how good he smelled.

"Have you?"

She met his gaze levelly. "Yes."

"And what have you changed your mind about?" he asked in a voice that Savannah thought sounded way too sexy.

"About my wedding night."

His eyebrows lifted. "*Your* wedding night?"

"Yes, I've decided that I want one."

He studied her. His gaze dark and heated. "Do you?"

"Yes." She was fully aware that he knew what she meant, but because he hadn't wanted to risk a misunderstanding, he had to be absolutely sure.

"Okay, I can handle that. Is there anything else that you want?"

She bit her lip a few times before saying, "I want for us to share a bed during the time we're married. I think we're mature enough to handle it, don't you?"

For a minute he seemed to absorb her words in silence before allowing a smile to touch his lips. "Sure, I don't see any problem in that. Do you mind telling me what made you change your mind?"

"I think it would be hard for us to share a house without sharing a bed. We're too attracted to each other and…"

He arched an eyebrow when she didn't finish. "And what?"

A smile touched the corners of her lips. "And I don't handle temptation very well, especially the Durango Westmoreland kind."

He reached out and placed his hand on her waist and

leaned forward slightly. "Can I let you in on a little secret?" he whispered against her lips.

"Sure."

"I don't handle temptation well, either. Especially the Savannah Claiborne kind, so I guess on some things we see eye to eye. That's a good sign."

"Is it?" She couldn't help but look at his mouth since it was so close to hers.

"Mmm, let me show you just how good it is."

And then he captured her lips and the moment he did so a wave of desire swept across her to settle in the pit of her stomach. He wrapped her tight into his arms and the intensity of the kiss made her bones melt. Moments later he reluctantly released her mouth.

"There is something I want to do, Savannah, and it's something I had intended to do at Chase and Jessica's wedding reception but never got around to doing," he said as his lips gently kissed the corners of her mouth and slowly moved to the side of her ear.

"What?" she asked softly, barely able to get the question out.

"Dance with you," he murmured in a low, sexy voice. He took a step back and held his hand out to her.

It was then that she heard the music, a melodic, soulful ballad by Anita Baker. The slow-tempo, easy-going jazzy sound of a saxophone in the background began flowing through her, touching all her senses, revving every nerve in her body and turning the heat up a notch more. Anticipation surged through her veins when she placed her hand in his.

Her pulse quickened when he pulled her closer into his arms, and she came into contact with his bare chest.

"Enjoy the dance," he said, his voice a sensuous whisper against her ear. He pulled her even closer and she knew the exact moment he dropped a kiss on the top of her head. Their bodies meshed together perfectly as they moved to the slow beat, making them fully conscious of the scanty clothing they were wearing. She could feel the heat deepening between them, and the way her flimsy negligee was clinging to her, shifting, parting with every movement of her body against his, she was certain he was aware of it, which only made her more aware of him. Especially the thick hardness of him that was pressed against her stomach.

Sighing deeply, she buried her face into his bare shoulder, absorbing his strength, his scent, the hard masculine feel of him. And as if on instinct, she gently licked his skin with her tongue. She knew he felt it when his arms tightened around her waist.

"If you lick me I get to lick you back," he murmured gently. "And in a place of my own choosing," he said in a low, sexy voice.

Savannah lifted her head and their eyes met, held. Deep down she anticipated and hungered for his next move, knowing it would be another kiss. And when he stopped moving and slowly lowered his head to hers, an urgent need took hold of her senses once again.

A mixture of need, greed and unadulterated longing flowed through her veins the moment their lips touched. His mouth fastened tight on hers and she instinctively absorbed everything there was about him. His tongue was unbelievably skillful when it came to giving her pleasure. It was like a magnet, clinging to whatever was in its path, attracting her own tongue, taking hold of it, dominating it, eliciting pressure, giving energy.

She heard herself whimper, while shiver after sensuous shiver coursed through her body. She was helpless to do anything but return the kiss with equal intensity while his body strained against hers.

And then she felt herself being lifted effortlessly into his arms and at that moment she knew that this was just the beginning.

Durango broke off the kiss the moment he placed Savannah on the huge bed in the bedroom she had chosen. Then he stood back and gazed down at her. Her negligee was feminine and enticing. Seeing her in it nearly sucked the very breath from his lungs.

Coming back to the bed he placed a knee on the pillow-top mattress and reached out and touched her breasts through the flimsy material. She made a low, sensuous sound the moment his hand came in contact with her and his fingers moved slowly, tracing a path around her nipples, feeling them harden beneath his fingertips.

His hand then slid down to her stomach. The flesh was exposed from the design of her lingerie, and he touched her bare skin, made circles around her navel, massaging it, caressing it, feeling the way her muscles tightened beneath his hand. Knowing his self-control was slipping, in one smooth sweep he removed the negligee completely, leaving her totally naked.

For the second time that night he actually felt the air he was breathing being sucked from his lungs. No woman, he quickly decided, should have a body this beautiful, this tempting, this seductive.

A slow, throbbing ache began inching its way through every part of him and as he stared at Savannah he felt an intense desire to possess her. Wanting to be sure she was ready for him, he reached out and touched the area between her legs, dipped his finger inside of her, stroked her, and saw she was indeed ready for him. She made a low moaning sound and he ceased what he was doing just long enough to remove his pajama bottoms.

"Durango."

His name was a whispered purr from her lips and he knew he was going to make love to her and not just have sex with her. The impact of that almost sent his mind spinning, but he refused to dwell on it now. He was too engrossed in how Savannah was making him feel and how his body was responding to the very essence of her. He was experiencing emotions he had not felt since the last time he had been with her. Nothing and he meant nothing would stop him from sharing this night with the woman who was now his wife.

Easing back on the bed with her, he kissed her, discovering again the sweetness that always awaited him in her mouth. And then he covered her body with his, lifted her hips and broke off the kiss to look deep into her eyes. He slowly entered her. The impact of their joining was so profound his body momentarily went still as their gazes locked.

"I know this might sound arrogant," he said in a low, husky tone. "But I think this," he said, pushing deeper into her body, "was made just for me."

Savannah smiled, adjusting her body to the intimate fit of his. "If you really believe that then who am I to argue? You definitely won't hear a peep out of me."

A sexy, amused chuckle rumpled from his lips. "Let's just see about that because I like the noises you make," he said, remembering the sounds she had made the last time they had come together.

He began moving, a slow pace, needing to feel himself thrusting deep inside her, needing to arouse even further that feminine hunger within her that he longed to release. He wanted to stir it up, whisk it to a level it had never been before and then give her what they both needed. He wanted her hungry for him, starving for him, desperate for him.

Durango refused to let her hold back on anything with him, especially his need to become one with her. His desire became even more feverish from the rhythmic movements of Savannah's hips.

He wanted it all and more than anything he needed to hear her express her satisfaction. And with that goal in mind, he continued to move against her, sliding back and forth, stroking in and out between her legs, letting her feel the workings of his solid shaft within her as his hand lifted her hips for better contact, more intense pleasure. Several times his body nearly shuddered with the force of his own release but he found the strength to hold back, keep himself in check.

But the moment Savannah cried out in ecstasy, and he felt her body tighten around his, using every feminine muscle she possessed to aggressively claim what she wanted, he gave in and succumbed to his powerful release that pushed him over the edge.

And when he leaned down and captured her mouth, clung to it, devoured it like a starving man, he tightened his arms and legs around her, tilted her body at an angle that would increase their pleasure. Durango knew at that moment if he lived to be a hundred years old, he would only find this degree of pleasure here, in Savannah's arms.

He was forced to admit that only with this woman could he claim complete sexual fulfillment. Only with her.

Ten

Durango shook his head as he raised his eyes to the ceiling. He and Savannah had returned to his ranch that morning and he had decided to wait until late afternoon to make the call to his family.

"Yes, Mom, I'm telling you the truth. I got married on Friday, and yes, I married Jessica's sister, Savannah."

He gazed across the room at Savannah, who was walking out of the bathroom. She had just showered and was wearing a beautiful blue silk bathrobe. A towel was wrapped around her head because she'd also washed her hair.

"Mom, Savannah and I eloped and got married in Lake Tahoe. Ian knew about it but I swore him to secrecy, so he was right not to tell you."

He nodded moments later. "Yes, it's okay for you and Savannah's mom to get together and plan a reception, but I'll have to get back to you and let you know when we can come to Atlanta. It won't be for another three to four weeks."

After a few moments of nodding, he then said, "Savannah and I met at Chase's wedding, fell in love and decided to get married quietly. Without any hoopla," he tacked on, borrowing Savannah's words.

He turned and watched as she removed the towel from her head, and he saw how the mass of dark, curly hair tumbled around her shoulders. He watched as she lifted her arms and began drying her hair. Doing so stretched her silk robe, showing off her generous curves. There was something about watching her dry her hair that was a total turn-on. He hoped it had nothing to do with the fact that this was his bedroom and she looked so damn good in it. Even her clothes that were hanging next to his in the closet looked right.

He frowned, not liking the thought of that. And then he cleared his throat, trying to concentrate on what his mother was saying. "Yes, Mom, you can tell the rest of the family, and yes, Savannah is here. Would you like to speak with her?" he asked, eager to get off the phone.

He could last only so long under his mother's intense inquisition. Just like Ian had said, their mother had been angry at first, but the news that another of her sons had married had smoothed her ruffled feathers. And it amused him that already she had her sights on the next of her sons who she felt was ready for matrimony. He chuckled, thinking Ian, Spencer, Quade and Reggie had better watch out.

"Okay, Mom, and I love you, too. Give Dad my best. Now here's Savannah."

"Be prepared," he whispered, before handing her the phone.

He then watched and listened while Savannah began talking to his mother. She first apologized, and accepted all blame for their decision to elope. Then told Sarah Westmoreland in an excited voice that she would love for her to plan a reception, and agreed with the older woman that it would be a wonderful idea to get Savannah's mother involved, too.

Durango was about to walk out of the room when Savannah promised to send his mother digital pictures taken at the wedding. Sending pictures was a nice touch that was sure to win Savannah brownie points with his mom.

When Durango returned twenty minutes later after taking a shower, Savannah was still on the phone with his mother. He gave Savannah an apologetic smile as he sat on the bed beside her. After another ten minutes he'd had enough and surprised Savannah by taking the phone out of her hand.

"Mom, I think you've talked to my wife long enough. It's our bedtime. We're newlyweds, remember?"

"Durango!"

He placed a finger to his lips, prompting Savannah to silence. "Thanks, Mom, for understanding. And yes, I'll make sure Savannah sends those photos to you tonight before she…ahh, goes to sleep. Good night, Mom." He chuckled as he quickly hung up the phone.

Savannah glared at him. "Durango Westmoreland, how could you embarrass me that way by insinuating that we—"

He kissed her mouth shut and then tugged her backward on the bed, removing her robe in the process. "I didn't imply anything that isn't true," he said, after releasing her lips.

He kissed her again, then pulled back and said, "Mmm, this is how I like you—naked and submissive." He knew his words would definitely get a rise out of her.

She pushed against his chest. "And just who do you think is submissive? I want you to know that…"

He kissed her again, thinking how dull his life had been before she came into it. Then just as quickly he decided that kind of thinking sounded like he was getting attached—and he didn't do attachments. But then again, he had to be honest enough and admit that for a man who'd always liked his privacy, he was thoroughly enjoying having Savannah around…even if she would only be there on a temporary basis.

When he finally released her mouth, she looked at him as desire darkened her eyes and said softly, "You aren't playing fair."

He met her gaze with an intensity he felt all the way to his toes and said hoarsely, "Sweetheart, I'm not playing at all."

Durango then stripped off his robe and stretched his naked body out beside her, pulling her into his arms and kissing her again. When he finally broke off the kiss he smiled down at her. "So, did you enjoy our trip to Lake Tahoe?"

She reached up and ran her fingers through the hairs on his chest, thinking about all the things they had done together, especially the time they had spent in bed. Durango, she had discovered, had extraordinary stamina. "Yes," she finally said, thinking just how much she had liked spending time at the Rolling Cascade with him. "It was a very rewarding experience."

"And you didn't once have morning sickness," he pointed out.

She grinned. "And I did enjoy the break. Maybe this bracelet works after all."

He lifted her hand and kissed her wrist. Then he smoothed his hands over her stomach, massaging gently, liking the thought that his child rested there. "And I take it our baby is well?"

"Yes, she's doing just fine."

"That's good to know. Now I can turn my full attention to the mother." He whispered the words in her ear and the sound was so low and seductive that it made every muscle in her body quiver.

"And how will you do that?" she asked innocently, knowing the answer but wanting him to expound anyway.

"I can show you better than I can tell you."

Cocking her head, and with a seductive glint in the depths of her hazel eyes, she said, "Then show me."

And he did that night. Numerous times.

"That's it. Move a little to the right. Oooh, yes. Now tilt your head a little back. Just a little. That's perfect, now hold it right there."

It was at that moment that Savannah took Durango's picture, just one of several she had taken already that day after he'd come in from work. She had convinced him that she needed to use up the rest of her film and that he would make the perfect model.

"Now open your shirt and let me see your chest."

He frowned. "Hey, just what kinds of photos are you taking?"

She grinned. "I told you. I want to sell my boss on the idea of doing a calendar on park rangers. They do them on firemen and policemen all the time. It's about time we honor American heroes."

He crossed his hand over his chest, ignoring the fact that Savannah and her camera were still clicking. "And just who will be buying these calendars?" he asked, thinking about a calendar that his cousin Thorn had done for charity a couple of years ago. They had sold like hotcakes.

. She chuckled. "Anyone who appreciates good art… as well as a good-looking man. Besides, I think it would be a great idea for a charity fund-raiser. I can see you as Mr. February."

He lifted a brow. "Why Mr. February?"

She shrugged, and then said, "I think of you as Mr. February because that's the month this is, and so far it's been a good one—morning sickness and all. Also, February makes you think of hearts, and it was this month I heard a heart…the one belonging to our baby… so, you being Mr. February makes sense even if what I just said doesn't."

Durango looked at her with understanding because to him everything she said *did* make sense. No matter how long their marriage lasted or when it ended, the month of February would always have a special meaning to them. Without saying anything else he undid the top button while she snapped away with her camera.

"Sexy. Yes, that was one sexy pose," she said, looking up at him, deciding she'd taken enough pictures of him for now. Just then her pulse quickened due to the totally male look he was giving her.

"You think so?"

"Yes," she said, unzipping the case to put her camera in.

"I have to admit it was fun. When did you decide to get into photography?" he asked, leaning against the wooden rail of the outside deck.

Savannah glanced up at him. A great expanse of mountain range was in the background and for a heartbeat of a minute she was tempted to pull her camera out again. He was giving her another sexy pose.

"When I was a teen...sixteen, I think," she said. "My grandparents bought me my first camera and I drove everybody crazy with it by taking pictures whether I had their permission or not. I caught Mom, Rico and Jessica in some very embarrassing moments."

"Um, should I be worried?" he asked, grinning.

Savannah laughed. "No, I've grown up a lot since that time. Now I'm harmless."

Harmless? Durango wasn't so sure about that. Since Savannah had come into his life, nothing had been the same. The people he worked with couldn't believe it when he'd made the announcement that morning that he had gotten married. A number of them thought he was joking until Savannah had shown up at the ranger station at noon for their lunch date. Then he'd seen both understanding and envy in a lot of the guys' eyes. He wondered what those same coworkers would think a year from now when he and Savannah went their separate ways.

"I hope you like what I cooked for dinner."

Savannah's words intruded, reclaiming his thoughts.

"I'm sure I will. But you didn't have to go to any trouble. I could have fixed something when I got in."

She laughed. "It's the least I can do while you're at work every day. I'm not used to being home all day. In fact, I pitched the calendar idea to my boss. If he approves the project, I'll be busy. Do you think your coworkers will mind having their pictures taken?"

Durango shook his head and grinned. "No, they'll probably get a kick out of it. The thought of being featured on a calendar will boost a few of their egos, I'm sure."

He studied her, sensing something was bothering her. He hadn't picked up on it earlier, but now without a camera in her hand it was becoming obvious. He couldn't help wondering if she oftentimes used her camera as an emotional shield.

"Did something happen today that I should know about, Savannah? Does it have anything to do with your mother or your brother?"

He knew her mother was still in Paris and Savannah had spoken to her the day before. She hadn't reached her brother until later in the day. He had been surprised but happy with her news and was looking forward to their visit to Philly.

Durango watched as she took a deep breath and said, "No, it's not about my family."

He nodded. That could only mean one thing. It was about *his*. "Did someone in my family call you today?"

"Yes."

"Who?"

He saw the small smile that touched her lips before she said, "It would probably be easier to ask who didn't. You have a rather large family."

Large and overwhelming, Durango thought, giving her his full attention. "And?"

"And…er…everyone, although surprised by the news we had gotten married, seemed genuinely sincere in wishing us the best, which made me feel like a phony."

He understood her ambivalence because he'd felt the same way at work today. "You're not a phony. Our decision to have a temporary marriage is our business and no one else's."

"Yes, I know…but."

He lifted an eyebrow. "But what?"

"But everyone was so nice. Even your cousin Delaney called all the way from the Middle East. And all the Westmoreland spouses, those married to your cousins and brother, called to welcome me into the family. They said from this day forward we would all be sisters. It was the same welcome Jessica told me they gave her. Do you know how that made me feel?"

She was staring at him with a strained expression on her face. He smiled at her. "No, how did that made you feel?"

"Special. I've always dreamed of belonging to a huge family, but it's not for real. Do you know what I'm saying? Am I making much sense?"

Yes, he knew what she was saying and she was making plenty of sense. He remembered that one of the main reasons she had agreed to marry him was that she wanted their child to have something she'd never had— a chance to belong to a large family; a family who would always be there for you through the good times or bad; a family who stuck together no matter what; a family that instilled strong values in future generations and a family who proved time and time again that when the going got tough, they didn't get going. They rallied around each other and gave their support.

"Yes, I understand," he said, after expelling a deep breath. "No matter what, there will always be a bond between us because of our child. You know that, don't you?"

"Yes, I know it, but I still feel like I'm being deceitful and that bothers me."

Not for the first time, Durango compared Savannah with Tricia. The more he did so, the more he was discovering there was no comparison. Both were city girls for sure, but where being deceitful actually bothered Savannah, Tricia hadn't shown any remorse when she'd looked him dead in the eyes and told him that she'd played him for a fool.

"I'm going to put dinner on the table now, Durango. I'll let you know when everything is ready."

Feeling her need to change the subject, he asked, "Need my help?"

"No. I can manage."

Moments after Savannah left, Durango turned to gaze out at the mountains. Today was a clear winter day and what he saw was breathtaking, a sight to behold, and it provided such a picturesque view that it made him appreciate his decision to settle down in these parts years ago.

He'd always found comfort in looking at the mountains when something weighed heavily on his mind and today Savannah was weighing heavily on his mind.

Although he had decided that Tricia's and Savannah's characters weren't anything alike, he still felt as though he was reliving the past. It had been so quick, too easy to fall in love with Tricia, and he had done so, proudly wearing his heart on his sleeve. But once she had ripped that sleeve, he had decided it could never be repaired. Under no circumstances would he allow himself to be that vulnerable again.

Durango knew the difference between lust and love and right now what he felt for Savannah was nothing more than lust. She had caught his eye from the first; they had made love, made a baby, and now they were married. But still the very thing that had drawn them together from the start was good old-fashioned lust. And they were taking it to a whole other level. Just the thought of what they had shared over the past few days made his breath catch, and last night, through the wee hours of the morning, had been the epitome of perfection.

He would be the first to admit that during one of those moments, a part of him had analyzed, fantasized, even had gone so far as to consider the idea of more than a year with her. But then that rip in his sleeve, that deep gash in his heart, had reminded him that there were some things in life that a man never got over. The pain he had suffered that one time had completely closed his mind to the prospect of ever loving again.

That's the way it was and that's the way it would stay.

Later that night Durango and Savannah sat cross-legged on the floor in front of the fireplace. They had eaten and showered and were ready to relax.

"Dinner tasted wonderful tonight, Savannah."

She smiled over at him. "Thanks. That's my grand-mother's favorite dish," she said of the steak and baked potatoes she had prepared.

"So," Durango said, stretching out to lie on his side. "How do you suggest we spend the rest of the evening?"

She grinned at him and said teasingly, "I could take more pictures."

"I don't think so. Let's think of doing something else."

"Something like what?"

"Something like finding out just how hot things can get between us."

His words made her pulse quicken and she watched his mouth tilt into a very seductive smile. "Um, what do you have in mind?" she asked, meeting his gaze and holding it tight.

"Come here and let me show you," he said, reaching out and gently snagging her wrist to bring her on the floor beside him. She watched his every movement as he removed her robe. "Aren't you curious about the next step?" he asked.

She glanced down at his lap and saw the size of his arousal through his robe and immediately, her feminine muscles clenched in appreciation and anticipation. "No, I have an idea how this is going to get played out," she said, her breath almost catching in her throat.

"Good."

"But I do have one request," she said, wrapping her arms around his neck.

"What?"

"Let me take off your robe."

He smiled. "Go for it."

When she had removed his robe she took her tongue and licked a section of his shoulder before she drew back and looked at him. "You have a beautiful body."

He chuckled. "You think so?"

"Yes."

"Thanks, and I think you have a beautiful body, as well, and it's a body that I want to get all into."

"Well, in that case…"

He moved closer to her, growled low in his throat as he nudged her on her back. Like a leopard on the prowl, he cornered his prey and when he had her just where he wanted her he whispered softly, "Now it's my turn to lick."

And he did just that, starting with the insides of her thighs before moving to savor another part of her.

"Durango!"

Only when he was nearly intoxicated with the taste of her did he ease his body over hers to take her hard and fast, putting everything he had into each mind-wrenching thrust and watching her features glow with the pleasure he was giving her. And when he felt the quivering deep in her womb where his child nestled, he threw his head back and rocked furiously against her the same way she was rocking against him.

It pleased him immensely to know she was on fire, but only *for* him and *with* him. And when she arched against him and groaned from deep within her throat, he felt those same sensations that engulfed her rip through him as one hell of an orgasm slammed into him, lifting him to a place he'd never been before, pushing him high above the clouds, the earth, the entire universe.

And when he drove into her again and then again, he was met with an immense feeling of satisfaction. Knowing she was reaching the same level of mind-shattering pleasure as he was put him in total awe of everything they were sharing. He couldn't get enough of her. She was simply amazing. A city girl by day and a mountain wildcat by night.

And as she continued to pull everything out of him, take what he'd never given another female, he could only think of the remaining months they would be together and knew when she left, his life would never be the same.

"Get some rest, baby. I'm going to my office for a while," Durango whispered in Savannah's ear. After making love in front of the fireplace, he had picked her up in his arms to carry her into the bedroom and tucked her into bed. Quietly closing the door behind him, he went downstairs to his office.

He immediately walked over to the window. The moon's light cast a beautiful glow on the mountains, giving him a feeling of warmth, and for a while he stood there thinking that things couldn't get any better than this. He loved where he lived, he enjoyed his job and for a short while he wasn't living alone.

Sharing dinner with Savannah had been wonderful and afterward they had showered together as if it was the most natural thing to do. But nothing could top the lovemaking that had come later. It seemed that each and every time they came together was better than the last, and that thought was beginning to bother him.

Deciding he didn't want to dwell on it any longer, he was about to take a seat behind his huge desk when the phone rang. So it wouldn't disturb Savannah, he quickly picked it up, not bothering to check caller ID as he normally did. "Hello."

"What the hell is going on, Durango?"

He leaned back in his chair, recognizing his oldest brother's voice immediately. "Jared. And how are things with you?"

"Cut the crap and answer my question."

Durango rolled his eyes. Jared, the attorney, was his no-nonsense brother. Marriage had softened him some, but he was still a hard case. "What makes you think something is going on?"

"You got married."

Durango smiled. Yes, that would say it all. "It was time, don't you think? You seemed happy, so I decided to try it."

"And you want me to believe that?"

"That would be nice."

"Well, I don't."

"Figures."

"And Ian isn't talking."

Durango smiled. "That's good."

"Mom's overjoyed, of course," Jared Westmoreland went on to say. "I think she e-mailed every single family member those pictures she got over the Internet."

"Okay, Ian's not talking, but Mom's happy, so what's your problem, Jared?"

"I want to know why you did it."

"The reason I told you earlier wasn't good enough?"

"No."

He wasn't surprised. Of his five brothers, it was Jared who knew him the best. He could never pull anything over the brother who was nearly three years older and to Durango's way of thinking, plenty wiser. Whereas other relatives would cautiously buy the story that he and Savannah had fabricated, he immediately thought of three members of the Westmoreland family who would not. Jared and his cousins Dare and Stone.

The attorney in Jared would put up an argument no matter what Durango said, and because Dare—the current sheriff of College Park, Georgia—was a former FBI agent, he had a tendency to be suspicious of just about everything.

And Durango dreaded the call he knew he would eventually get from his cousin Stone. He and Stone were only months apart in age and had always been close. Durango figured the only reason Stone hadn't called yet to give him hell was because he and his wife, Madison, were somewhere in Europe on a book promotion tour.

"Are you going to tell me what I want to know, or will I have to take drastic measures and start an investigation?" Jared asked, breaking into Durango's thoughts.

"Um, what drastic measures would those be?"

"How does catching the next plane to Montana to check out things for myself sound?"

Not too good. Durango sighed, knowing Jared was dead serious and because of that he decided to come clean. "Savannah is pregnant."

He heard his brother's deep sigh. Then for a few moments Jared was silent, evidently taking it all in.

"How far along?" Jared finally asked.

"Going into her third month."

Silence again. Then Jared said, "It happened Christmas night."

Durango lifted an eyebrow. "How did you know?"

"For Pete's sake, Durango, do you think you weren't missed at the card game that night? Hell, we'd all been counting on winning all your money. And besides that,

I couldn't help but notice you were attracted to the woman and we all saw you leave the reception to walk her to her room."

Durango smiled, remembering. "You all saw too much that night."

"Whatever." Then moments later Jared asked, "The two of you made a decision to get married for the baby's sake?"

"Yeah, that just about sums it up. But our marriage is only temporary."

"Temporary?"

"Yes, until the baby is around six months old. I didn't want my child born illegitimate and I wanted to be around during Savannah's pregnancy to bond with it and spend some time with them for a while afterward."

"And what happens after that?"

"Then we part ways. But Savannah and I have agreed to always be there for the baby. She knows I want to be a part of its life and Savannah wants that, too. It won't be easy with us living so far apart, but we'll manage."

There was another long pause and then Jared asked, "And you're okay with the temporary setup?"

Durango frowned. "Why wouldn't I be?"

"I saw those pictures Mom is so proudly brandishing about town. At your wedding, you and Savannah looked good together, actually happy. If I didn't know better, then I—"

"But you do know better, which is why you made this call. Don't let those pictures fool you, Jared. The only thing going on between the two of us is the baby. Six months after it's born Savannah will go her way and I'll go mine."

"And until then the two of you will live together happily as man and wife?"

"More or less." And at the moment he was thinking more because he was discovering that Savannah was such a giving person, he couldn't imagine her giving less.

"Be careful, Durango."

Durango's eyebrow lifted higher. "Be careful of what?"

"Discovering the fact that your heart isn't really made of stone and that it might be putty in the right woman's hands."

Durango frowned. "Trust me, it won't happen to me."

Jared laughed. "I thought the same thing. Although I'm not complaining now, mind you. I discovered the hard way that the worst types of affairs are the pretended kind."

"What are you talking about?"

There was another pause and Durango thought he heard the sound of his brother sipping something. Probably a glass of the finest wine. He could imagine Jared doing so in that million-dollar home he owned. Jared was a hotshot Atlanta attorney who over the years had made a name for himself by handling high-profile cases involving celebrity clients. Up until a year ago, Jared had been determined to stay a bachelor like Durango, and then Dana Rollins happened, surprising the hell out of everyone in the Westmoreland family who'd known Jared's stand on marriage. He'd always claimed it wasn't for him. He was a divorce attorney who ended marriages, not put them together. But now he was a happily married man who didn't care if the world knew how much he loved his wife.

"My engagement to Dana," Jared finally said, pulling

Durango's thoughts to the present then tumbling them back to the past when he remembered Jared's surprised announcement of his engagement at their father's birthday party last Easter.

"What about your engagement?"

"There never was one, at least not a real one."

Durango frowned, wondering what the hell his brother was saying. He was too tired, not in the right frame of mind to try to figure out anything tonight. "What do you mean there never was one? I was there when you announced it."

"I never announced anything. Mom did."

Jared's words made him think. Jared was right. Their mother had been the one who'd made a big fuss about Jared's engagement. Jared hadn't really said much. But then he hadn't spoken up to deny it, either.

"Are you saying you went along with an engagement because Mom put you on the spot?"

"There was more to it than that, Durango. If you recall, soon after that we found out about that lump in Mom's breast. She'd made it up in her mind I was getting married and the last thing I wanted to do was to burst her bubble, considering everything."

Durango nodded. "So you pretended an engagement? And you actually got Dana to go along with doing something like that?"

"Yes, but in the midst of it all we fell in love."

Durango shook his head, thinking how his brother had effectively pulled the wool over their eyes. "Who else knew the truth?"

"Dare. No one else needed to know. The only reason I'm even telling you is that I want you to see how things can happen."

"Things like what?"

"How you can enter into a situation thinking one way and in the end, your thinking can change. The more I got to know Dana and spent time with her, the more I wanted more out of our relationship. I saw Savannah that night and I sensed the attraction between the two of you. She's a woman a man can easily fall in love with. I could see that happening to you."

Durango sat up straight in his chair. "Well, I can't," he snapped. "I'm happy things turned out that way for you and Dana, but it won't for me and Savannah."

"Can you be sure of that?"

"Yes, I can be sure. You were evidently capable of loving someone. I'm not. At least not now. If I had met Savannah before Tricia, then I—"

"When will you let go of what she did to you?"

"I have let go, but that doesn't mean I want to open myself up to the same kind of hurt again."

"And you think that you will be?"

"I'm thinking that I'm not willing to take the risk."

"And what about Savannah?"

"What about her?"

"What if she feels differently?"

"She doesn't and she won't. She was more against us marrying than I was. In fact, I had to convince her it was the right thing to do. She only agreed to do it for the baby's sake. She'll stay for six months and then she's out of here."

"And the two of you have agreed to all of this?"

Durango rolled his eyes. "Yes, but we haven't put it in writing, if that's what that attorney's mind of yours is driving at. Hey, maybe that isn't such a bad idea. I want her to know I will continue to do right by her even after the baby is born. Draw me up something, will you?"

"Draw you up what?"

"I don't know. Some legal document that spells out that I will continue to support her and the baby after the time is up. I want to set up a college fund and I intend to provide generous monthly allotments for my child, which I'll be able to afford thanks to that business venture I'm in with McKinnon."

"Are you sure you want to bring a legal document into the picture now?"

"Why not? I'd think she would appreciate knowing I will support her, something her father didn't. She has this thing about how her old man treated her pregnant mother when they got married and he never did right by her, Jessica and her brother. I want to assure Savannah that I have no intentions of treating her that way."

A half hour later Durango ended the call with Jared after telling him everything he wanted to put in the document. Whether his brother wanted to accept it or not, his marriage to Savannah was only temporary and Durango did not intend to ever forget that fact.

Eleven

The next two weeks were busy ones for Savannah. It helped tremendously that her bouts of morning sickness were infrequent and she woke each day seeing it as another adventure.

Her boss was excited about the idea of a calendar to commemorate Yellowstone National Park and the men who protected its boundaries. In addition to the calendar, he also envisioned something bigger and he had suggested a documentary film. She was excited about the idea and spent most of her days shooting footage that might be used for the project.

Her nights belonged to Durango. After dinner she would read to him from the baby book, keep him abreast of all the changes that were taking place within her body, and then they went to bed. Each night Durango did his own investigation, getting firsthand knowledge by going deep inside her body. And each time he entered her, after bringing her to a feverish pitch, she was fully aware that the private moments they shared would remain a part of her, even after they had parted ways. But then she realized that something had happened that she hadn't counted on.

She had fallen in love with Durango.

As she stood looking out the window, a part of her wondered at what point it had happened. Had it been just last night, when they had showered together and he had made love to her in such a beautiful way that had brought tears to her eyes? Or had it been last week, when he had taken her on a hike up the mountain, and they had stopped at the hunting cabin that he and McKinnon had built and had enjoyed the packed lunch he'd made for them. Or later, before coming back down the mountain, when they had enjoyed each other, making love outside near a beautiful stream under a beautiful Montana sky. She would always relish the tender, loving moments they shared and knew that deep down she would miss Durango.

She turned when she heard the phone ring, and quickly crossed the room, thinking it was Durango, but the caller ID indicated it was her brother, Rico, instead.

"Hello."

"I know, Savannah."

Savannah lifted a brow having an idea of what he knew. Evidently her mother had let something slip. "You know what?" she asked innocently.

"That you're pregnant."

Savannah smiled wryly. That was Rico for you. Straight to the point. "I had planned to tell you when I thought the time was right."

There was silence for a moment and then he asked, "Are you okay with it?"

Savannah chuckled. "I'm more than okay with it. I'm ecstatic. Of course, I wasn't at first because I was nervous and scared more than anything. Then I decided since I never planned to marry anyway, at least I'd have a baby. I always wanted one."

"But you *did* get married."

"Only for the baby."

"Which is something you swore you'd never do."

She sighed deeply. Leave it to Rico to remind her of that. "This is different. Durango and I went into this marriage with our eyes open. We want what's best for our child and we'll do whatever it takes to make sure that happens."

"Even if it means sentencing yourselves to a loveless marriage?"

"Yes, but in our case it will only be temporary. We've agreed to a divorce when the child is six months old."

"And you're okay with that?"

"Sure. Why wouldn't I be?" she asked simply.

"No reason, I guess. When are you coming home?"

She shrugged. "Not sure. I had thought of coming to Philly to check on things, but all my bills are paid up, so there's no rush. Besides, I like it out here."

"And your husband?"

"What about him?"

"How's he treating you?"

In all the right ways that a man should treat a woman. That very thought came to the tip of Savannah's tongue and she hesitated, thinking of just how true it was. Maybe it was because they knew that things between them were only temporary, but whatever the reason, she enjoyed every second, every moment she spent with Durango.

But then it would be easy for her to do so anyway, because she'd fallen in love with him, and could now admit that she had done so the first time she had seen him at Jessica and Chase's wedding.

"Savannah?"

"Durango is treating me well, so don't worry yourself by thinking anything different. He's a good man."

"He got you pregnant."

She heard the anger in Rico's voice. "And he wasn't in that bed alone, remember that," she replied tersely. "Nor did he have my hands tied behind my back. Remember that, too," she added. "I'm a big girl, Rico."

He chuckled. "And you'll be getting even bigger in the coming months."

She smiled, glad the tension between them had passed. "Yes, and multiple births run in the Westmoreland family. So we might be getting double."

"Finding out that you're pregnant and the possibility of you having twins. That's a lot for me to deal with, Savannah."

Her smile deepened. "But I'm more than certain that you will."

"It was really nice of your coworkers to give this party in our honor," Savannah whispered to Durango while glancing around the room. Beth Manning, one of the female park rangers, had contacted her at the beginning of the week to tell her of the rangers' plans to host a postwedding party for her and Durango.

At first Savannah had felt dishonest, but then, like Durango had said, the terms of their marriage were nobody's business.

"Yes, it was nice of them," he agreed, placing his arm around her shoulders to pull her closer to his side. They were at the home of Beth and her husband, Paul. Paul was a veterinarian in the area.

Savannah thought that Beth and Paul had a beautiful house that was located not far from Durango's ranch, on the other side of the mountains. Inside the decor was different from Durango's. Instead of it having two stories, the rooms were spacious and spread out on one level. And one side of the living room was a huge picture window that had no curtains, blinds or shades to block the beautiful panoramic view of the mountains.

Savannah had met most of the park rangers who worked with Durango when she had joined him for lunch one day, but this was the first chance she'd gotten to meet their spouses. Already she liked everyone. She thought they were genuinely friendly and appreciated them for making her feel welcome and at home.

Everyone had brought a covered dish and they were enjoying themselves, having a good time basking in the decent weather as well as the delicious food. One thing Savannah noticed was that Durango rarely left her side. He was always there, either holding her hand or placing his arms around her shoulders. She knew to everyone who observed them they appeared to be a very happy couple.

"Are the two of you ready to open the gifts now?" A smiling and exuberant blond-haired, blue-eyed Beth came up to them and asked.

Durango glanced at his watch. It was nearing midnight. "Now would be good. It's getting late."

"When did you ever care about time, Durango? I've known you since college and you've never been known to leave a party early," Beth's husband Paul came to join them and asked with twinkling green eyes and a charming smile.

"Oh, but he's a married man now, Paul," Beth reminded her husband, grinning. "We're seeing a new Durango Westmoreland."

Savannah could only imagine how the old Durango had been. She'd known the first moment she'd seen him that he was irresistible to women. Any man with his dark, striking good looks and strong, masculine body had to be. She wasn't naive to assume that before she'd met him he had lived a quiet life that hadn't included women. In fact, Jessica had been quick to tell her that he was a playboy and chances were once he regained his freedom he would revert to his womanizer ways.

A short while later she and Durango found themselves seated in chairs that were in the middle of a circle. Everyone else sat around them.

One by one Beth handed Savannah a gift that she excitedly opened. She and Durango received wineglasses, bath towels, plants, throw rugs and various other gifts. Durango had watched the happy enthusiasm on Savannah's face as she opened each present. But it was the huge, beautiful blue satin bedspread that had caught everyone's attention, including his.

The lower part of his body actually stirred when Savannah unwrapped it. Immediately, he could envision it on his bed with them buried beneath it while they made love. He met her gaze and knew she had had the same vision, and that made his body stir even more. Lucky for him that was the last gift that needed to be opened.

"I'm going to load everything in my truck and Savannah and I are going to call it a night," he said to everyone while glancing at his watch again. "It's officially Sunday morning."

Paul chuckled. "Nobody made you the time keeper, Durango, but I understand. I've been married four years longer than you have."

Savannah didn't know what to say other than thanks and good night to everyone once the guys had helped Durango load all the packages into his truck.

"I never thought I'd live to see the day that Durango Westmoreland fell so hard for a woman," Penny Washington, another park ranger, came and whispered in Savannah's ear. "The two of you look so happy together."

It was on the tip of Savannah's tongue to say that looks were deceiving, but then she changed her mind. She wasn't sure how Durango actually felt about being with her, but she could inwardly admit she was very happy being with him. And that, she thought, was beginning to be the root of a very serious problem. It was all fine and dandy when the two of them had wanted the same thing out of their marriage—no emotional ties. But now she loved him, and it was getting harder and harder to pretend otherwise.

"Ready?"

She glanced up and noticed Durango had come back inside the house. She saw the look in his eyes. She recognized it. She was becoming used to it. But still, that didn't stop the sensation of air being ripped right out of her lungs. Already she felt her entire body melting.

She cleared her throat. "Yes," she said.

"Wait a minute, Durango. You know how these types of gatherings are supposed to end. You have to kiss your bride for us," one of the rangers called out.

Durango smiled and hollered back, "Hey, that's no problem." And then he leaned down and kissed her in front of everyone, taking her mouth as passionately and as thoroughly as he'd done when they'd been alone. His kiss made her want and desire him…and love him even more. The cheers, catcalls and whistles went unnoticed. She was too busy drowning in the taste of the man who was her temporary husband.

Durango had only made it partway to the ranch when he couldn't take it any longer. Pulling his truck over to the side off the road, he cut off the ignition then, after unsnapping their seat belts, he reached across the seat and pulled Savannah into his arms. He needed another kiss.

Her lips parted instantly, eagerly. She was full of fire and heat and the more he devoured her mouth, the more she returned his passion.

He liked the sound of her whimpering in pleasure; he liked the feel of her wiggling in his lap, trying to get even closer; and he liked the scent of her scintillating perfume.

He reluctantly withdrew his mouth from hers. If he didn't stop now they would wind up making love in his truck and he didn't want that. He wanted a bed. "As soon as we get home I'm going to teach you a skill every woman should know."

A quick surge of heat rushed through Savannah at his words. "And what skill is that?"

He gently squeezed her nipples through her blouse and grinned ruefully. "You'll find out soon enough." He then placed her back in her seat and snapped her seat belt in place.

Sitting beside him the rest of the way to the ranch was torture for Savannah. He had turned her on and there was no way she could get turned off. In silence she glanced over at him. It was a moonless night but the glow from the SUV's console was all the light she needed to study his profile and note the intensity that lined his features. She quickly realized that he was as turned on as she was.

When they reached the ranch he brought the truck to a stop, got out, strode over to the passenger side, opened the door, unsnapped her seat belt and lifted her into his arms. Walking swiftly, he headed for the house.

"What about the gifts?" she asked, pressing her face into his chest, relishing the masculine scent of him.

"I'll unload everything tomorrow. There's no time tonight."

She smiled, thinking he was certainly making time for something. He opened the door and, after kicking it back shut with the heel of his boot, he carried her up the stairs to his bedroom.

She didn't have to wonder what would happen next.

Durango undressed her in record time and then proceeded to undress. Soon he had her on her back and purring like a cat.

He touched her everywhere, with his hands and then with his mouth, first tugging gently on her nipples, letting his tongue bathe them as he licked away. She heard herself moan, groan and whisper his name several times.

Her legs felt weak. Her body ached. And her mind was being blown to smithereens.

No man could touch her and make her feel the way Durango was making her feel. She was certain of it. He could stroke her desire and fill all of her needs and only with him could she give her entire being, and share the very essence of her soul. Her love.

At the thought of how much she loved him, a pulse began beating deep inside of her, close to her heart. And when his mouth released her breasts to move lower, she nearly stopped breathing.

He touched her intimately and her body responded immediately. Her back arched and her hips bucked the moment his fingers slipped inside of her. His fingers stroked her, expertly, seductively, intently, and moments later, when his mouth replaced his fingers, her entire body nearly jumped off the bed at the same time that a small, hoarse, gurgle of pleasure found its way up her throat. If she could be granted one wish for them, besides wanting a healthy baby, she wanted this. Him. For the rest of her life.

"You make me think crazy stuff, Savannah," he whispered when he covered her body with his own and swiftly entered her, making her breath catch. She wondered what crazy stuff he was thinking because he was making her think crazy stuff as well. And the craziest was that she didn't want their marriage to end. But she knew there was no permanent future for them. She loved him, but he didn't love her. But tonight, she wanted it all and if she couldn't have the real thing, then she would pretend.

They had made love plenty of times but something

about tonight was different. She felt it in his every stroke, his every thrust into her hot and responsive body. Whatever fever that was consuming him began consuming her, as well.

And she couldn't take it anymore.

A deep-rooted scream tore from her lips and she felt it, the smoothness of his engorged flesh as it jetted a hot thickness deep inside her, getting absorbed in her muscles, every hollow and every inch of her womb. And when he leaned down and kissed her, the urgency of that kiss melted her further. She knew if she lived to be a hundred, Durango was the only man who would ever have her heart.

A short while later, bathed in the room's soft lamplight, she exhaled a satiated sigh as he pulled her closer into his arms. He kissed her gently as one hand possessively cupped her breast. "I can't get enough of you," he whispered huskily.

She couldn't get enough of him, either, and knew she never would. "What skill did you want to show me?" she asked, barely able to get the words out.

He shifted on his back, lifted her, smiled and said, "Now I want you on top."

"Tell me about your brothers," she said, bending her head toward his and whispering against his lips. After several hours of practicing her new skills, she couldn't move an inch even if she needed to.

He wrapped his arms around her waist, keeping her there, on top of him with their bodies connected. "I guess you should know something about them as you'll get to see them soon. I found out today that I'll be able to take two weeks off now that Lonnie is back at work," he said.

"That means we can fly to Atlanta and Philly?"

"Yes, within a week's time."

She snuggled closer. "I met all your brothers at Chase and Jessica's wedding, but I don't know much about them and I want to be prepared."

"Okay, then let me prepare you," he said. "At thirty-eight, Jared is the oldest and the only one who's married. He's the attorney in the family. Next comes Spencer. He's only eleven months younger than Jared. He's a financial planner. I always admired his ability to keep both his profession and personal life from falling apart a few years ago when his fiancée drowned. He took Lynette's death hard, and I doubt to this day that he has fully recovered. Spence lives in California and is the CEO of a large financial firm there."

He looked at her and gave her his disarming smile and said, "I'm the third oldest and you know everything there's to know about me. But if there's more you think you need to know, then I rather show you than tell you."

"No, I think I have a pretty good idea of what you're all about," she said, determined not to be sidetracked. "What about the others?"

His smile widened to touch the corners of his lips. "Then there are the twins, Ian and Quade. They're thirty-three. You spent time with Ian at our wedding. He was seriously involved a few years ago with a woman who worked as a deputy for Dare, but they broke up. I don't know the reason they split, and as far as I know, he hasn't gotten serious about another woman since then."

He shifted their bodies and placed her on top of him. She felt his staff had grown as he entered her. She felt stretched, hot and ready. "My brother Quade works for the Secret Service. We barely know where he is most of the time, and when he comes home we know not to ask any questions. And last but not least, there is Reginald, whom we call Reggie. He'll be turning thirty later this year. He owns his own accounting firm in downtown Atlanta."

Savannah lifted her head. She had heard the love, the respect and the closeness in Durango's voice when he'd spoken of his brothers. "Now what about your—"

"I'm through talking for a while."

She raised an eyebrow. "Are you?"

"Yes."

She smiled. "So what would you like to do?"

He grinned and the sexual chemistry between them was immediate and powerful. "I'd like you to perfect that skill I taught you earlier."

Twelve

Durango woke up on Monday morning with an ache in his right knee. Although a glance out the window indicated a clear day he knew the ache was a sign that a snowstorm was coming.

Being careful not to wake Savannah he eased out the bed and went into the bathroom. The moment the door closed behind him he took a deep breath and met his dark gaze in the vanity mirror. Except for the remnants of sleep still clinging to his eyes, he looked the same. Okay, he admitted he did need a shave. But there was something going on inside him that he couldn't see. It was something he could feel and it was something the depth of which he had never felt before.

Not even for Tricia.

At the thought of the one woman who had caused him so much pain, he felt...nothing. Not that ache that

used to surround his heart, nor the little reminders of the
heartbreak that he had survived. What he felt now was
an indescribable fulfillment, one that was new but welcome. It was a fulfillment that Savannah had given him.
A warm feeling that she had miraculously placed in his
heart.

In a short period of time, being around her, spending
time with her and getting to know her, Savannah Claiborne had done something no other woman had been
able to do. She had taken his heartache away. She had
opened new doors for him, passionate doors, doors filled
with trust, faith, hope and love.

Love.

That one word suddenly made him feel disoriented.
But just as quickly, he came to the realization that he
did love Savannah. He loved everything about her, including the baby she was carrying. And he wanted them
both, here with him, and not just temporarily, but for
always. He didn't want their marriage to end. Ever.

He sighed deeply, admitting that Jared had been right.
His heart had been putty in the hands of the right woman.

Savannah's hands.

Now, the big question was, what was he going to do
about it? He'd had a hard enough job selling her the idea
of a temporary marriage; she would probably fight him
tooth and nail if he brought up the idea of a permanent
one. But he would. Tonight. If he had to he would catch
her at one of her weakest moments.

He would do whatever it took to win Savannah's heart.

Savannah waited for the mail with excitement. Her
boss had indicated that he would be sending the contract

for her to sign for the proposal she had submitted for the calendar and documentary. Already, several of Durango's coworkers, eager to participate, had volunteered.

As she sat at the table and sipped her tea she thought about the phone calls she had gotten from Durango. He'd called twice to warn her about a snowstorm that was headed their way. In the second call, he had informed her that he wanted to talk with her about something important when he got home. Although he wouldn't go into any details, she could tell by the tone of his voice that whatever he wanted to discuss was serious.

She heard the mail truck pull up and quickly placed her teacup aside and grabbed her coat off the rack. As soon as she stepped outside, she felt the change in the weather.

After getting all the mail out of the mailbox, she quickly went back inside to the warmth. Tossing all the letters aside that were addressed to Durango, she came across two that were addressed to her.

The first was the one she'd been waiting for, from the company where she worked. The second, however, caused her to lift an eyebrow. It was a letter from Jared Westmoreland's law firm. Curious, she ripped into the letter Durango's brother had sent her and pulled out the legal-looking document.

Tears began forming in her eyes when she read it. In his ever efficient way, Durango was taking every precaution by reminding her of the terms of their agreement, as well as putting in writing what he intended to do for her and the baby after their marriage ended. The purpose of the paper she held in her hand was to remind her of their agreement. Their marriage was nothing more than a business arrangement.

She wondered if that was what he wanted to talk to her about when he got home. Had he detected the change in her? Had she not been able to hide the fact that she loved him? Maybe he wanted to get everything out in the open, and back into perspective? Was the document his way of letting her know he was beginning to feel smothered and wanted her to leave?

A sudden pain filled her heart and she knew she could never stay where she wasn't wanted…or loved. Her mother had remained in such a situation, but Savannah had vowed that she never would. Tossing the document on the table, she went into the bedroom to pack. If she was lucky, she would be able to catch a plane to Philadelphia before the bad weather set in.

She was going home.

Durango glanced up at his office door and saw Beth standing there. He smiled. He hadn't had a chance to thank her for hosting the party the past weekend.

Before he could open his mouth, she quickly said, "Paul just called and said that an SUV resembling yours passed him on the road."

Durango lifted an eyebrow and sat up straight in his chair and frowned. He had begun using one of the park's SUVs so that Savannah wouldn't be without transportation at the ranch. "And he thinks he saw my Durango?"

"He said it looked a lot like yours and that it was headed toward Bozeman. He was concerned with the storm coming in."

So was Durango. He had called Savannah twice earlier to tell her about the bad weather coming their way and she hadn't mentioned anything about going out. Why on earth would she drive to town?

"Maybe it wasn't your truck, but one that looked like yours."

Durango knew Beth was trying to keep him from worrying, but he was already reaching for the phone to call home. Most people around these parts knew his truck when they saw it because of the custom chrome rims.

He began to panic when no one answered the phone at his place. He then tried Savannah's cell phone. When he didn't get an answer he hung up the phone and glanced back at Beth, who had a worried look on her face. A snowstorm in Montana wasn't anything to play with and the thought of Savannah out in one wasn't good. He stood, already moving toward the door. "I'm out of here. I need to find Savannah before the storm hits."

"Call me when you do."

"I will." He tossed the words over his shoulder as he quickly left.

No need to panic now, Savannah told herself as she continued to drive although she could barely see the road through the snow. It seemed the huge flakes had begun coming all at once, blanketing everything, decreasing her sight to zero visibility.

Knowing it was no longer safe to move Durango's truck another foot, she pulled to the shoulder of the road and killed the engine. She reached into her purse for her cell phone and tried several times without success to reach Durango. Without the heat in the truck, she soon began to feel chilled. She reached for the blanket Durango kept under the seat. Savannah wrapped it around her shoulders, grateful for the warmth it provided, but knew it was only a temporary measure. She wasn't sure how long she could sit here like this, but she also knew to get out of the truck in this type of weather would be suicidal. She wasn't far from the ranch but she wasn't familiar enough with the area to venture out on foot. She decided to stay put.

The best thing to do would be to wait and turn on the engine for heat every so often. She hoped and prayed that the storm would let up or that someone would find her.

Durango drove the road that led from Bozeman to his ranch. Within eight miles of his home he spotted his truck on the side of the road. Pulling up beside it, he quickly got out of the Jeep, ignoring the snowflakes that clung to his face. His heart was beating rapidly as he ran to his SUV.

His heart leaped in his chest the moment he opened the door. Savannah was wrapped in his blanket and curled up on the seat. He reached out and touched her and the first thing he noticed was that she was cold as ice. The second thing he noticed was her overnight bag and camera case on the floor. *Where was she going? Why was she leaving?*

"Savannah? Baby, are you okay? What's going on?"

When she didn't respond he panicked. He pulled her gently into his arms, sheltering her face in his thick, fur-lined parka.

His first inclination was to get her to a hospital and fast. But that was a fifteen-mile trip. He was adequately trained in first aid and made a quick decision to get Savannah to a warm place.

Since they were close to the ranch, he decided to go there. Once at home he would call Trina. He had spoken to her earlier and knew she was at the Marshalls' place on a medical call. The Marshalls' baby had picked the day of what looked to be one of the biggest snowstorms of the year to be born on.

Trina would have to pass by his place on the way home. If she hadn't left already, he would have her stop at his ranch. As he slogged through the deep snow to the SUV, he couldn't help worrying about his wife and child.

He didn't know why she had tried leaving him, but now that he had found her, there was no way he would ever let her go.

"And you're sure Savannah and the baby are going to be all right, Trina?"

Trina motioned for them to step out in the hallway before she began speaking. "Yes, they are both doing fine. I checked the baby's heartbeat and it's as strong as ever. That's a tough kid the two of you are going to have."

Durango had nearly been a basket case when she'd arrived. Any assumption she'd had that the only reason he had gotten married was because Savannah was pregnant had gotten blown out the window, smothered in the snow. What she saw in Durango was a man who truly loved his wife.

Seeing that her words had relaxed him somewhat, Trina continued by saying, "You did the right thing by bringing her here and getting her warm. Giving her that tea really did the trick. But I'm glad you found her when you did. I don't want to think about what would have happened if you hadn't. She knew the risk of carbon monoxide poisoning which is why she hadn't kept the truck's heater running and I'm glad she didn't."

Durango nodded. He was glad, as well. "How long will she be sleeping?"

"For another couple of hours or so. Just let her rest," Trina said, slipping into her coat.

"Are you sure you want to go out in this? You can stay and wait for things to clear up."

Trina smiled. "Thanks, but I know my way around these parts pretty good. Have you forgotten that I grew up here? I only live a few miles away. I'll be fine. And I promise to call you when I get home."

Durango nodded, knowing there was nothing he could say to Patrina Foreman that would make her change her mind. Perry had always said that stubborn was her middle name. "Thanks for everything, Trina. How can I repay you?"

"You already have, Durango. From the day you moved into the area, you were always a true friend to me and Perry, and then, after I lost him, you, McKinnon, Beth and everyone else in these parts were there for me, giving me the shoulder I needed to cry on and helping me keep the ranch running. For that I will always be grateful."

She smiled and continued by saying, "Perry and I were married for five happy years, and my only regret is that we didn't have a child together. Then I would have something of his that would always be with me. But you have that, Durango. You got the best of both worlds. You have a wife you love and the child she is giving you. Take care of them both."

An hour or so later, Durango stood at the window, barely able to see the mountains for the snow. It was falling thicker and faster. At least Trina had called to let him know she had made it home and he was glad of that. He had also called the rangers' station to let everyone know Savannah was safe and doing fine.

He sighed deeply and lifted the document he held in his hand and reread it. It had included all the things he had told Jared he wanted in it, and now after reading it he could just imagine what Savannah had thought, what she had assumed after reading it herself. How would he ever convince her to stay now?

He glanced around the room. The house would be cold, empty and lifeless without Savannah there. No matter what he needed to do, get on his knees and beg if he had to, he refused to let the woman he loved walk out of his life.

Savannah forced her eyes open although she wasn't ready to end her dream just yet. In it Durango had just removed her clothes, had begun kissing her. But a sound made her come awake.

She glanced across the room, and there he was, the man she loved, kneeling in front of the fireplace, working the flames and keeping her warm. She breathed in deeply as pain clutched at her heart. She recalled packing, trying to make it to the airport before the storm hit. How had she gotten back here, to a place where she wasn't wanted? That agonizing question made her moan deep in her throat and it was then that Durango turned around and stared at her, holding her gaze with his and with a force that left her breathless.

She watched as he stood and slowly came over to the bed, his gaze still locked on hers. "You were leaving me," he said in a low, accusing tone. "You were actually leaving me."

Savannah sighed. Evidently he wasn't used to women leaving him and the thought of her abandoning him hurt his pride. "You didn't want me anymore," she said softly, not knowing what else to say. "I thought it would be best if I left."

"Did you think that I didn't want you anymore because of that document Jared sent?" When she didn't respond to his question quickly enough, he said, "You assumed the wrong thing, Mrs. Westmoreland."

Savannah blinked. In all the weeks they had married, he had never called her that, mainly because they'd both known the name was only temporary. So why was he calling her that now? "Did I?"

"Yes, you did. I thought having everything spelled out in a document was what you'd want. I guess I was wrong."

"It doesn't matter," she said softly, trying to hold back her tears.

He came and sat on the side of the bed and took her hand in his. "Yes, it does matter, Savannah. It matters a lot because you matter. You matter to me."

She shrugged, weakly. "The baby matters to you."

"Yes, and the baby matters to you, too. But you also matter to me. *You* matter because I love you."

She blinked again and those beautiful hazel eyes of hers stared at him with disbelief in their depth. He was determined to make her believe and accept him. "I do love you. It would be a waste of time to ask exactly when it happened, but since we have all the time in the world you can go ahead and ask me anyway," he said, smiling and stretching out beside her on the bed.

"When?" she asked, barely able to get the single word out.

He paused, as if searching for the right words. "I think it was when I arrived late at the rehearsal dinner and saw you standing there talking to Jessica. And when you looked up and met my gaze, something hit me. I assumed it was lust, but now I know it was love. Lust would not have driven me to have unprotected sex with any woman, tipsy or not, Savannah. But when we made love I was driven with an urgency I'd never felt before to be inside you and feel the full impact of exploding inside you."

He grinned. "Pill or no Pill, no wonder you got pregnant. Now when I think about it, it would have really surprised the hell out of me if you hadn't. I was hot that night and so were you. Mating the way we did was just a pregnancy waiting to happen. It wasn't intentional, but it was meant to be. And regardless of how you feel about me, I love you."

He shifted a little to get closer to her. "A few weeks ago, before we married, you asked why I had an aversion to city girls and I never gave you an answer. Maybe it's time that I did."

And then he spent the next twenty minutes or so telling her about Tricia, the one woman he'd actually thought he'd loved and how she had used him and tossed his love back in his face. "And I actually thought I could never love another woman for fear of getting hurt that way all over again, especially a female who was a city woman."

He chuckled in spite of himself, remembering the first night he'd seen her. "The moment I saw you I knew you were a city girl and as much as I didn't want to, I couldn't help falling in love with you anyway, Savannah."

He looked down at her, held her gaze. "And no matter what that document says, I do love you. I love you very much."

Savannah felt her cheeks getting wet and tried furiously to wipe at them. But Durango took over, and leaned down and licked them dry. When he pulled back his dark eyebrows rose, clearly astonished. "I thought all tears were salty but yours are sweet. Is there anything that's not perfect about you?"

Savannah let out a small cry and threw her arms around Durango's neck and whispered, "I love you, too, and I fell in love the exact moment that you did."

He chuckled softly and eased from the bed. "Then that leaves only one thing to do," he said, reaching to retrieve the legal document off the nightstand.

Savannah watched as he stood and walked over to the fireplace and tossed it in, and watched with him as the flames engulfed it, burning it to ashes.

"Now that is taken care of," he said.

Savannah kept her eyes on Durango as he slowly removed his shirt. Her heartbeat quickened when he then proceeded to take off his jeans. "I know you're probably too exhausted to make love, but I need to hold you in my arms, Savannah. I need your warmth, I need your love and I need your promise that you won't ever leave me."

She swallowed thickly when he came back to the bed and slipped under the covers with her. She turned to him when he pulled her into his arms. "I won't leave you, Durango. I want forever if you do…and I'm not tired."

He smiled. "I want forever, too, and you are tired. You just don't know it."

He captured her lips with his, kissing her with all the

intensity of a man who had found love by first having an affair—The Durango Affair. It was definitely his last.

"So, Mrs. Westmoreland, will you stay married to me? For better or for worse?"

She smiled through her tears. "Yes, I'll stay married to you, but I have a feeling all my days will be for the better."

He leaned over and kissed her after whispering, "I'll make sure of that."

Epilogue

Savannah glanced around the room. There were more Westmorelands than she remembered from Jessica's wedding. She'd known Durango's family was big but she had no idea it was this large.

The wedding reception given in their honor had turned out to be a beautiful affair. To Savannah's surprise, even her grandparents from Philly had come to be a part of it.

"I know how you feel," Dana Rollins Westmoreland eased up by her side to say. "The first time Jared took me to meet them I thought that this wasn't a family, it was a whole whopping village."

Savannah smiled, thinking the very same thing. She glanced around the room again and it was Tara Westmoreland, who was married to Durango's cousin Thorn, who came up and said, "It seems that Durango called a meeting with the menfolk."

"Oh," Savannah said, wondering the reason why.

Upon seeing her concern, Tara said, "I'm sure whatever they need to talk about won't take long. In the meantime, has anyone ever told you how I met Thorn?"

Savannah smiled. "No, but after meeting him I'm sure it was very interesting."

"Yes, it was. Come on, let me, you and Dana grab the others and go into the kitchen for a talk. If the guys can have a little chat time then so can we."

After gathering Delaney, Shelly, Madison, Jessica, Casey and Jayla up in their wake, the Westmoreland women headed for the kitchen. The married women would tell Savannah how they met their husbands and fell in love.

"Okay, I can see all of you have questions, so what is it you want to know?" Durango asked the men who had cornered him and demanded this meeting.

It was Stone who spoke up. "I know it's really none of our business, Durango, but we know you. What's the real reason you got married?"

Durango shook his head. He'd known his marriage would be hard for a lot of his family to believe, so he decided to be up-front with them, since he suspected a few had their suspicions anyway.

"Savannah is pregnant. However," he went on to say before unnecessary conversation could get started, "although her pregnancy might have been the reason we married initially, it's not now."

Spencer Westmoreland raised a dark eyebrow. "It's not?"

"No. I'm in love with her. She's in love with me. We're having a baby in September and we're happy."

The men in the room stared at him. A few, those who knew how easy it was to fall in love if the right woman came alone, accepted his words. But Durango saw a few skeptical gazes.

"And you want us to believe that just like that, a die-hard bachelor can fall in love?" Quade Westmoreland asked.

"It can happen," Durango said, smiling.

"I agree," added the man who'd once been such a confirmed bachelor that the women had pegged him the *Perfect Storm*. Storm Westmoreland met the gazes of his brothers and cousins and one lone brother-in-law, Sheikh Jamal Yasir. "All of you know my history and yet Jayla was able to capture my heart," he reminded them.

Thorn Westmoreland chuckled. "And all of you know what Tara did to me."

The men in the room doubted they would ever forget. Tara had been Thorn's challenge and had lived up to the task.

"And you're really happy about being married, Durango? No regrets?" Reggie Westmoreland asked, needing to be certain.

Durango met all the men's gazes. "Yes and there aren't any regrets. You've all seen Savannah. What man wouldn't be happy married to her? But her beauty isn't just on the outside. It's on the inside, as well. I need her in my life and she has single-handedly opened my heart to love."

All the men in the room finally believed him. As miraculous as it seemed, Durango Westmoreland had fallen in love. Unfortunately that didn't bode well for the remaining single Westmorelands, who didn't have falling in love on their agendas. The thought of doing so was as foreign to them as a six-legged bear.

"Congratulations and welcome to wedded bliss," Chase Westmoreland said, clapping Durango on the back.

"Thanks, Chase."

Other congratulations followed. It was Ian who had a serious question to ask. "What about us? The ones who have no desire to follow down that path?"

Durango grinned at his brother and said, "I hate to tell you this, but I doubt any man is safe. I'm going to tell it to you like someone older and wiser told it to me. No matter how much your heart is made of stone, it can turn to putty in the right woman's hands."

Jared Westmoreland grinned and raised his wine-glass up in the air and said, "With that said, gentlemen, I rest my case."

Dare Westmoreland, who had been quiet all this time, smiled and said after glancing around the room at the remaining six Westmoreland bachelors, "Now we're faced with that burning question again. Which one of you will be next?"

* * * * *

SOS

DON'T MISS...

the books in this mini-series:

SUMMER OF SECRETS

Expecting Lonergan's Baby
Maureen Child
May 2006

Strictly Lonergan's Business
Maureen Child
June 2006

Satisfying Lonergan's Honour
Maureen Child
July 2006

AVAILABLE FROM

Target • K-Mart • Big W
• selected supermarkets
• bookstores • newsagents

OR

Call Harlequin Mills & Boon
on 1300 659 500 to order now
for the cost of a local call.
NZ customers call (09) 837 1553.

Shop on-line at www.eHarlequin.com.au

Books only available from Harlequin Mills & Boon
for 3 months after the publishing date.
Release dates may be subject to change.

Available Next Month

Heiress Beware
Charlene Sands

A Convenient Proposition
Cindy Gerard

The Soon-To-Be-Disinherited Wife
Jennifer Greene

Paying The Playboy's Price
Emilie Rose

Satisfying Lonergan's Honour
Maureen Child

Forced To The Altar
Susan Crosby

AVAILABLE FROM

Target • K-Mart • Big W • Borders • selected supermarkets
• bookstores • newsagents

OR

Call Harlequin Mills & Boon on 1300 659 500 to order
for the cost of a local call. NZ customers call (09) 837 1553.

Shop on-line at www.eHarlequin.com.au

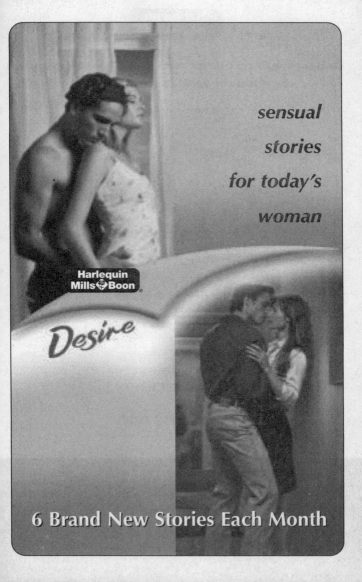

sensual stories for today's woman

Harlequin
Mills & Boon®

Desire

6 Brand New Stories Each Month

Snuggle up this winter with exciting new romance by some of your favourite authors

Plus a bonus book by DEBRA WEBB!

Includes books by:

Susan Meier

Tori Carrington

Kathryn Shay

DON'T MISS OUT!

OUT NOW

AVAILABLE FROM BIG W, KMART, TARGET, BORDERS
NEWSAGENCIES AND SELECTED BOOKSTORES.

Shop online at www.eHarlequin.com.au
or call 1300 659 500 (AU), 09 837 1553 (NZ) for home delivery

WC0606

*n a glitzy Vegas casino, a daredevil professional gambler and a cautious,
shy statistician learn to stack the deck in favour of true love...*

**Don't miss this fabulous book from
Jayne Ann Krentz, writing as Stephanie James.**

Includes the stories:
GAMBLER'S WOMAN and BATTLE PRIZE

AVAILABLE IN ALL GOOD BOOKSTORES
JULY 2006

Shop online at www.eHarlequin.com.au
or call 1300 659 500 (AU), 09 837 1553 (NZ) for home delivery

GW0606

MIRA

New York Times bestselling author

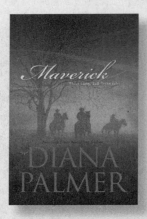

DIANA PALMER brings you three more brand new irresistible
Long, Tall Texan tales:

LUKE, CHRISTOPHER & GUY

They're long and lean...and impossible to resist. Mavericks
through and through. And they have all the ladies in
Jacobsville swooning.

AVAILABLE IN ALL GOOD BOOKSTORES
JULY 2006

Shop online at www.eHarlequin.com.au
or call 1300 659 500 (AU) 09 837 1553 (NZ) for home delivery

**Candace Camp enchants readers once again
with this brand new tale of love and friendship**

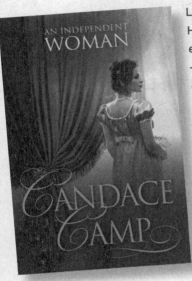

Lady's companion Juliana Holcott fears she will never experience true happiness – until she encounters a childhood friend, Lord Nicholas Barre. What begins as a renewal of friendship soon bears the brunt of society's wrath, leaving Juliana unemployed, compelling Nicholas to offer what he can – a marriage of convenience.

NEW YORK TIMES **BESTSELLING AUTHOR**

AVAILABLE IN ALL GOOD BOOKSTORES
JULY 2006

Shop online at www.eHarlequin.com.au
or call 1300 659 500 (AU), 09 837 1553 (NZ) for home delivery

IW0606

Experience all the action, adventure and **thrills**
romance has to offer each month with
Harlequin Mills & Boon

INTRIGUE

6 edge-of-the-seat romantic suspense stories

Intimate

6 stories each month packed with adventure,
suspense, melodrama and glamour

AVAILABLE FROM BIG W, KMART, TARGET, BORDERS
NEWSAGENCIES AND SELECTED BOOKSTORES.

Shop online at www.eHarlequin.com.au
or call 1300 659 500 (AU), 09 837 1553 (NZ) for home delivery

Experience the very best of life and love each month with Harlequin Mills & Boon

Sweet

6 romances that prove some love affairs really do last a lifetime

Special Edition

6 emotionally compelling stories that explore
the dramas of living and loving

Super *Romance*

6 intense, true-to-life contemporary romances
that celebrate life and love

6 on-the-pulse medical romances that explore the drama
and passion of busy city hospitals and intimate
country practices around the world

AVAILABLE FROM BIG W, KMART, TARGET, BORDERS
NEWSAGENCIES AND SELECTED BOOKSTORES.

Shop online at www.eHarlequin.com.au
or call 1300 659 500 (AU), 09 837 1553 (NZ) for home delivery

**Experience the passion each month with
Harlequin Mills & Boon**

Sexy

8 powerful romances packed with passion

Desire

6 sensual stories for today's woman

Temptation

2 sexy, sassy and seductive new stories

Blaze®

4 red-hot reads that really turn up the heat

AVAILABLE FROM BIG W, KMART, TARGET, BORDERS
NEWSAGENCIES AND SELECTED BOOKSTORES.

Shop online at www.eHarlequin.com.au
or call 1300 659 500 (AU), 09 837 1553 (NZ) for home delivery

Rich and vivid historical romances *that will capture your heart and imagination*

From the high-society of Regency England to the passion and peril of Medieval Europe, Harlequin Mills & Boon is offering you three tantalising period romances each month.

AVAILABLE FROM BIG W, KMART, TARGET, BORDERS NEWSAGENCIES AND SELECTED BOOKSTORES.

Shop online at www.eHarlequin.com.au
or call 1300 659 500 (AU), 09 837 1553 (NZ) for home delivery

HC0206

Classic Romances that are too good
to be forgotten

Each month Harlequin Mills & Boon offers four stories from our
very bestselling authors, reprinted by popular demand.

AVAILABLE FROM BIG W, KMART, TARGET, BORDERS
NEWSAGENCIES AND SELECTED BOOKSTORES.

Shop online at www.eHarlequin.com.au
or call 1300 659 500 (AU), 09 837 1553 (NZ) for home delivery

UC0206